# A BEST BOOK OF THE YEAR

New York Times Book Review
Washington Post • People
Entertainment Weekly • USA Today
Time • A.V. Club • BuzzFeed • PopSugar

"What dazzles most are the warmly rendered dynamics
of an ad hoc, dysfunctional family that
desperately wants to work."
—USA Today

"An incendiary, exuberant romp."
—O, The Oprah Magazine

"A deadpan, hilarious modern fairy tale."
—Newsday

"Laugh-out-loud funny. I love the way Kevin Wilson writes."
—Jacqueline Woodson, National Book Award winner

"There's hardly a sentence that feels like anything you've
read before; that's how fresh his voice is."
—Entertainment Weekly

"A pleasing blend of tartness and tenderness. . . .
Wilson's ability to capture such tangled sentiments makes
him a thoroughly engaging and appealing writer."
—Boston Globe

## Praise for
## Nothing to See Here

"Good Lord, I can't believe how good this book is. . . . It's wholly original. It's also perfect. . . . Wilson writes with such a light touch that it seems fairly impossible for the book to have a big emotional payoff. But there is, and that's the brilliance of the novel—that it distracts you with these weirdo characters and mesmerizing and funny sentences and then hits you in a way you didn't see coming. You're laughing so hard you don't even realize that you've suddenly caught fire."
—Taffy Brodesser-Akner, *New York Times Book Review*

"[Wilson's] most perfect novel. Paradoxically light and melancholy, it hews to the border of fantasy but stays in the land of realism. . . . You can sense the real heat radiating off these pages. . . . This novel may seem slight and quirky, but don't be fooled. There's a lot to see here." —*Washington Post*

"Darkly funny yet quietly devastating. . . . Wilson crafts a stunning portrait of the push and pull of parenthood."
—*Time*

"Funny and even eerily beautiful. . . . It's the sweetness of this novel that will melt you." —NPR

"It's a giddily lunatic premise, one that author Kevin Wilson grounds with humor and deadpan matter-of-factness. . . . Wilson's observational humor is riotous in its specificity. . . . The writing dazzles. . . . But what dazzles most are the warmly rendered dynamics of an ad hoc, dysfunctional family that desperately wants to work."  —*USA Today*

"Weird, funny, but also unexpectedly moving. . . . An affecting reflection on the blithe cruelty of the rich and what it means to be a good parent."  —BuzzFeed

"There's hardly a sentence . . . that feels like anything you've read before; that's how fresh his voice is. . . . Witty, confiding, breezily profane. . . . That the supernatural elements . . . feel so right is a testament to Wilson's innate skill as a storyteller."
—*Entertainment Weekly*

"Wilson's latest is outlandish *and* laugh-out-loud funny."
—*Parade*

"Quirky and insightful, strange and delightful."  —PopSugar

"Perennially weird and wonderful. . . . Wilson's portrayal of these fire children conveys more emotional truth about life with a difficult or neurodivergent kid than any of those parenting guides. . . . Funny and affecting."
—*Minneapolis Star Tribune*

"Wilson captures the wrenching emotions of caring for children in this exceptional, and exceptionally hilarious, novel."
—*Publishers Weekly* (starred review)

"Lillian tells the story, revealing immediately that she's another of Wilson's normal extraordinary protagonists. . . . She fills the book with her wry humor and large, embracing heart."

—*Booklist*

"A love letter to the weirdness and difficulties of children and of parenting, with or without spontaneous human combustion. . . . [With] an easy, engaging voice, cynical and funny without being caustic. Like the author's *The Family Fang*, this is another story of a family that is as delightfully bizarre as it is heartfelt and true."

—*Library Journal*

"Wilson is a remarkable writer. . . . A funny and touching fable about love for kids, even the ones on fire."

—*Kirkus Reviews*

# Nothing to See Here

# Nothing to See Here

# Kevin Wilson

*An Imprint of* **HarperCollins***Publishers*

HarperCollins books may be purchased for educational, business, or sales promotional use. For information, please email the Special Markets Department at SPsales@harpercollins.com.

A hardcover edition of this book was published in 2019 by Ecco, an imprint of HarperCollins Publishers.

FIRST ECCO PAPERBACK EDITION PUBLISHED 2020

*Designed by Renata De Oliveira*

Library of Congress Cataloging-in-Publication Data

Names: Wilson, Kevin, 1978– author.
Title: Nothing to see here / Kevin Wilson.
Description: New York : Ecco, 2019.
Identifiers: LCCN 2019008256 (print) | LCCN 2019009387
 (ebook) | ISBN 9780062913487 () | ISBN 9780062913463
 (hardcover) | ISBN 9780062944870 (softcover)
Subjects: LCSH: Domestic fiction. | BISAC: FICTION / Family
 Life. | FICTION / Literary. | FICTION / Humorous. | GSAFD:
 Humorous fiction.
Classification: LCC PS3623.I58546 (ebook) | LCC PS3623.I58546
 N68 2019 (print) | DDC 813/.6—dc23
LC record available at https://lccn.loc.gov/2019008256

ISBN 978-0-06-291349-4 (pbk.)

20 21 22 23 24  LSC  10 9 8 7 6 5 4 3 2

*For Ann Patchett and Julie Barer*

# Nothing to See Here

# One

IN THE LATE SPRING OF 1995, JUST A FEW WEEKS AFTER I'D
turned twenty-eight, I got a letter from my friend Madison
Roberts. I still thought of her as Madison Billings. I heard from
Madison four or five times a year, updates on her life that were
as foreign to me as reports from the moon, her existence the
kind you only read about in magazines. She was married to an
older man, a senator, and she had a little boy whom she dressed
in nautical suits and who looked like an expensive teddy bear
that had turned human. I was working two cashier jobs at com-
peting grocery stores, smoking weed in the attic of my mother's
house because when I had turned eighteen, she had immediately turned my childhood bedroom into a workout room, a
huge NordicTrack filling the place where I'd unhappily grown
up. I sporadically dated people who didn't deserve me but
thought they did. You can imagine how Madison's letters were
a hundred times more interesting than mine, but we stayed in
touch.

This letter had broken up the natural spacing of her correspondence, precise and expected. But that didn't give me
pause. Madison and I did not communicate except on paper. I
didn't even have her phone number.

I was on break at the Save-A-Lot, the first chance I'd had
to read the thing, and I opened it to find that Madison wanted
me to come to Franklin, Tennessee, where she lived on her husband's estate, because she had an interesting job opportunity
for me. She'd included a fifty-dollar bill for bus fare, because
she knew that my car wasn't great with more than fifteen-mile
distances. She wouldn't say what the job was, though it couldn't
be worse than dealing with food stamps and getting the fucking scale to properly weigh the bruised apples. I used the last
five minutes of my break to ask Derek, my boss, if I could have
a few days off. I knew he'd say no, and I didn't begrudge him
this refusal. I'd never been the most responsible employee. It
was the hard thing about having two jobs: you had to disap-
point them at different times and sometimes you lost track of
who you'd fucked over worse. I thought about Madison, maybe
the most beautiful woman I'd ever met in real life, who was
also so weirdly smart, always considering the odds of every sce-
nario. If she had a job for me, I'd take it. I'd leave my mom's attic. I'd empty out my life because I was honest enough to know
that I didn't have much that I'd miss when it disappeared.

**A WEEK AFTER I WROTE BACK TO MADISON WITH A DATE THAT**
I'd arrive, a man in a polo shirt and sunglasses was waiting
inside the bus station in Nashville. He looked like a man who
was really into watches. "Lillian Breaker?" he asked, and I nodded. "Mrs. Roberts asked me to escort you back to the Roberts
estate. My name is Carl."

"Are you their driver?" I asked, curious as to the particu-
lars of wealth. I knew rich people on TV had drivers, but it
seemed like a Hollywood absurdity that didn't connect to the
real world.

"No, not exactly. I'm just kind of a jack-of-all-trades. I help Senator Roberts, and Mrs. Roberts by extension, when things come up."

"Do you know what I'm doing here?" I asked. I knew what cops sounded like, and Carl sounded like a cop. I wasn't super jazzed about law enforcement, so I was feeling him out.

"I believe I do, but I'll let Mrs. Roberts talk to you. I think she would prefer that."

"What kind of car are you driving?" I asked him. "Is it your own car?" I had been on a bus for a couple of hours with people who communicated only in hacking coughs and weird sniffs. I just wanted to hear my own voice go out into the open air.

"It's a Miata. It's mine. Are you ready to go, ma'am? May I take your luggage?" Carl asked, clearly ready to successfully complete this portion of his task. He had that cop-like tic where he tried to hide his impatience with a tight formality.

"I didn't bring anything," I said.

"Excellent. If you'll follow me, I'll get you to Mrs. Roberts ASAP."

When we got to the Miata, a hot red number that seemed too small to be on the road, I asked if we could ride with the top down, but he said it wasn't such a great idea. It looked like it pained him to refuse. But it also looked like maybe it pained him to be asked. I couldn't quite figure out Carl, so I settled into the car and let everything move past me.

"Mrs. Roberts says that you're her oldest friend," Carl said, making conversation.

"That might be right," I said. "We've known each other a while." I didn't say that Madison probably didn't have any other real friends. I didn't hold it against her. I didn't have any real friends, either. What I also didn't say was that I wasn't even sure that we were actually friends at all. What we were was something weirder. But Carl didn't want to hear any of that, so we just rode in silence the rest of the way, the radio playing easy listening that made me want to slip into a hot bath and dream about killing everyone I knew.

I MET MADISON AT A FANCY GIRLS' SCHOOL HIDDEN ON A mountain in the middle of nowhere. A hundred or so years ago, maybe even longer, all the men who had managed to make enough money in such a barren landscape decided that they needed a school to prepare their daughters for the eventuality of marrying some other rich men, moving up in life until no one remembered a time when they had been anything other than exemplary. They brought some British guy to Tennessee, and he ran the place like a school for princesses, and soon other rich men from other barren landscapes sent their daughters. And then, after this happened enough times, rich people in real cities, like New York and Chicago, started hearing about this school and started sending their own daughters. And if you can catch that kind of good luck, it holds for centuries.

I grew up in the valley of that mountain, just poor enough that I could imagine a way out. I lived with my mom and a rotating cast of her boyfriends, my father either dead or just checked out. My mother was vague about him, not a single picture. It seemed like maybe some Greek god had assumed the form of a stallion and impregnated her before returning to his home atop Mount Olympus. More likely it was just a pervert in one of the fancy homes that my mom cleaned. Maybe he was some alderman in town, and I'd seen him all my life without knowing it. But I preferred to think he was dead, that he was wholly incapable of saving me from my unhappiness.

The school, the Iron Mountain Girls Preparatory School, offered one or two full scholarships each year to girls in the valley who showed promise. And, though it might be hard to believe now, I showed a fucking lot of promise. I had spent my childhood gritting my teeth and smashing everything to bits in the name of excellence. I taught myself to read at three years old, matching the storybooks that came with records to the words the narrator spoke through the little speaker. When I was eight, my mother put me in charge of our finances, the weekly budgeting from the envelopes of cash that she brought home at night. I made straight As. At first, it was purely out of an instinctual desire to be superlative, as if I suspected that I was a superhero and was merely testing the limits of my powers. But once teachers started to tell me about Iron Mountain and the scholarship, information that my mother could not have cared less about, I redirected my efforts. I didn't know that the school was just some ribbon that rich girls obtained on their way to a destined future. I thought it was a training ground for Amazons. I made other students cry at the spelling bee. I plagiarized scientific studies and dumbed them down just enough to win county science fairs. I memorized poems about Harlem and awkwardly recited them to my mom's boyfriends, who thought I was some weird demon speaking in tongues. I played point guard on the boys' traveling basketball team because there wasn't one for girls. I made people in my town, whether they were poor or middle class, especially upper middle class, feel good, like I was something they could agree on, a sterling representative of this little backwoods county. I wasn't destined for greatness; I knew this. But I was figuring out how to steal it from someone stupid enough to relax their grip on it.

I got the scholarship, and some of my teachers even raised

enough money to help cover expenses for books and food, since my mother told me flat-out that she couldn't afford any of it. When it was time to start school, I put on some ugly-ass jumper, the only nice thing I owned, and my mother dropped me off with a duffel bag filled with my stuff, including three changes of the school's uniform black skirts and white blouses. Other parents were there in their BMWs and cars so fancy I didn't know the names of them. "God, look at this place," my mom said, heavy metal on the radio, fidgeting with an unlit cigarette because I asked her not to smoke so it wouldn't get in my hair. "Lillian, this is going to sound so mean, but you don't belong here. It don't mean they're better than you. It just means you're gonna have a rough go of it."

"It's a good opportunity," I told her.

"You got shit, I understand that," she said, as patient as she'd ever been with me, though the engine was still idling. "You got shit and I know that you want better than shit. But you're going from shit to gold, and it's going to be real tough to handle that. I hope you make it."

I didn't get angry with her. I knew that my mom loved me, though maybe not in ways that were obvious, that other people would understand. She wanted me to be okay, at least that. But I also knew that my mom didn't exactly like me. I weirded her out. I cramped her style. It was fine with me. I didn't hate her for that. Or maybe I did, but I was a teenager. I hated everyone.

She pushed in the car's cigarette lighter and while she waited for it to fire up, she kissed me softly and gave me a hug. "You can come back home anytime, sweetie," she said, but I imagined that I'd kill myself if I had to do that. I got out of the car, and she drove off. As I walked to my dorm, I realized that the other girls didn't even look at me, and I could tell that it wasn't out of meanness. I don't think they even saw me; their eyes had been trained since birth to recognize importance. I wasn't that.

And then I found Madison in my room, the room we were going to share. All the information that I had on her had been provided in a brief letter during the summer, informing me that my roommate would be Madison Billings and that she was from Atlanta, Georgia. Chet, an ex-boyfriend of my mom's who still hung around the house when she wasn't dating someone else, had seen the letter and said, "I bet she's from the Billings Department Stores. That's Atlanta, too. That's big money."

"How would you know, Chet?" I asked. I didn't mind Chet so much. He was goofy, which was better than the alternative. He had a tattoo of Betty Boop on his forearm.

"You gotta pick up on little clues," he told me. He drove a forklift. "Information is power."

Madison had shoulder-length blond hair and was wearing a yellow summer dress with hundreds of little orange goldfish printed on it. Even in flip-flops, she was model tall, and I could tell that the soles of her feet would be so fucking soft. She had a perfect nose, blue eyes, enough freckles to look wholesome without looking like God had blasted her with bad skin. The whole room smelled of jasmine. She'd already arranged the space, had chosen the bed farthest from the door. When she saw me, she smiled like we were friends. "Are you Lillian?" she asked, and I could only nod. I felt like a kid on *The Bozo Show* in my shitty jumper.

"I'm Madison," she told me. "It's nice to meet you." She held out her hand, her nails painted a faint pink, like the nose of a bunny rabbit.

"I'm Lillian," I said, and I shook her hand. I'd never shaken the hand of someone my own age.

"They told me that you're a scholarship kid," she then informed me, though there wasn't any judgment in her voice. She seemed to just want to make it clear that she knew.

"Why did they tell you that?" I asked her, my face reddening.

"I don't know. They told me, though. Maybe they wanted to make sure that I'd be polite about it."

"Well, okay, I guess," I said. I felt like I was forty, fifty steps behind Madison, and the school was already making it harder for me to catch up.

"Doesn't matter to me," she told me. "I prefer it. Rich girls are the worst."

"Are you not a rich girl?" I asked, hopeful.

"I'm a rich girl," she said. "But I'm not like most rich girls. I think that's why they put me with you."

"Well, good," I said. I was sweating so hard.

"Why are you here?" she asked. "Why did you want to come to this place?"

"I don't know. It's a good school, right?" I said. Madison had a kind of directness that I'd not experienced before, where shit that should get her killed somehow seemed okay because her eyes were so blue and she didn't seem to be joking.

"Yeah, I guess. But, like, what do you want to get out of this place?" she asked.

"Can I put down my bag?" I asked. I touched my face and sweat was beading up and starting to trickle down my neck. She gently took my bag from me and placed it on the floor. Then she gestured to my bed, unmade, and I sat on it. She sat beside me, closer than I'd prefer.

"What do you want to be?" she asked me.

"I don't know. Jesus, I don't know," I said. I thought Madison was going to kiss me.

"My parents want me to get amazing grades and go to Vanderbilt and then marry some university president and have beautiful babies. My dad was so specific. *We'd love it if you married a university president*. But I'm not doing that."

"Why not?" I said. If the university president was sexy, I'd jump right into the life that Madison's parents imagined for her.

"I want to be powerful. I want to be the person who makes big things happen, where people owe me so many favors that they can never pay me back. I want to be so important that if I fuck up, I'll never get punished."

She looked psychotic as she said this; I wanted to make out with her. She flipped her hair in such a way that it could only have been instinctual, evolution. "I feel like I can tell you this."

"Why?" I asked.

"Because you're poor, right? But you're here. You want power, too."

"I just want to go to college, to get out of here," I said, but I felt like maybe she was right. I'd learn to want all that stuff she said. I could go for power.

"I think we'll be friends," she said. "I hope so, at least."

"God," I said, trying to keep my whole body from convulsing, "I hope so, too."

And we did become friends, I guess you could say. She had to tamp down her weirdness in public because it scared people when beautiful people didn't act a certain way, made themselves ugly. And I had to tamp down my weirdness because people already suspected that I was supremely strange because I was a scholarship kid. A few days into my time there, another scholarship girl, from a town that bordered mine, came up to me and said, not in a mean way, "Please don't talk to me the entire time that we're here," and I agreed immediately. It was better this way.

The point is, we had to be composed in public, so it was nice to come to our shared space and cut out pictures of Bo and Luke Duke and rub them all over our bodies. It was nice to hear Madison talk about being a lawyer who sends the most evil man in the world to the electric chair. I told her that I wanted to grow up and be able to eat a Milky Way bar every single morning for breakfast. She said that was better than wanting to be the president of the United States of America, which Madison kind of wanted to be.

We also played on the basketball team, the only two freshmen to start in years and years. The team was no joke, had won a few state titles. At Iron Mountain, basketball and cross-country were hugely important to the school's identity; I suspected that, for most girls, they were a great way to add complexity to their college applications, but there were girls like me who just really liked being badasses all over weaker people. I played point guard and Madison, so damn tall, played power forward. We spent a lot of time in the gym, just the two of us, running full-court sprints, shooting with our nondominant hands. I had always been good, but I got better with Madison on my team. She gave me some kind of extrasensory court vision; she was so beautiful that I could find her without even looking. We were Magic and Kareem. We told our coach that we wanted to wear black high-tops, but he refused. "Jesus, girls, you act like you're New York playground legends," he said. "Just don't get in foul trouble or turn the ball over."

There were times when Madison left me behind, but I

didn't take it personally. I think if I'd been a different kind of person—and I don't mean wealthy—I could have been a part of it, but I had no interest. She and the other beautiful girls would sit together at lunch. Sometimes they would sneak off campus and hang out at a bar near this experimental art college where boys hit on them. Sometimes they bought cocaine from some super-sketchy dude named Panda. Madison would show up in our room at three in the morning, somehow eluding the dorm parents who watched over us, and sit on the floor, drinking a huge bottle of water. "God, I hate myself for being so damn predictable," she would say.

"It looks fun," I said, lying.

"It can be," she said, her pupils crazy big. "But it's just a phase."

School was more complicated there than in the valley, but the classes weren't hard. I made straight As. So did Madison. I won a poetry contest when I wrote about growing up poor; Madison had told me to do it after I showed her my first poem, which was about a fucking tulip. "Use it at the right time," she told me, by which I think she meant my bad upbringing, "and you'll get a lot out of it." I think I understood. I mean, here I was at Iron Mountain, thriving. I got here. Madison sometimes slept in my little bed, the two of us wrapped around each other. I had good things, and it wasn't as hard to admit to where I'd been before I ended up right where I belonged.

And then one of Madison's beautiful friends—the least beautiful of the six of them, if you want to be cruel—got upset at a joke that Madison had made, a moment when Madison's weirdness had spilled out beyond the confines of our dorm room, and so the girl told the dorm parent that Madison had a bag of coke in her desk drawer. The dorm parent checked, and there it was. Iron Mountain was a place for rich people, and it depended on those rich people, so Madison hoped, in bed with me one night as we talked it over, that the school would go easy on her. But I was not rich, and what I understood was that sometimes a place like Iron Mountain made an example of one rich person in order to gain the trust of a bunch of other rich people. It was almost the end of the year, just a few weeks till final exams, and the headmaster of the school, no longer some British dude but a Southern woman named Ms. Lipton with a white shell of a hairstyle and a maroon pantsuit, called Madison and her parents to meet with her in her office, the invitation sent on official letterhead. Ms. Lipton called everyone "daughter" but had never married.

Madison's father drove up the night before; her mother was unable to come, "so overwhelmed with disappointment," Mr. Billings told Madison over the phone. He wanted to take us out to dinner, a kind of farewell for Madison and me, although I thought that seemed weird. He picked us up in a brand-new Jaguar. He was older than I'd expected, and he looked like Andy Griffith, with that winking way of acknowledging you. "Hello, girls," he said, opening the door to the car. Madison just grunted and hopped in, but Mr. Billings took my hand and kissed it. "Madison has told me so much about you, Miss Lillian," he said.

"Okay," I said. I was still unsteady with adults. I thought maybe he wanted to sleep with me.

We drove to a steakhouse and there was a table reserved for us, though Mr. Billings said it was for four. And then I saw my mom, dressed up for her, but not dressed up enough for this place. She looked at me with this kind of *what the fuck have you done* look on her face, but she then quickly smiled at Mr. Billings, who introduced himself and then kissed her hand, which my mother was so jazzed about, clearly.

"A drink, ma'am?" he asked my mom, who ordered a gin and tonic. He ordered a bourbon, neat. It felt like we had instantly become a new family. I kept looking at Madison for some kind of clue as to whether she was freaked out, too, but she wouldn't even look at me, just kept running her eyes up and down the menu.

"I'm happy you two could join Madison and myself on this night," Mr. Billings said after we ordered. My mother had chosen a filet that was listed at twenty-five dollars, but I got chicken fettuccine, which was the cheapest thing on the menu. As much as I try to remember, I have no idea what Madison and her dad ordered.

"Thank you for inviting me," my mom said. She had lived a hard life, smoked too much, but she had been a cheerleader and a beauty queen in high school. She was still beautiful, I had to admit, a beauty that she'd not passed on to me, and I could see how she just might, in this setting, seduce Mr. Billings for a night.

"I'm afraid the reason for our gathering is not so happy," he said, looking at Madison, who was now staring at the tablecloth in front of her. "I'm afraid Madison has gotten herself into some trouble, because she is headstrong. I have five children, but Madison is the youngest and she is more trouble than the other four put together."

"Four boys," Madison said, a little flash of anger.

"Anyway, Madison has made a mistake and she is going to be punished for it. Or that seems to be what awaits us tomorrow morning. And that is why I wanted to talk to you and Lillian here."

"Dad—" Madison began, but he froze her with a hard stare.

"Did Lillian do something wrong?" my mom asked. She already had her second gin and tonic.

"No, my dear," Mr. Billings continued. "Lillian has been an exemplary woman while at Iron Mountain. I'm sure you're quite proud of her."

"I am," my mother said, but it sounded like a question.

"Well, here's the situation. I'm a businessman, and as such, I'm always looking at things from a different angle, seeing all the possibilities. Now, my wife refused to come here; she thinks that Madison needs to accept her punishment and aspire to do better with what's left to her. But my wife, though I love her, hasn't fully considered the ramifications of Madison's expulsion. The effect it would have on her future is more than I can state."

"Well, kids make mistakes," my mother said. "That's how they learn."

Mr. Billings's smile slipped for the briefest of moments. Then he recovered. "That's right," he said. "They learn. They make a mistake and then they learn never to do it again. But in Madison's case, it won't matter that she won't ever do it again. Her fate has been sealed. And so I come to you with an offer."

And I knew. I fucking knew right then. And I was so angry that I hadn't known it hours before. I looked at Madison, and of course she wouldn't look at me. I grabbed her arm under the table and squeezed the shit out of it, but she didn't even flinch.

"What's the offer?" my mom said, slightly drunk, very interested.

"I believe that the headmistress would be more forgiving if the student were someone other than Madison," he said. "I think if, for instance, it were your daughter, a virtuous girl who has made so much of herself while dealing with such hardship, the headmistress would offer only a cursory punishment, at most a semester's suspension."

"Why?" my mother asked, and I wanted to kick her in the face. I wanted to sober her up, but I knew it wouldn't matter.

"It's complicated, ma'am," Mr. Billings said. "But I do believe this. I believe that if you and Lillian marched into that woman's office tomorrow morning and told her that the drugs were actually Lillian's, the punishment would be quite lenient."

"That's a big maybe," my mother said. Maybe she wasn't as drunk as I thought.

"Well, it is a risk, I admit that. Which is why I would be willing to reimburse you for your troubles. In fact, I have a check, made out to you, Ms. Breaker, for ten thousand dollars. I believe that would help toward Miss Lillian's continuing education. I believe there's enough in that gift to cover some of your own expenses."

"Ten thousand dollars?" my mom repeated.

"That's correct."

"Mom," I said, just as Madison was saying, "Dad," but they both shut us up. Right then, Madison looked at me. Her eyes were so blue, even in the dim light of this shitty steakhouse. It was such a strange feeling, to hate someone and yet love them at the same time. I wondered if this was normal for adults.

Mr. Billings and my mom kept talking; the food came, and Madison and I didn't eat a single bite of our dishes. I stopped listening to anything. Madison grabbed my hand under the table and held on to it right up until her father paid the bill and escorted us out of the restaurant, his check in my mom's purse.

That night, after he'd dropped us off at our dorm and we'd signed ourselves back in, Madison asked if she could sleep in my bed with me, but I told her to fuck off. I brushed my teeth and then, while she sat in her bed and read Shakespeare for some paper she had to write, since she wasn't going to be expelled after all, I packed up my duffel bag. How in the world did it hold less than it had when I arrived? What was my life? I got into bed and shut off my light. A few minutes later, Madison turned off her light and we both sat there in the dark, not saying anything. I don't know how long it took, but she finally crept over to my side of the room and stood over me. She was my only friend. I scooted over, and she crawled into my bed. She wrapped her arms around me and I could feel her chest press against my back. "I'm sorry," she said.

"Madison" was all I could manage. I'd wanted something, and I didn't get it. Or it was going to be harder to get it when I got another chance.

"You're my best friend," she said, but I couldn't say anything else. I lay there until I fell asleep, and when the dorm parent knocked on our door in the morning to say that my mother was outside waiting for me, I realized that, sometime in the night, Madison had gone back to her own bed.

THE HEADMISTRESS SEEMED TO KNOW THAT I WAS LYING; SHE tried several times to get me to alter my story, but my mother kept butting in, saying how hard my life had been. And then Ms. Lipton expelled me. My mother didn't even seem that shocked. I'd never even smoked one of my mom's cigarettes at this point, and I was kicked out of school for drugs. I felt like I'd been good for nothing.

When I went to the room to get my duffel bag, Madison was gone. On the drive back to the valley, my mother said that she would set aside money for my college tuition, but I knew that money was already gone. It had vaporized the moment it touched her hands.

Four months later, I got a letter from Madison. She told me about her summer vacation in Maine. She told me how awful the last weeks of school had been without me there, and how she so badly wanted me to come visit her in Atlanta. There was no mention of what had happened to me, what I'd done for her. She told me about a boy she'd met in Maine and how much stuff she'd let him do. I could hear her voice in the letter. It was a pretty voice. I wrote back, and I didn't mention the awful shit between us. We became pen pals.

I went back to my awful public high school, which felt like returning to sea level after spending a year on the highest mountain peak. All the teachers and students, everyone in the town, had heard about my expulsion, the cocaine, the fact that I had fucked up my one chance to improve my circumstances. They invented little twists on the basic story to make it seem even worse. And they blamed me. They were so angry, like, fuck, why had they ever thought that someone like me could have handled such an experience? And so they gave up on me, stopped talking about college, about scholarships. I turned into a ghost, this story that lived in the town, a cautionary tale, but who would it scare? Who would listen?

Everything was so easy, and nobody cared, and I lost interest. I started working after school, helping my mom clean houses. I started hanging out with idiot boys and girls who had access to weed and pills, and I'd stay with them as long as they didn't expect anything from me. Then, when they did expect things, I just bought weed myself and smoked joints on the back porch of my house all alone, feeling the world flatten out. I started to care less about the future. I cared more about making the present tolerable. And time passed. And that was my life.

**AS WE NEARED THE ESTATE, ALL I COULD SEE WERE GREEN** pastures and what felt like miles and miles of white fence. I couldn't understand what the fence was there for, because it wouldn't keep anything in or out. It was purely ornamental, and then, like, *duh,* I realized that if you had this much money, you could make gestures that were purely ornamental. I reminded myself to be smarter. I was smart. I just had a thick layer of stupid that had settled on top of me. But I was still wild when I needed to be. I'd get smarter. Whatever Madison had, I'd get it easily.

The fucking driveway felt like it was a mile long, and it looked like it would lead you straight to the gates of heaven, that's how perfectly maintained it was. It could have ended at a run-down pizza joint with bars on the windows and you'd still be so thrilled.

"Almost there," Carl said.

"What's the mail situation like?" I said.

"What do you mean?" he asked.

"Do they have to walk all the way to the end of this driveway just to get the mail? Or do they have, like, a golf cart? Or does someone get it for them?" I didn't ask if he was the one who got the mail for them, but I feel like maybe he knew that I was wondering.

"Well, the postman just brings it to the door," he said.

"Oh, okay," I said. I thought about Madison sitting on her porch, drinking sweet tea and waiting patiently while the postman crept up the driveway, bearing a letter from me about my ideas for a tattoo on my ankle.

I had often fantasized about Madison's home. It seemed weird to ask her for a photo of the mansion, like, *Hey, I could live without another photo of your teddy bear son but please send me pictures of every single one of the bathrooms in your mansion.* When she sent photos, I could make out parts of the house, expensive and well maintained. Maybe if I'd cut them into pieces and reassembled them, I could have seen the whole mansion. Sometimes it was simpler to just believe that Madison lived in the White House. That made sense to me at the time. Madison lived in the fucking White House.

Now, as we pulled up to the estate, I felt this diamond form in my throat, and I almost grabbed Carl's hand for support. The house was three stories, maybe more. I couldn't crane my neck enough to see the top of it; for all I knew at that moment, it went all the way up to space. It was blindingly white, not one trace of mold or dirt, a house that you build in your dreams. There was a huge porch that seemed to wrap around the entire structure; it must have been a mile if you walked it. I had been prepared for wealth, but clearly my life had left me ill prepared for what wealth could be. And was Madison's husband even really all that rich? He hadn't invented computers or owned a fast-food empire. And yet his level of wealth had given him this house. It had given him Madison, who suddenly appeared in the front doorway, and she was waving, so beautiful that I knew I'd take her over the house every single time I had a choice.

Carl pulled the car around the fountain in the middle of the driveway and stopped right at the front door of the house. While the car idled, he swiftly ducked out of his seat and came around to open my door. I couldn't get up. I couldn't make my legs work. Madison suddenly walked down the stairs and held out her arms for an embrace. But I couldn't meet her. I felt like if I moved one muscle, the whole thing would evaporate and I would wake up back on my futon, the A/C broken again. Carl finally had to haul me up, rag-dolling me as if I were a gift for Madison's birthday, and then I fell into her arms. She was so tall, so strong, that she held me until I smelled the scent of her, until I remembered her, the two of us in bed in that dorm room, and everything was tangible again. It was real. I straightened up, and there I was, standing there. It was the first time in almost fifteen years that I'd seen Madison, but she looked the same. She'd just gotten a little tanner and filled out in a way that suggested adulthood. She didn't look like a robot. She didn't look soulless.

"You look so beautiful," she said, and I believed her.

"Well, you look like a supermodel," I replied.

"I wish I were a supermodel," she said. "I wish I had a calendar that was nothing but me." And like that, it was the two of us again, me being weird and her revealing that, by god, she was weird, too.

Carl checked his watch, did this little bow, and then hopped back in the car and drove away. We could have spent the rest of the day watching him drive away. I kind of wanted to. I kept waiting for his car to turn into some dumb gourd and him to turn into a mouse. I waited for magic, and I didn't think I would be disappointed.

"It's so hot out here," she said. "Come inside."

"This is your house?" I asked.

Madison smiled. "It's one of them," she said, and her nose wrinkled and her eyes got all twinkly. She couldn't talk like this with her husband, none of the other women who lived in luxury. This was good. She couldn't believe her good fortune, either.

Inside the house, I don't know what I'd expected, but it was pretty plain. There wasn't a lot of crazy art on the walls, and I guess I thought maybe there would be space-age furniture, but this was the kind of wealth where things were so plain that you didn't realize how expensive they were until you touched them or got closer and saw how they were made with great care and with super-fancy materials. In the hallway was a huge portrait of Madison and her husband from their wedding. She looked like she'd just been crowned Miss America and he looked like the emcee who had once been famous. I couldn't tell if it was love, but I also knew that I was no real judge of love, having never experienced it or even witnessed it a single time in my life.

**MADISON HAD MET SENATOR JASPER ROBERTS WHEN SHE'D** worked on his reelection campaign right after she'd graduated from Vanderbilt University with a degree in political science. She'd started at the lowest rung, brought on because the normally untouchable senator had recently left his wife and two kids and started dating one of his biggest donors, some heiress who was obsessed with horses and wore crazy hats. They wanted to get a woman's perspective on things, I guess. The dudes at the top, who had the senator's ear, had told him that he had to be super dignified about it and never talk about it and harrumph like a Muppet if anyone even brought it up. I remember her letter to me around this time. *Jesus, these guys are so stupid,* she wrote. *It's like they've never followed up on a single stupid-ass thing they've ever done so they could just fix it.* Because Madison was brilliant and because she had that slightly skewed way of saying things in a straightforward manner that broke you in half, the senator ended up putting her in charge of the campaign. And, of course, he did this because he was falling in love with her, like everyone did, and because the heiress wouldn't shut the fuck up about some horse that she wanted to buy.

Madison made him conciliatory. She wrote his speeches, every single one. He confessed to his failings, that his desire to make his constituency prosperous, to help every single person he represented, had caused him to lose sight of what made his own family happy. And now that he'd lost that family, he could not lose his larger family, the voters of the great state of Tennessee. It wasn't that hard. He was a political legacy, generations of Roberts men running things, so much wealth that people just assumed they had to vote for him. He merely had to show that he was aware that he'd done a fucked-up thing.

And he won. And Madison got kind of famous in these political circles. *It's really all because his stupid fucking opponent didn't know what he was doing,* she'd admitted in another letter. *If I'd been on that side of things, Jasper would have lost.* And then they got married. And then she got pregnant. And now she had this life.

**WE SAT ON THE SOFA, AND IT WAS LIKE SITTING ON A CLOUD,** the exact opposite of my ratty futon, which felt like getting stuck in a hole in the floor, just trapped there for all eternity. I wondered how much of this decor had been Madison's choosing and how much of it was left over from her husband's previous wife. There were sandwiches on a tiered tray, lots of mayo and cucumber, so tiny that they looked like dollhouse food. There was a pitcher of sweet tea and two glasses with big solid chunks of pristine ice in them. The ice hadn't even begun to melt, and

I realized that they must have materialized just seconds before we'd entered the room.

"Do you remember that day we first met?" Madison asked.

"Of course I do," I said. It hadn't been that long ago. Had it been a long time ago to her? "You had a dress with goldfish on it."

"My dad had that dress made for me by a dressmaker in Atlanta. I hated it. Goldfish? He was clueless."

"Wait, is he dead?" I asked, suddenly suspicious.

"No, he's still alive," she said.

"Oh, good," I said, but I didn't mean it. It just came out. "Good," I added, just in case.

"I remember that maybe you hadn't even brushed your hair," she said.

"No, I'd definitely brushed my hair," I told her.

"I remember when you walked into the room, like a lightning bolt, I knew that I was going to love you."

I wondered where her husband was. I felt like we were about to make out. I felt like maybe the job was to be her secret lover. My pulse was racing, as it always did in her presence.

When I didn't respond, her eyes turned a little glassy all of a sudden, and she said, "I always felt like I missed out on something really wonderful when you left Iron Mountain."

We weren't going to have a reckoning, not really. Not yet. She wasn't going to bring up the fact that her not-dead father had paid me off to take the fall for her, so that she could have this mansion, this senatorial husband, and all these expensive things. We were, I understood, being polite.

"But now you're here!" she said. She poured sweet tea, and I drank it down in, like, two gulps. She didn't even look surprised, just filled my glass up again. I ate one of the sandwiches, and it was gross, but I was hungry. I ate two more. I didn't even realize that there were tiny plates stacked on the tray. I'd held the sandwiches in my dumb hands. I didn't even want to look down at my lap because I knew there were crumbs there.

"Where is Timothy?" I asked, expecting to see her son walk into the room with a coonskin cap and a wooden popgun, his skin pale like old royalty's.

"He's taking a nap," she said. "He loves naps. He's lazy, like me."

"I love naps, too," I said. How many sandwiches did you eat at something like this? There were nearly twenty more on the trays. Did you leave some for propriety's sake? She hadn't touched them. Wait, were they decorative?

"I bet you want to know why I asked you to come all this way," she said.

It sank in that this was temporary, that I'd have to leave, so I became curious as to what had been so important that we finally had to see each other face-to-face after so many years of correspondence.

"You said there was an opportunity for me?" I continued. "Like a job, maybe?"

"I thought of you because, Lillian, this is honestly very private, what I'm about to tell you, regardless of what you decide to do. I needed someone who could be discreet, who knew how to keep a secret."

"I can be discreet," I said. I loved this stuff, bad stuff.

"I know," she said, almost blushing, but not really.

"Is everything okay?" I asked.

"Yes and no," she said, twisting her mouth like she was rinsing it out. "Yes and no. Did I ever tell you about Jasper's first family?"

"I don't think so. I read about them, I think. Do you mean his first wife?"

She looked apologetic, like she knew she was pulling me into something that might ruin me. But she didn't stop. She didn't send me back to my mom's house. She held on to me.

"Well, he had a first wife, a childhood sweetheart, but she died. She had a rare kind of cancer, I think. He doesn't talk about her at all. I know he loves me, but I know he loved her the most. Anyway, after that, there was a long period of grieving. And then he ended up marrying Jane, who was the youngest daughter of a really powerful man in Tennessee politics. Jane was—well, she was strange. She had darkness inside of her. But, not to speak ill of my husband, it was politically advantageous to be married to her. She knew the world he moved in and could do the things that he needed done. And they had twins, a girl and a boy. And that was their life, you know? Until he met that horse woman, and everything went to shit."

"But then you met him," I offered. "It all worked out."

She didn't even smile. She was in this now. She was doing it. "It did. We had Timothy. I still get to be involved in politics, just from a different angle, a kind of support position. And it's nice. Jasper listens to me. Honestly, policy kind of bores him. It's just his family's legacy. He likes the fame, but he's not big on laws. Anyway, things were fine."

"What happened?" I asked.

"Okay, well, Jane died. She died a few months ago."

"I'm sorry," I said. I tried to figure out what kind of grief Jane's death would inspire in Madison. None, probably. But I still said that I was sorry.

"It's tragic," she said. "She never really recovered from the divorce. She had always been so brittle, so strange. Honestly, she went a little crazy. She'd call late at night saying the most awful things. Jasper never really understood how to deal with her. I'd have to talk to her all night long, walking her through her new reality. I'm good at that stuff, you know?"

"What happened to her?" I asked.

Madison frowned. Her freckles were so beautiful. "Here's what I need to tell you, okay, Lillian? Here's where I need you to promise to keep a secret."

"Okay," I said, growing a little irritated. I'd already said I'd keep the fucking secret. I needed the secret. I needed to eat it, for it to live inside me.

"Now that Jane has passed away," she continued, "there is the matter of Jasper's children. They're ten years old. Twins. Bessie and Roland. Sweet kids— Shit, no, I don't know why I said that. I don't know them. But, you know, they're kids. And now, well, they're Jasper's kids. They're his responsibility. And so we're making adjustments in our lives in order to accommodate them."

"Wait," I asked, "you've never even met your husband's kids? Has he seen them?"

"Lillian? Please," she said, "can we not focus on this?"

"Are they not already here?" I asked.

"Not yet," she admitted.

"But if the mom died a while ago, what are they doing? Are they on their own?" I asked.

"No, of course not. Jeez. They're with Jane's parents, super-old people and not good with kids. We just needed time to get everything prepared for their arrival. In just over a week, they'll be here with us. Living with us."

"Okay," I said.

"They've been through a lot, Lillian. They've not had the

best life. Jane was a difficult person. She kept the children in the house with her and never left. She homeschooled them, but I can't imagine what she taught them. They're not used to people. They're not prepared for change."

"What do you want me to do about it?" I asked.

"I want you to take care of them," Madison finally said, the whole reason I'd taken a bus to see her.

"Like a nanny?" I asked. "I don't understand."

"Like a nanny, I guess; okay," Madison said, more to herself than to me. "I thought maybe more like a governess, like more old-fashioned."

"How is it different?" I asked.

"I think it's mostly just the way it sounds. Really, though, you'd handle all aspects of their care. You'd make sure they were happy; you'd teach them so that they can get up to speed with their lessons. You'd monitor their progress. Make sure they exercise. Make sure they stay clean."

"Madison, are they, like, mole people or something? What's wrong with them?" I wanted so badly for something to be wrong with them. I wanted them to be mutants.

"They're just kids. But kids are so fucking wild, Lillian. You have no idea. You don't even know."

"Timothy seems pretty easy," I offered, so dumb.

"That's just pictures," Madison said, suddenly wired. "I've trained him, though. I kind of had to break him in."

"Well, he's cute," I said.

"These kids are cute, too, Lillian," Madison replied.

"What's wrong with them?" I asked again.

Madison hadn't touched her tea during the entire conversation, since we sat down, and now, to buy some time, she drank a whole glass. Finally, she looked at me with great seriousness.

"Here is the thing," she said. "Jasper is up for secretary of state. It's all very hush-hush right now, okay? The other guy is sick and he's going to step down. And some of the president's people have reached out to Jasper to see about him and to start the process of vetting him. It's all happening this summer."

"That's crazy," I said.

"This could lead to big things. Like, vice-president stuff. Or president even, if everything went just right."

"Well, that's cool," I said. I imagined Madison as the first lady of the United States of America. I remembered the time during a basketball game when she elbowed this girl in the throat in order to get a rebound and got kicked out of the game. I smiled.

"So, you see what's going on, right? Jane's dead and these kids are coming to stay with us, right when this is all going down. It's crazy. It's very stressful. Vetting. That's serious shit, Lillian. They look at everything. They already know about the adultery stuff, which they're obviously not thrilled about. But they like Jasper. People like Jasper. I think this might all work out. But these kids. Who knows what their lives have been like? I don't want them to mess this up for Jasper. He would be so angry. God, like super angry."

"You just want me to watch over them and keep them safe?" I asked.

"Make sure they're safe and they don't do anything crazy," she replied, her eyes so bright, so hopeful.

I knew how to keep order. I knew all the ways to make bad things happen and how to avoid them. I was wise to how people tried to ruin you. These kids, they would not beat me.

And I realized that I was already thinking like I had taken the job. I didn't know the first thing about kids, for fuck's sake. I didn't know how to take care of them. What did kids like? What did they eat? What dances were popular with them? I didn't have the slightest idea how to teach children. If I failed spectacularly at this task, that would be the end of things with Madison. I'd never get to visit her in the White House. It'd be like we'd never even met.

"I guess I can do it," I offered, so lame. I made my voice harden. I made my body turn into steel. "I'll do it, Madison. I can do it."

She reached across the sandwiches and hugged me, hard. "I can't tell you how much I need you," she said. "I don't have anyone. I need you."

"Okay," I said. My whole life, maybe I was just biding time until Madison needed me again, until I was called into service and I made everything good. It honestly wasn't a bad life, if that's all it was.

Madison's body, which had been tense and vibrating, re-laxed. I finally felt calm, knew the depth of the situation, saw the bottom and knew I could climb into and out of it without incident. I leaned back into the comfort of this sofa, which held me in just the right position. Then I quickly leaned forward and ate two more sandwiches.

"Lillian?" Madison said.

"What?" I asked.

"There's more, actually," she said, grimacing.

"What?" I asked.

"The kids. Bessie and Roland. There's something I have to tell you about them."

I had a quick flash of what might come. It was sexual, some kind of abuse that had left them hollowed-out shells. That notion transformed into some kind of disability: missing limbs, horrific facial scars. A sensitivity to sunlight, a mouth without any teeth at all. And then it moved to homicidal impulses, kittens drowned in the bathtub, knives at the ready. Of course Madison would wait until I had given myself to her.

"They have a unique—I don't know what to call it—kind of affliction," she began, but I couldn't keep quiet.

"Do they not have any teeth?" I asked, not frightened but merely wanting to get it over with. "Did they kill a kitten?"

"What? No, just . . . just listen to me, okay? They have this affliction where they get really overheated."

"Oh, okay," I said. They were delicate little kids. Didn't like exercise. Fine.

"Their bodies, for some reason that doctors haven't quite nailed down, can quickly rise in temperature. Alarming increases in temperature."

"Okay," I said. There was more. I just spoke to make Madison keep talking.

"They catch on fire," she finally said. "They can—rarely, of course—burst into flames."

"Are you joking?" I asked.

"No! God, of course not, Lillian. Why would I joke about something like this?" she said.

"Well, 'cause I've never heard of anything like this. 'Cause it just seems like a joke."

"Well, it's not a joke. It's a serious condition."

"Jesus, Madison, that's wild," I said.

"I haven't seen it, okay?" she replied. "But Jasper has. I

guess the kids get really hot when they're agitated and they can just catch fire."

I was in shock, but the images felt easy in my brain, honestly. Children made of fire. That seemed like something I wanted to see.

"How are they still alive?" I asked.

"It doesn't hurt them at all," she said, shrugging to highlight how dumbfounded she was. "They just get really red, like a bad sunburn, but they're not hurt."

"What about their clothes?" I asked.

"I'm still figuring this out, Lillian," she said. "I guess their clothes burn off."

"So they're just these naked kids on fire?"

"I think so. So you can understand why we're worried. I mean, Jasper is their father, though I'm fairly certain that this comes from Jane's family. It only started once she was raising them on her own. She was a real handful; I wouldn't be surprised if she was some weird pyromaniac. But Jasper is stepping up. He's going to take care of these kids, but we have to be smart about this. We've got a guesthouse on the property. Well, it used to be something else, but whatever. Jasper spent a fortune to have it renovated and properly safeguarded for the children. That's where you and the kids will live. It's really nice, Lillian. It's beautiful. I'd rather live there than in this huge house, if I'm being honest."

"I'd live with the kids?" I asked.

"Twenty-four hours a day, seven days a week," she said, and she could see on my face that this sucked. "We can arrange for a few days off, to have someone else watch them if you need a break one day. And it's just for the summer, until we can figure out a more permanent solution, okay? Once the vetting is done and the nomination comes through, it'll all be easier."

"This is weird, Madison. You want me to raise your husband's fire children."

"Don't call them 'fire children.' Don't even joke about it. We can't really talk about it. The doctors have been very discreet, thanks to Jasper's connections, and they're not going to say anything, but we have to get a handle on the situation so that we can figure out how to solve this problem."

This was Madison, campaign manager. She looked at the children setting my fucking hair on fire, these naked fire starters, and she saw only a problem that could be solved with a press release or a photo op.

"I just don't know," I said. Those weird cucumber sandwiches were now making my stomach ache something fierce. My teeth hurt from the sweet tea. Where was Carl? Could he drive me back to my mom's house? Would Madison even let me leave?

"Lillian, please. I need you. And I've read your letters, okay? I know your life. Do you really feel like you're giving up much of anything? That friend who stole your television? Your mom making you drive her to some casino in Mississippi? We're going to pay you, okay? A ton of money. And, yeah, it's a lot of work, but Jasper is a powerful person. We can help you. After this is all over, you'll be free of your life and you'll have something better."

"Don't act like you're the one doing me a favor," I said, a little angry.

"No, I know that I'm asking a lot from you. I didn't want any of this, you know? But you're my friend, okay? I'm asking for you to be my friend and help me."

She wasn't wrong. My life sucked. It was bad, and it hurt because I had envisioned a life that was, if not Madison's fate, at least something that could sustain me. Really, truly, I still believed that I was destined for an amazing life. And if I tamed these children, if I cured their weird fire sickness? Wasn't that the start of an amazing life? Wasn't that something that got optioned for a prestigious biopic?

"Okay," I said. "Okay, I'll watch these kids. I'll be their . . . what did you call it?"

"Governess," she said, delighted.

"Yeah, I'll be that."

"I promise you that I will never forget this. Never."

"I'd better get home," I said. "Is Carl gone? Can somebody drive me to the bus station?"

"No," Madison said, shaking her head, standing up. "You aren't going home tonight. You're staying here. You'll spend the night. In fact, you don't have to go home if you don't want to. We're buying you everything you need. All new clothes! The best computer. Whatever you want."

"Okay," I said, so tired all of a sudden.

"What do you want for dinner tonight? Our cook can make anything."

"I don't know," I said. "Maybe pizza or something like that."

"We have a pizza oven!" she said. "The best pizza you've ever had."

We stared at each other. It was three in the afternoon. What did we do until dinner?

"Is Timothy still napping?" I asked, trying to break the awkwardness.

"Oh, yeah, I'd better go check on him. Do you want a drink or anything?"

"Maybe I can take a nap?" I asked.

I barely took note of how huge the house was now that I was able to move through it. We went up a spiral staircase, like in some big-budget musical. Madison was telling me some nonsense about how during the Civil War they took horses up these stairs and hid them in the attic from the Union army. It's possible I imagined this, some kind of fever dream in the aftermath of making a life-altering decision.

She led me to a room that looked like there should be an exiled princess in the bed. Every single piece of furniture seemed like it weighed a thousand pounds. Probably some nineteenth-century carpenter had built the desk right in the room and it had been here ever since. There was a chandelier. I'd lived in apartments that were one-third the size of this single room. I made a mental note that I needed to stop being so awed by Madison's wealth. I was going to live inside this place. Everything that she owned was now mine. I would need to get used to touching it and not being electrocuted.

"Do you need a nightgown?" she asked.

"I'll just sleep in this stuff," I replied.

"Sweet dreams," she said, kissing me on the forehead. She was so tall; I'd forgotten how she'd kiss me on the forehead in high school, how soft her lips were. And then she was gone; the house had swallowed her up. I couldn't even hear footsteps.

It was almost too much to get into the bed. I felt like the dirtiest thing this house had ever seen. I felt like an orphan who had broken in to the mansion. I kicked off my shoes and then delicately lined them up next to the bed. I got onto the bed, which took actual effort, it was so high up. I closed my eyes and willed myself to sleep. I thought about those two kids, on fire, beckoning me with open arms. I watched them burn. They were smiling. I wasn't even asleep. I wasn't dreaming. This was my waking life now. They stood in front of me. And I pulled them into my arms. And I burst into flames.

# Two

I NEVER WENT BACK HOME. I CALLED MY MOM THE NEXT morning to tell her that I was staying in Franklin. I had an elaborate lie cooked up, something about being hired as a paralegal and working on a big class-action lawsuit involving toxic waste, but she didn't even really care. "What do you want me to do with your stuff?" was all she asked.

I didn't really have stuff, nothing that I needed. There were some magazines that I'd stolen from the grocery store, this one T-shirt that I really liked, and a pair of basketball shoes that I'd saved up for six months to buy and wore only when I played pickup games at the YMCA. But Madison had said they'd buy me anything I wanted.

"Just keep it there," I said. "Maybe I'll come get it later."

"You're with Madison?" she asked.

"Yeah, I'm staying with her," I told her.

"She's always been good to you for some reason," she said, like she was dumbfounded by unnecessary kindness.

"Well, you know, I did a good thing for her," I told her, heating up, ready for a fight.

"Ancient history," she said.

"I'm actually going to be a governess," I told her suddenly.

"Okay, then," she said, and she hung up before I could explain what that was.

MADISON WAS DOWNSTAIRS IN THE BREAKFAST NOOK, A smooth leather bench that curved all the way around the table. There was a huge bay window and I could see squirrels hopping around the lawn, scavenging nuts. It took me a second to realize that Timothy was there, holding a sterling silver fork that fit perfectly in his little hand. I tried to remember how old he was. Three? Four? No, three. He was beautiful, but it was a different kind of beauty than what Madison possessed. On Timothy it was unnatural, cartoonish. His eyes were so large that they seemed to take up seventy-five percent of his face, like a collectible figurine in some old lady's house. He was wearing pajamas that were red and patterned with the insignia of the Tennessee state flag.

"Hello," I said to him, but he kept staring at me. He didn't seem shy. He just couldn't figure out whether I was someone he should talk to.

"Say hi to Lillian," Madison finally said. She was eating cottage cheese topped with blueberries.

"Hello," Timothy said, but he immediately turned back to his scrambled eggs. He was done with me.

"Do you want coffee?" Madison asked, like I was one of her children, like this wasn't the first time in years that we'd even seen each other.

I was startled when some lady appeared right behind me, holding a pot of steaming coffee. She was Asian, very small, age indeterminate.

"This is Mary," Madison said.

"I can make anything you want," the woman said, her accent possibly British. Or maybe just so elegant that it felt European. It wasn't Southern, that's all I knew. She wasn't smiling, but maybe she wasn't supposed to smile. I kind of wished she were smiling. It would make it easier to ask her for a giant bacon sandwich.

"Just coffee is fine," I said, and Mary poured me a cup and then returned to the kitchen. I wondered how many people were employed by Jasper Roberts. Was it ten? Or maybe fifty? Or was it a hundred or more? Any of these seemed believable. Just then, as if conjured by my curiosity, a man wearing suspenders and a big floppy hat walked across the backyard; he was holding a rake like a soldier marching with a rifle.

"How many servants do you have?" I asked Madison, who stiffened. I couldn't tell if I was doing this on purpose, trying to make her feel bad about being so filthy rich.

"More than we probably need," she finally said. "But they're not servants. They're employees. It's like running a cruise ship or something like that. It's just that a place this big has a lot of things that have to get done and a lot of people who have specific abilities. But I know all their names. I can keep track of them."

"And now you have me," I said.

"You're not an employee," she said cheerfully. "You're my friend who is helping me out."

I drank the coffee and it was really good, the taste so complex that it made me realize that I was going to have to get rid of my expectations of how things worked. I was used to break-room coffee so thin that I had to dump a pound of sugar into it just to make it taste like something. The pizza we'd eaten the night before had been so fresh that I could taste the tomatoes in the sauce. The crust had been just slightly charred. I was finally, after twenty-eight years, going to experience things the way they had been intended. No more knockoffs.

"What do you have to do today?" I asked Madison, and then I added, "What do *I* have to do today?" which was more important to me.

"You can just relax. You can take a walk and get familiar with the grounds. This afternoon we'll go into Nashville and buy some clothes and necessities. Oh, and Jasper is going to be home this evening; he's flying back from D.C. I wanted him to meet you."

"How often is he around here?" I asked.

"Less than you'd think," she said. "He has a lot of work in Washington; he has an apartment there. But I see him enough; he's big on family, you know."

I didn't know that at all. After all, the whole reason that I was here was to take care of his primitive, as-good-as-orphaned kids. Then I realized that this was just Madison going over talking points. She had a faraway look in her eyes. I knew that, over time, she'd forget herself and I'd learn what was wrong with Senator Roberts. I could wait.

"I'm going to take Timothy to day care and then when I come back, we'll go explore. Sound good?" she offered.

"That's cool," I said. I wanted another cup of coffee but didn't know if it was impolite to go get it myself. Or was it worse to call for Mary just to refill my cup? I knew that whatever I chose would be the wrong thing. I knew that until I truly believed that whatever I did was the exact right thing, I'd keep doing the wrong thing.

"Say goodbye to Lillian," Madison instructed Timothy.

The boy dabbed at his little mouth with a napkin, the most dainty and infuriating thing I'd seen in my life. Only then did he look at me and say, "Goodbye."

"Goodbye, Tim," I said, hoping that the boy would be annoyed by this abbreviating of his name. And already I was fucking up. I needed to get Timothy to like me. Or I needed to learn how to like him. He was practice. Until the twins arrived, he was my one shot to figure out how to talk to, how to behave around, how to tolerate a child.

I tried to think of the times when I had willingly interacted with children. One time, some little kid had gotten lost in the aisles of the Save-A-Lot. I was changing the price on some cereal boxes, and I suddenly noticed her, like a ghost had materialized just for me. She was doing that thing where her eyes were real wide while she put every bit of effort into trying not to cry. I cautiously held out my hand. She took it easily, without question, and we walked in silence through the store until we reached the last aisle and her dumbass fucking mother was standing in the freezer section, looking at Lean Cuisines, no clue her daughter had almost been abducted. Before I could mutter some real passive-aggressive stuff to the mom, the girl simply squeezed my hand so I'd look down at her. Then she kissed the top of my hand, slipped out of my grasp, and ran to her mother, leaving me there. For a few seconds, I wanted to scoop up the girl and keep her. I opened the freezer door to some Popsicles and held my head in the cold until I felt normal again, until the girl and her mom had moved out of sight. I was so out of it that I ended up stealing an entire country ham at the end of my shift just to take my mind off of that girl. For the next few weeks, I kept hoping she'd return, but I never saw her again. Maybe that's what children were, a desperate need that opened you up even if you didn't want it.

I stayed at the table, even after Madison and her son had left the room. I noticed that Madison hadn't eaten much of the cottage cheese, so I reached over and pulled the bowl to me. Just as I took my first bite, Mary reappeared, teleported probably, and was refilling my coffee cup. "I could have made you some food," she said. "You only have to ask."

"Oh, well, I just thought I'd eat this. You know, like, I didn't want it to go to waste."

"Scraps," Mary said. I couldn't tell if Mary was sympathizing with me or making fun of me. If I wasn't sure, I generally just assumed that someone was making fun of me. But I couldn't punch her. Not yet, not until I learned how essential she was to the whole operation. And then I took a sip of that amazing coffee, and I relaxed. *This is luxury,* I told myself. *Don't fuck it up by punching the help and getting your ass kicked out of paradise.*

"Could I have a bacon sandwich?" I asked Mary. She nodded and effortlessly reached around me and removed the bowl of cottage cheese and blueberries.

I took my coffee and walked behind Mary to the kitchen. "I'll bring it to you," she said, looking over her shoulder.

"I'll come with you," I told her. "I feel weird at the table by myself."

She opened a refrigerator that was as big as a car and removed a huge package of bacon. She slapped so many strips in a pan; it must have been a pound. Without ever looking at me, she sliced a loaf of fresh bread and put two pieces in a toaster that looked like both the fifties and the future.

"How long have you been working for Madison?" I asked Mary.

She didn't respond until the toast popped up. "I have worked for Jasper Roberts for eleven years."

"Do you like it?" I asked.

"Do I like work?" she asked, frowning. There was an edge to her, but I understood why. Every time the supermarket hired some new doofus, all I wanted to know was how much extra work I was going to have to do to make up for what they didn't know, how many of their fuckups might blow back on me. But I'd win Mary over. My fuckups affected only me. She'd be safe.

"I mean, is it okay here?"

"It's work. It's fine. Senator Roberts is a nice enough man." She placed the bacon on a paper towel to collect the grease. "What do you want on the bread? Anything?"

"Mayonnaise?" I asked.

When the sandwich was prepared, she placed it on a plate that looked like something you'd use at a wedding, like it would break if you breathed on it. "Can I eat it at the counter?" I asked, and Mary shrugged. Of course, of course, it was the best sandwich I'd ever eaten. I first thought it was just because someone had made it for me, but my mom had made some sorry sandwiches for me in my life, so maybe it was the atmosphere. I tried not to overthink it. "This is so good," I told Mary, who just nodded. I ate it in three bites and then looked at the plate, unsure what to do with it. Mary took it and washed it right in front of me. I let it happen. That's how easy it was, I guess.

"So you were here when Mr. Roberts was married to his second wife?" I asked Mary.

"Yes, of course," she said.

"What were the kids like?" I asked.

"What are kids like?" she replied. "They are kids. Wild."

"Like Timothy?" I asked, and I thought I almost made her smile.

"No, not like Timothy," she said. Her posture relaxed as she tried to explain. "Wild. In a good way. Sweet, wild kids. They would make a mess, but I didn't mind cleaning it up."

"I'm going to take care of them," I said.

"I know," she said, but I wasn't entirely sure that she already knew this. She was good. She'd been doing this awhile.

"Madison is my best friend," I said, so stupid, and Mary knew it was stupid because she didn't dignify it with a response. "Thank you for the sandwich," I said, and she turned in the exact direction of work that was waiting for her.

I walked around the house, checking all the rooms, just getting used to the sensation of my body being inside this mansion, this estate. I tried to guess what each room was for, what distinguished it from another one. The floor of the hallway was marble, and I hated the way it felt on my socked feet, but the rooms all had beautiful hardwood floors with giant rugs from, I don't know, Civil War times. There was a game room, but that wasn't the right word. I remembered the board game Clue: the Billiards Room. There was a pool table in the middle and a pinball game against one wall, a chessboard with two cushy chairs on either side. There was a bar in the corner with all manner of dusty liquors. I reached into one of the pockets of the pool table, removed a ball, and hid it in an empty ice bucket. I pushed the start button on the pinball game, Monster Bash, and it lit right up, no quarters required. I immediately slammed the side of the machine and the word

TILT appeared and the game went dead. I took the white queen from the chessboard and was going to take it with me, but I got sheepish and put it back.

I went back to my own room to get my shoes so I could walk around the grounds. There was a woman in the room, and she was making up the bed. I instantly felt guilty that I hadn't done it after I woke up. "Hey," I said, and she startled, but then relaxed.

"Hello, ma'am," she said.

"Thank you for making up the bed," I told her, but she looked embarrassed. I grabbed my shoes and hustled out of there. I still hadn't brushed my hair or my teeth. I hadn't brought anything with me. I knew that if I asked, a hairbrush would appear, a toothbrush and four different kinds of toothpaste, but I tried to pretend I was self-sufficient. A lot of times when I think I'm being self-sufficient, I'm really just learning to live without the things that I need.

I followed a stone path to the guesthouse, where I'd be living with the kids. It was a two-story wooden house, white with dark red shutters. The door didn't even have a lock on it; I walked right in. The walls were painted with orange and yellow polka dots on a white background. The floors were made of a kind of spongy material, bright blue. There were lots of beanbag chairs, primary school furniture. The whole place felt like *Sesame Street* mixed with a mental health facility. But it wasn't bad. It was clean, like someone had designed a scientific experiment, but inviting enough that I could live in it. There was so much space that I thought I'd have places to hide when I felt like strangling the kids.

When I looked up, I saw an unbelievably complicated sprinkler system and blinking red lights from smoke detectors. I wondered if the house had been stuffed full of asbestos. How did one prepare a house for the possibility of fire children?

"Do you like it?" someone behind me suddenly said.

"Fuck!" I shouted, whirling around, my leg involuntarily doing this little judo kick. Carl was standing there, his arms crossed. He wasn't even looking at me; he was staring at the sprinkler system.

"I'm sorry," he said, but he actually didn't seem all that sorry. It felt like this had been a test, to see how badly I could be scared. I had pegged Carl as a cop, but now I reconsidered. He seemed like one of those faceless suits in sunglasses who tracks down E.T. He was the bad guy in an eighties movie.

"You scared the shit out of me," I told him.

"The door was open," he said. "I was just checking it out."

"This is where I'm going to live," I said.

"Yes, for now," he said. "And Mrs. Roberts has informed you of the situation?"

I stared at him because it felt good to make him work for it.

"The children?" he finally said. "Their . . . situation?"

"They catch on fire," I said. "I know."

"May I ask you something, Ms. Breaker?"

"What is it?" I asked.

"Do you have any experience with childcare? Do you have medical training? Do you have a degree in child psychology?"

"I can take care of two kids," I told him.

"I'm not trying to be rude. For instance, do you know CPR?"

"Jesus, Carl, yes, I know CPR," I said. "I have a certificate, even. I'm certified. I can bring the kids back to life." Two years ago, an old lady had died in the produce section while I knelt over her, waiting for the ambulance. After that, the owner of the store made everyone get trained in CPR and first aid.

"Okay, that's good," he said, smiling.

"I took a class in fire safety, too," I said. "I know how to use a fire extinguisher."

"On a child?" he asked.

"If they're on fire," I told him.

He walked over to the kitchen and opened the door to what I thought was a pantry. Instead, it was filled top to bottom with gleaming red fire extinguishers. "Well, then I guess you'll be fine."

"Carl?" I said.

"Yes?" he replied.

"Do you think I came up with this idea? Do you think I scammed Madison into giving me a job taking care of these weird fucking kids?"

"No, not at all. I think Senator Roberts and Mrs. Roberts have been placed in an unusual situation. I think they are doing the best that they can; they are trying to be responsible and empathetic, considering the circumstances. And I think you are simply a part of that larger desire to help these children. But I do not think this is the correct response. I think this is going to be a disaster."

"They're just kids," I said.

"I'm here to assist in any way that I can," he told me. "Think of me as someone who can help you when you run into unforeseen problems."

Just then, Madison appeared in the doorway. "Don't you love it?" she asked me. "The polka dots?"

Carl somehow found a way to stand even straighter than he had been, like his bones locked into some unknown posture that not even soldiers could achieve.

I nodded, looking around the house. "Carl," I said, "what do you think of the polka dots? Do you love it?"

He smiled. "It's very appropriate for children," he finally said. "Very . . . festive."

"Carl likes it," I said to Madison.

"We need to get you some clothes," Madison said to me. "Let's go shopping."

"Sounds good," I said, and she linked arms with me and we left Carl standing there, like it was his birthday and not one person had dreamed of coming to his party.

"He creeps me out a little, Madison," I told her as we walked to the garage.

"I guess that's kind of his job?" she replied. "Like, he makes people uncomfortable or super comfortable, based on the situation."

"I don't think he likes me," I said.

"Well, I'm not sure that he even likes me," she told me. "Who cares?"

WE DROVE IN MADISON'S BMW TO NASHVILLE, TO A MALL where one of the anchors was a Billings Department Store, the *B* on the building all huge and fancy, the letters golden. She reached into her purse and produced a gold credit card from the store, something her father must have given her. "Everything is free here," she said, "so get whatever you want."

There wasn't much that I wanted. Everything was so delicate and sparkly; I tried on a pair of satin pants and wanted to kill myself. "Madison," I said, "I'm taking care of kids. I'm a nanny. I don't need stuff for dinner parties."

"You never know what you might need," she said. She picked out a bright green dress, strapless, and held it up to me like I was a doll that she was dressing.

"I don't have enough boobs to hold that dress up," I said. I had no boobs at all, which I'd appreciated when I was growing up, and then in high school I got sad about it, and then I stopped caring again.

"I'm buying it for you," she said. "One fancy thing. That's it. Now you can get whatever you want."

I bought six pairs of pretty amazing Calvin Klein jeans in various states of distress and a bunch of T-shirts, stuff that looked comfortable without being trashy. Stuff that, if it caught on fire, it wouldn't be the end of the world. I bought some tracksuits that were meant for either much older or much younger people, but I loved them, green and silver rayon like I was an assassin. I bought four pairs of Chuck Taylors and a really expensive pair of Nike basketball shoes. I got some underwear and bras, a bathing suit like Olympic athletes wore, and a cool bucket hat to keep the sun out of my eyes. I felt like some mermaid who had suddenly grown legs and was now living among the humans.

Madison found some dude with slicked-back hair who was wearing a crummy suit to follow us around and we weighed him down with stuff. When he couldn't hold it any longer, he took it back to a register and added it to the total. When I wasn't looking, Madison picked out some heels and a pantsuit and even some pretty sexy lingerie. I didn't stop her. I'd take everything. She bought me some perfume called Sense and

Sensibility that was in a bottle that looked so much like a dick that I thought it was a joke.

When we were done, she sent me into the mall, to the food court, because I think she didn't want me to see how much it all cost. Not that I would have cared. Or maybe I would have, Madison so tall and perfect, handing him that gold card, me in my dirty clothes like some orphan. I guess I'd never know how it felt, because not too long after, Madison was standing there, all the clothes already stuffed into the trunk of her BMW, ready to take me back to my new home.

"Tell me about Jasper," I asked her, turning off the Emmylou Harris CD that was making me crazy, her voice too good to concentrate.

"What do you want me to tell you about him?" she replied. She was barely touching the steering wheel, the car just doing whatever she wanted based solely on her desire.

"What's he like?" I asked. "No, I mean, I guess I want to know if you love him."

"You think I don't love my husband?" she said, smiling.

"Well, do you?" I asked, genuinely curious.

"I guess I love him," she finally said. "He's the perfect man for me because he's very responsible and he treats me like an equal and he's got his own interests and he lets me do whatever I want."

"But what's he like? What do you like about him on a personal level?" I asked, not willing to give up. I thought about my mom's boyfriends, thousands of them, and how each one had been a mystery to me, why my mom thought he added anything to her life. I thought about my own boyfriends, the way I mostly wanted them to just be in the same room with me, the way I didn't expect anything from them. I thought about

Senator Roberts. The pictures of him that I'd seen made him look handsome enough, silver hair and ice-blue eyes, but old enough that I would have left him for dead.

"He's intense. He's not Southern in the way that makes you embarrassed. You know, at Vanderbilt, there was a kind of boy who wore pastel shorts and boat shoes. They wore seersucker, like they were racist lawyers from the forties. I hated them. They seemed like children but they already looked like middle-aged men. I called them Mint Julep Boys, like they missed the Old South because, even if there was horrible racism, it was worth it if it meant that they could be important by default."

"It sounds like you're describing your brothers," I said. Madison sometimes wrote about them, all of them bankers or CEOs. She always said that nothing she did was ever treated by her parents with the same enthusiasm as her brothers' accomplishments, even though the brothers were functioning alcoholics, all divorced and remarried.

"Yeah, like my brothers. Mint Julep Boys, like they would drink a mint julep on a regular day and they wouldn't think it was weird. I don't know. I'm rambling. I'm not talking about Jasper. I don't know how to describe him. He's quiet and principled and he's intense. He understands people and that makes him slightly impatient with them, like they're too stupid to protect themselves, so he has to do it for them. He's not funny, but he has a good sense of humor."

"Why did you marry him?" I asked.

"Because he wanted to marry me," she said. "He wanted me, and he was older and experienced, and I liked that he'd already fucked up with the heiress and leaving his family. I liked that he was flawed but still principled. I guess that was important to me."

"I'm scared to meet him," I admitted.

"I'm a little scared for you to meet him," she said. "I hope you don't hate him."

I didn't say anything because I was pretty sure that, just on principle, I was going to hate him. I didn't like men all that much, found them tiring. But I was willing to give him a chance. I was open to new things, I guessed. If it meant living in that house, I could handle talking to the senator every once in a while. I mean, his job required him to serve my interests, since I was a resident of his state. I didn't vote, but he didn't have to know that.

WHILE MADISON WENT TO PICK UP TIMOTHY FROM DAY CARE, I showered and then changed into new clothes, leaving my old ratty stuff in a hamper that I knew would be spirited away when I wasn't looking, my clothes laundered and folded and then returned with maybe even a ribbon tied around them. I put on some of the perfume Madison had picked out for me, which smelled like old silver and honeysuckle. When I finally went downstairs, I saw Timothy standing there, no sign of any adults. "Where's your mom?" I asked, and he simply turned away and started walking down the hallway. I followed him, and we ended up in his room, which I hadn't seen earlier that day. His bed was bigger than any bed I'd ever owned, so fluffy that I wondered how he didn't suffocate instantly when he got into it. "So this is your room?" I asked him.

"Yes," he said. "Do you want to see my stuffed animals?"

"I mean, I guess," I said. "Sure."

There was a big chest and, with some effort, he lifted the lid. And then, like clowns from a VW Bug, out came so many stuffed animals that I felt like I'd dropped acid. Timothy pulled out a red fox with a bow tie. "This is Geoffrey," he said, no emotion on his face.

"Hello, Geoffrey," I said.

He pulled out an elephant with a thick pair of black eye-glasses. "This is Bartholomew."

"Oh, okay; hi, Bartholomew."

He pulled out a frog with a crown on its head. "This is Calvin," he said, presenting him to me.

"Are you sure his name's not Froggy?" I asked.

"It's Calvin," he said.

"Well, jeez; hey, Calvin."

There was a teddy bear with a pink dress on. "This is Emily," he said.

"Are these from some TV show or something?" I asked, trying desperately to understand this boy.

"No. They're just for me."

"What do you do with them?" I asked.

"I line them up."

"Is that it? You just line them up?"

"Then I pick the best one," he said.

When I was six years old, I used my birthday money to buy this giant box filled with action figures for boys at a yard sale. Barbies were too expensive, and so I played with these guys, all decked out in camo, interesting facial hair. I just made them stand-ins for the people in my town, and I worked my way through imaginary scenes about the life I wished I had. My figure was a doll of the Fonz from *Happy Days,* his plastic hands formed into thumbs-up signs. And my mom was this bearded dude with muscles and a denim vest and shorts.

One time, I was playing in my room and the mom doll said, "Lil, the mayor's cat is missing," and then my doll said,

"C'mon, Mom, the Breaker Detective Agency is ON IT!" and I heard my mom's actual voice say, "What are you doing?"

I looked up and my mom was standing in the doorway, staring at me.

"The mayor's cat is missing?" I said, confused.

"Is that supposed to be you?" she asked, pointing to the Fonz. I nodded.

"And that's me?" she asked, pointing to the Big Josh doll. I nodded again, but now I felt like maybe I'd done something wrong.

My mom looked at me with this strange expression, and now, thinking back, I feel like this was the exact moment when she realized that I wasn't her, that I was a mystery to her and maybe always would be. I could see this flash in her eyes. And she said, kind of dumbfounded, "God, Lil, what's in that head?" And she walked off. And I felt like a freak, even though what I was doing, pretending, was what all kids did. But my mom had no use for pretending. I think she thought it was stupid, was a kind of weakness. From that point on, I guess I sort of realized that my imagination, which made life tolerable, needed to be kept a secret from the rest of the world. But if you keep something hidden away, all tied up, it's hard to summon it when you really need it.

And, so, maybe I understood Timothy a little. Or maybe I was jealous of him. "Can I play, too?" I asked him. He nodded and produced twelve more stuffed animals, lining them up along the floor.

"Okay, so I just pick the best one?" I asked.

"It has to be the best one," he said.

There was a panda bear with a little guitar stitched to his paw. "I think this one."

Timothy's eyes kind of flashed with recognition, as if the seventeenth-century ghost who lived inside him had suddenly awakened.

"That's Bruce," he said, and I laughed a little at the name, so ridiculous for a stuffed animal.

"Is he the best one?" I asked.

He looked at the others, took his time. Finally, he said, "Today, Bruce is the best one." He handed the panda over to me and I hugged it. It smelled so good, so clean.

While I held Bruce, Timothy gathered up the other stuffed animals and then put them away. He seemed pleased. I felt like I'd passed a test. Timothy touched my head, and I resisted the urge to swat his hand away.

"You're good," he said, and he smiled a little. Just then, Madison showed up. "Oh, are you two playing?" she asked.

"Kind of," I said.

"Did you pick Bruce?" she asked.

"I did. He's the best one," I told her.

"The best one *today*," Timothy clarified.

"Daddy's home!" Madison suddenly said, and Timothy started to vibrate with, what, happiness? Excitement? Fear? "Daddy," he said, now smiling, and he stumbled out of the room.

"Jasper's here," Madison said to me.

"Yikes," I said. "Okay."

I walked as close to Madison as I could without it being a three-legged race, and we found Timothy lifted into the air by Senator Roberts. There was genuine happiness on the man's face, and this softened me temporarily, which was exactly what I needed to get through this moment.

"Daddy's here!" Timothy said, and I could see the pride radiating off of his tiny body.

"I'm here," Jasper said, not smiling, but not frowning.

Senator Roberts was tall, just enough to make him seem important. His hair was silver, not gray, like he was the emperor of some distant, icy planet. And his eyes were so blue, just beautiful. He was a handsome man. He wore a beige suit that fit him perfectly, a light blue tie with a silver donkey tie clip. He looked a little weary, like being important was a Herculean task. If any aspect of his appearance had been off by even a few degrees, he would have seemed evil. But he had the ratio perfect. I wouldn't have married him, even with his money, but I understood why Madison would.

"Honey," Madison said once Timothy had received his father's full attention, "this is Lillian."

He kept holding on to Timothy, who had hidden his face against Jasper's chest. "Hello, Lillian," he said.

"Senator Roberts," I said.

"Oh, Jasper, please," he said, though he looked pleased at the formality.

"It's nice to meet you, Jasper," I then said.

"You are almost mythical in this house," he said, his voice so measured, so hypnotic, the right amount of Southern accent. It wasn't Foghorn Leghorn and it wasn't a newscaster in Atlanta. It was lyrical and honeyed and entirely natural. It sounded nice. "Madison thinks the world of you," he continued.

"Oh, okay," I said, embarrassed. What would Madison have told him? Did he know about the fact that I'd kept Madison from being kicked out of a fancy boarding school? Was it better or worse if she'd told him?

"We are so happy to have you here," he said; he didn't blink. I didn't know if this was something necessary for a politician, if blinking was a sign of weakness or something. As a result, I began blinking so much that I almost started crying.

"I'm happy to be here," I finally said, like I was in a play and I'd finally remembered my next line.

"Dinner?" Jasper then said, not to anyone in particular, like a magic spell. I knew that when we walked into the dining room, there would be food that had not been there before Jasper said that single word.

"Yes!" Madison said. "Are you hungry?"

"I am," he said, still not smiling. Maybe he was thinking about his fire children. Maybe he was thinking about me, this strange woman, taking up space in his house. Or maybe he was just thinking about the steps necessary for him to become the president. The point was, I didn't know what he was thinking, and that made me nervous.

"Are you hungry, Lillian?" Madison asked, and I wondered what would happen if I said no. Sometimes I didn't eat dinner until one or two in the morning. It was six o'clock in the evening. If I said no, would everyone go to their room and wait until I was ready? It wasn't worth finding out. I was actually pretty damn hungry.

"Yeah, I'm hungry, too," I finally said, and we all walked into the dining room. I marveled at how easily I had been absorbed into the rhythm of this family's life. It didn't feel natural, but it also didn't feel like I was expending all my energy trying to make it work. It made me think that wealth, as of course I already knew without firsthand experience, could normalize just about anything.

It made me think that these two children who were coming over the horizon like twin suns would not do a thing to this place, that they would be purified. I didn't think about it then, but later I remembered that these kids had already been in this very house, had called it home, but had been expelled. I didn't know what the lesson was. I didn't think about it.

After dinner, which Mary had prepared—angel hair pasta with olive oil and lemon chicken, bread that cracked open like a geode, icy-cold wine, and some kind of spongy cake spiked with alcohol—we all went outside, the sun still out, a perfect evening. Madison wanted to show me something, and we walked through the grass, which honest-to-god squeaked under my feet, until we reached a basketball court, the surface shiny onyx asphalt and the lines painted in sparkling white, regulation. Madison flicked a switch and lights crackled to life and illuminated the court.

"Oh my god," I said, unable to really take it in.

"It used to be boring tennis courts," Madison said, "but I had it converted."

"It's beautiful," I said. Honestly, it was more impressive than the mansion.

"Basketball isn't really a refined pastime," Madison said, frowning. "No one ever wants to play."

"I do," I said. "I want to play."

Jasper, as if this had all been planned in advance, took Timothy by the hand and led him to a modest set of bleachers. Madison went to a waterproof chest and produced a ball that looked like it had never once been bounced. She flicked a pass to me, and I caught it and then dribbled it three times and sent up a lazy jumper that, thank god, fell right through the hoop, with that sexy sound the net made when you'd hit it just right. If I'd missed that shot, I think I would have cried.

Madison caught the ball before it hit the ground and then

posted up against an imaginary defender, spun to her left, and executed an old-school hook shot that banked into the hoop.

"Do you play a lot?" I asked. If I had this court at my disposal, I'd sleep on top of the rim.

"Not as much as I'd like. You know, it's boring to just shoot free throws. I miss five-on-five."

"You can't just get your employees to play?" I asked. Why did you need a gardener, I wondered; why not hire the Washington Generals to live in the guesthouse?

"They wouldn't be able to hang with me," she said. She wasn't being arrogant. It was probably true. Iron Mountain had won state in her junior and senior years, and she'd been All-State both times. She'd played at Vanderbilt. She hadn't started, but I knew how good you had to be to ride the bench on an SEC team.

And I knew that she was happy to have me here. I'd been All-State my senior year, though it was mostly because our team was so crappy that I had to do everything on my own, which drove my stats through the roof. We didn't even make it out of the region. I could never decide if I was happy or sad that my high school and Iron Mountain were in different classes, that I'd never get a chance to drive on Madison and see what she'd do to stop me.

But we didn't play one-on-one that night. We just shot, hypnotized by the sound of the ball smacking against the asphalt. I felt my muscles loosen up, and I found my rhythm. I couldn't miss. And Madison even stepped back and hit three after three. When I was a kid, I'd been so angry that I was a girl and couldn't dunk, but this was so much better. You found your spot, lined it up, and knocked it down. The rim had a nice amount of play in it, a playground assist, and we shot for about forty-five minutes. The sun was going down, and Timothy shouted when fireflies started blinking around us. I drove to the bucket and hit a layup, and then Madison put the ball away. Timothy held his hands in front of him, awkwardly trying to catch a firefly, and then Jasper gently snatched one out of the air and let it rest on his open palm. We all gathered around him and watched as the bug seemed to be breathing, the glow emanating from inside it once, twice, and then it flew away.

"Bath time," Madison finally said, and I thought she meant me, but then I saw Timothy nod and start walking back to the mansion. Madison took his hand in hers, and then Jasper touched my right elbow and I froze.

"I appreciate what you're doing for us," he said.

"It's no big deal," I said. I had no idea what I was doing. Until I knew how hard it was going to be, I didn't want his gratitude.

"My children . . ." he said, but then seemed to let the thought drift away. "I've always tried to be a good man," he finally said, finding a new way to say what he wanted to say. "But I haven't always been successful. Madison has helped me find the way to something true. I'm lucky to have her."

"Okay," I said.

"I made too many mistakes with my kids, with Roland and Bessie. I let them get away from me. I lost sight of them. And that's my fault. Whatever happened while they were with Jane, it's still my fault. But I hope you understand that I'm trying to make it right."

He looked like every word slightly pained him, and I wasn't sure how to make it easier for him. I didn't actually want it to be easy for him.

"I know this is asking a lot of you," Jasper said. "I know

you're only doing this because you care for Madison, but I want you to know how much it means to me to have you here."

I understood that he wasn't hitting on me. I could tell he wasn't interested in me romantically, and that calmed me. "Madison says that someday you might be president," I said.

Jasper got a funny look on his face, like Madison amused him more often than not. "Well," he said, "it's a possibility, yes."

"President Jasper Roberts," I offered.

"Well, not anytime soon. There are more important things to think about right now," he said.

He simply started walking to the house, and I let him get twenty yards away from me before I followed him. I watched him, his posture slightly crooked. He looked like he had no idea how anything in his life had fallen out the way that it had. I felt the same way.

# Three

WE WERE HUMMING DOWN THE HIGHWAY IN A WHITE FIFTEEN-passenger van with the last two rows of seats removed and an air mattress slapped down in the back. To make it more inviting, there were Charlie Brown bedsheets and two stuffed animals, identical Smokey hound dogs. At the moment, it was just Carl and me, the unhappiest couple in the history of the world, on our way to pick up the children, Roland and Bessie.

I don't know why, but I had just assumed that the kids would one day appear at the estate, maybe stuffed inside a giant wooden crate, packing peanuts pressed against their rickety bodies. I thought I'd just take them in my arms and place them in our new home like dolls in a dollhouse. But no, we had to go on a road trip, six fucking hours round-trip, and Carl made it seem like we'd have to tie them up, pull them screaming from the crawl space of some bombed-out building, a kind of kidnapping. "These children are not used to transitions," he said. "They're already dealing with the death of their mother. From what I understand from their grandparents, they've been . . . agitated."

"Well, then maybe the police should get them," I offered. I hated the way I always tried to get out of hard work, but, Jesus, hard work sucked. I'd been sleeping on a feather bed and drinking chamomile tea. I wasn't up for snatching some feral kids.

"No police," he said. "That's not what we need right now. This all needs to be private, a personal matter. We don't want social services or hospitals or police. It's just you and me. It's an easy enough task."

"What does Madison say?" I asked him, hoping to gain a reprieve.

"This is what you're being paid to do," he said, exasperated. "You're to care for these children. So you're coming with me to get them. Once they're here, you can do whatever you think is necessary to keep them safe and happy."

"What should I wear?" I said. I was still in my pajamas, drinking coffee and reading the *New York Times* while Mary fried some eggs for me. It was already ten thirty in the morning. It made more sense to go early the next day.

"Just wear normal clothes," Carl said. I appreciated that he no longer tried to hide his impatience with me. It meant that I didn't have to hide my irritation with him.

"Okay, okay. Chill out," I told him. "After I eat my eggs, we'll leave."

"I have some granola bars and a thermos of coffee. We need to get going. I already let you sleep in," he said.

"Mary is already making the eggs," I said. "I don't want to waste them."

Carl sat down on the bench next to me and leaned forward, whispering, "Do you think Mary cares if you don't eat those eggs? Do you think you would hurt her feelings?"

"You're too close to me," I told him, and he seemed to suddenly realize how threatening he might seem to me, that my fucking with him had made him overplay his authority. He got all stiff and embarrassed, and he stood back up.

"I'll be waiting in the van," he said. "Meet me in ten minutes."

"Should we sync our watches?" I asked, but I don't think he heard me because he was already in the hallway. I stood up and went over to the kitchen counter. Mary, not saying a single word, set a plate of fried eggs in front of me, and I ate them so quickly it was like they hadn't ever existed. "Thank you, Mary," I said, and she nodded.

"Safe travels," she said, and she allowed just the slightest musicality into her normally monotone voice. I loved how expertly bitchy she was; I wanted to study her for a year.

Now we were almost to the vacation home where Jane's mother and father were keeping the children out of sight. From what Carl told me, the Cunningham family had long been a political force in East Tennessee, but not long after Jane's marriage to Jasper, her father, Richard Cunningham, had been implicated in some complicated Ponzi scheme and pretty much lost the entire family fortune in litigation. Jasper had kept him out of jail, but the Cunninghams were ruined. Undeterred, Richard sold blue-green algae door-to-door, some kind of superfood that sounded like its own kind of Ponzi scheme. But they still had this vacation home near the Smoky Mountains, which was where they were watching over the children. Carl indicated that all they did was sit around while the kids splashed in the pool for hours at a time, occasionally calling them inside to eat fish sticks. I figured that, for their discretion, Jasper was going to pay them a tidy sum. There was an entire industry that had sprung up around these children.

As Carl tried to navigate the unmarked back roads, I grew antsy. "Were you in the military, Carl?" I asked him.

He turned his head, his sunglasses reflecting my image right back at me. He stopped at an empty four-way intersection and actually waited five seconds before continuing. He was probably in his late forties, lean but not handsome, his nose too big and his hair thinning. He was short, too, but there was an intensity about him that made up for it, the way he accepted his ugliness, which was a kind of virtue. "No," he finally said, "I'm not military."

"Did you used to be a cop?" I asked.

"No," he said.

"Well, what did you do before you worked for Jasper Roberts?" I asked, not willing to give up until I understood this man a little better.

"Different things," he said. "I worked for a newspaper as a junior reporter, and then I sold insurance, and then I got a license to be a private investigator. I was good at it, discreet, and I started running in political circles. And I did some work for Jasper, looked into the life of someone of interest to him, and I did a good job, I guess. He hired me to work for him full-time."

"Do you like working for him?" I asked.

"It's better than running down deadbeat dads," he said. "I grew up in a rough place. Sometimes I feel so far away from there that it seems like I must have done the right thing."

"I grew up in a rough place, too," I said, suddenly feeling tenderness for Carl, shocked that he had actually confided in me. I knew that we were nothing alike. He was too buttoned-up, too afraid to fuck up. I'm sure he thought I was a disaster waiting to happen, a problem that he was going to have to constantly manage. But for a moment, I could see him. He was good at his job, even if that job probably sucked. He handled things. You could depend on him.

"Oh, I know *all* about you," he said, and then he turned back into a starched suit, the way he tensed his jaw. So, okay, we wouldn't be best friends after all. Fine with me. "Where the fuck is this house?" he said, looking around, and he made a quick U-turn.

We finally pulled up to a cabin with all kinds of strange windows, the shape of it a triangle, and the front door was wide open. "Oh, Jesus," Carl said, removing his sunglasses and pinching the bridge of his nose.

"Do I just stay here in the van?" I asked, like, *Please just let me stay in the van.* Carl got out, opened the side door, and retrieved a cooler that was stocked with bottles of what looked like Kool-Aid and bars of Hershey's chocolate. I was kind of upset that all I'd had the whole trip were some dusty granola bars and weak coffee when there was this cache of sugar.

"This juice is laced with a sedative," he said. "It'll make things easier if we can get them to drink at least one of them on the drive home."

"We're gonna drug them?" I asked.

"Don't start, please," Carl said. "We're sedating them. Mildly. They are in a fragile state."

"Then why didn't Jasper come get them? I mean, he's their dad. That would calm them down."

"I don't know that it would," Carl admitted. "And Senator Roberts has work in D.C. right now. This is our job. You and me."

"Well, I don't want to drug them," I said. "That seems bogus."

"Have it your way," he said. "Let's go."

We walked into the cabin, which was dark, not a single light on, but we could see activity in the backyard. The sofa, some flowery abomination with plastic covering it, was burned black on one side, the ceiling above it dusted with soot. Carl slid open the glass door, and we saw Mr. Cunningham in a tiny swimsuit and some flip-flops, cooking a steak on a rickety old charcoal grill. His wife was dead asleep in a lawn chair.

"Carl!" Mr. Cunningham said. He was in his seventies, but he had curly gray hair like a wig. He looked like he was in the process of melting, his skin sunburned and sagging everywhere, hanging in folds. He had a huge dimple in his chin.

"What're you doing there, Mr. Cunningham?" Carl asked, adopting a very friendly tone.

"Living the life!" Mr. Cunningham said. "Cooking a steak."

"Looks good," Carl replied.

"Well, a man can't live entirely on blue-green algae, Carl," Mr. Cunningham continued. "Steak is a kind of superfood, I suppose."

"The kids in the pool?" Carl asked.

"Been there since this morning," he told us. "They like the water. Jane, you know, couldn't swim. But she made sure the kids knew how. That's the kind of mom that she was, giving her kids what she didn't have."

"She was an amazing woman," Carl replied.

"If Jasper hadn't fucked everything up . . ." But then Mr. Cunningham simply looked at his steak, which was sizzling, popping, just a single steak on the grill.

"He's going to take care of these kids," Carl reassured the man, but Mr. Cunningham wasn't listening.

"You have a check for me?" Mr. Cunningham finally asked. Carl handed him a cashier's check and then looked over at Mrs. Cunningham. "Would she like to say goodbye to the kids?" he asked.

"Let her sleep," Mr. Cunningham said.

"Is their stuff packed up?" Carl asked.

"It was the kids' responsibility," Mr. Cunningham said. "I don't think they ever did it. They're not entirely reasonable children."

Carl looked disgusted, but he simply nodded. "Okay," he told me, "I'm going to get their stuff together. You wait here with Mr. Cunningham and then we'll get the kids and head home."

"I kind of want to go see them," I said.

"Well, just wait a few minutes like an adult and then you can meet them," Carl said, and then he was off.

Mr. Cunningham didn't even seem to notice me. I don't know who he thought I was. "What does blue-green algae do for you?" I asked him.

He wouldn't look at me, but he replied, "Everything, dear."

We sat in silence for a few minutes, his wife snoring, and then I said, "I'm just going to go say hi to the kids." I needed time apart from Carl, so the kids would understand that I wasn't some narc, so I could hypnotize them with my own weirdness.

"Suit yourself," he said.

As I walked to the edge of the pool, I realized that the sounds of splashing had stopped. The kids, their faces obscured by giant goggles, were standing in the shallow end, the water lapping against them. It looked like they were staring at me, but with the goggles it was hard to tell. It was a little spooky, truthfully. I was working up this Mary Poppins kind of attitude, and the goggles were throwing me off.

"Hey, guys," I said, kind of casual cool, the tone where you act like you already know somebody so they'll be curious. "Bessie and Roland, right?"

In agonizing slow motion, the two of them began to slip beneath the surface of the water. They didn't swim away, just sat there, holding their breath, while I stood over them, my arms hanging at my sides. I didn't feel anything like Mary Poppins, that bitch. I needed a prop, some magic umbrella that played music or something. I wasn't counting, but it felt like they were under there for a good minute or so before they both stood back up, as if they thought I'd left.

"Bessie and Roland, right?" I asked, like maybe they just hadn't heard me.

"Who are you?" Bessie asked.

"Can you take those masks off?" I asked them. "I want to see what you look like."

"We're ugly," Bessie said.

"I doubt that," I said, but it was probably true.

"Our eyes get red in this chlorine," Bessie said. "Pop-Pop just dumps in these chemicals. He doesn't measure them or anything."

"Do you wanna come out?" I asked. I figured I had a few more minutes before Carl came back with their stuff and fucked everything up. As a kid, I'd had a lot of experience getting alley cats to trust me. I didn't do much with their trust, just gave them some scraps of food and light petting; it was all about getting them to come to me. I thought kids weren't much different from cats.

"We're not leaving this pool," Bessie said. She had on a black T-shirt and some swim trunks. Her haircut was severe, kind of like a bowl cut if you didn't have the bowl to make it uniform. She was sunburned, but not painfully. Her brother was crouched a little behind her, hiding from me. I figured if I could get Bessie on my side, Roland would come along.

"We have a pool at our place," I told them. "Bigger than this one."

"Does it have a slide?" Bessie asked, suddenly curious.

"Two slides," I lied.

"Do you have flippers?" she asked, Roland nudging her. "Pop-Pop says no flippers."

"I'll buy you flippers," I said.

"You want us to come with you?" Bessie asked.

"Yeah. Come see our place. It's a nice place. I think you'll like it. I like it," I said. Now I was kneeling at the edge of the pool. I put my fingers in the water and felt how warm it was.

"You're going to take care of us?" Bessie asked me. With each question she moved a little closer, leaving Roland out there by himself.

"If that's okay with you," I said.

"It sounds okay," Bessie said, trying not to sound too excited. "Two slides?"

"Two of them," I said, smiling. Bessie took off her goggles, and Roland did the same. They had crazy green eyes, emerald and shiny; even in the sun I could see them. Without the goggles, I could figure out their faces. I was a little surprised by how round they were. I had expected fire children to be thin and lanky, the fire burning all the weight off of them, but these kids still had baby fat. They looked like kids who hadn't been taken care of, a little wobbly and weird. But here came Bessie, right to the edge of the pool, wading over to me.

"Where are you going to take us?" she asked.

"Somewhere great," I said.

"Is our dad going to be there?" she asked.

"Sometimes," I said, wondering if that was the wrong thing to say.

"Help me out," she said, holding out her arms like a baby. I leaned forward to reach for her, and she slightly altered her posture. I watched her whole body turn electric and wild, and she grabbed my right arm by the wrist and pulled my entire hand into her mouth. She bit down so hard on my hand that I screamed with such force that the sound just disappeared, the kind of pain where time stops. I looked at Bessie, my hand still wriggling around in her mouth, and she looked like she was smiling.

I fell into the pool and Bessie held my head under the water, yanking my hair, scratching like crazy at my face. The alley cats from my youth had nothing on this wild, psychotic kid. I popped my head up and heard Bessie scream, "Run, Roland!" and I saw his form hop out of the water like he'd been shot from a cannon. He was running for the fence, but I was back under the water, Bessie's claws digging into the skin in the corner of my right eye, ripping at my cheek. I tried to grab her, to get some purchase on her squirmy body, slick from weeks in the pool, and she bit me again, and I felt like her tooth had cracked on my knuckle. I made it back to the surface, and I could see blood spinning in the water, riding the chlorine.

"Shit, Roland! Get out of here," she cried out, and I heard Carl screaming, "What the fuck is going on?" I had swallowed so much water, but I finally managed to get my arms around Bessie's waist, her legs kicking out in front of her while I held on from behind. She was scratching at my interlocked fingers, but I wasn't going to let go.

"Bessie, for fuck's sake. I'm going to be your best friend," I said, and I sounded so puny and whiny and like a fucking jerk. I hated myself.

And then, suddenly, I realized how hot Bessie was, even in the water, the heat rising up and reddening her skin, turning it almost purple. There was so much steam coming off of her. I panicked, I guess, and so I pulled her under the surface of the water. I counted to fifteen, then thirty, felt the heat recede from her skin, hoping I hadn't killed her. I lifted her up, carrying her to the steps. She went a little limp in my arms, had given up. "Where's Roland?" she asked. "Did he get away?"

I sat on the stairs, still holding her, and we looked over at Roland, who had tried to hop the fence and gotten snagged by his swim trunks, his pale white butt showing while he hung upside down, Carl muttering bullshit as he tried to free the fabric from the fencing.

"I'm not coming with you!" Bessie shouted, and she found some hidden strength inside her, pulled free of my arms, and started to run for the house. I grabbed her ankle and she fell, hard, skinning her knee. Her shirt started smoking, the fabric singeing along the neckline, but it was soaking wet and couldn't really catch fire. I realized there were delicate waves of yellow flame moving up and down Bessie's little arms. And then, like a crack of lightning, she burst fully into flames, her body a kind of firework, the fire white and blue and red all at once. It was beautiful, no lie, to watch a person burn.

I heard Carl shout, and I turned to see Roland now on fire, though not as bright as his sister. Carl simply kicked him into the pool, where he fell like a rock, extinguished.

I saw Mr. Cunningham holding a giant fork out for safety. Mrs. Cunningham was still asleep.

"You want to stay here?" I shouted back at Bessie. My hand was hurting so bad, the kind of pain where I didn't even want to look at it because I knew how fucking angry it would make me, how many times I would time-travel to think about all the ways I could have kept my finger from being bitten off by some feral child. "You want to stay with those old people who are boring and probably don't even know what things you like?"

"No," she said. Her skin was turning back to a normal shade, the fire already flickering out. It seemed like their bodies could only sustain the fire for a brief moment. Her shirt was in tatters, almost ash.

"Or do you want to be with me because I'm cool, and I'll keep being cool, and you'll like hanging out with me?" I just kept on going, didn't even wait for her to respond. "You want to stay here with your shitty grandparents and never get fed and scratch bug bites underneath sheets that haven't ever been washed? You want that?"

"No, I don't want that," Bessie said, not crying but wheezing from anger.

"Or do you want to come with me, and I'll take care of you and buy you all new clothes, and I'll feed you whatever you want and play games with you and watch movies with you and swim in the pool with you and rock you to bed and kiss you good night and sing you lullabies and then wake you up and let you watch cartoons?"

"That," she said, her teeth chattering. "We want that."

"Okay, then," I said. "Then you have to trust me that I'm going to take care of you. It's going to be weird, okay? It's going to make you angry sometimes. But I'll take care of you. It's what I'm going to do."

By this point, Carl had fished Roland out of the pool and was carrying him over to us; the boy was listening intently.

"Are you our stepmother?" Roland asked.

"No—Jesus Christ—no, I'm not your stepmother. I'm just—"

"She's like a babysitter that never leaves," Carl suddenly said.

"Never?" Bessie and Roland said at the same time, and I realized how this could go bad so quickly.

"Never," I said, smiling. Bessie still had a little trail of my blood running down her chin.

"We catch on fire," Bessie told me.

"I know," I said. "It's okay."

"We just go with you?" she asked, and I nodded, exhausted.

Bessie looked at Roland, who simply nodded his assent. "We'll go with you," they both said at the same time.

"I've packed up your belongings," Carl told them.

Roland shrugged. "We don't have that much stuff to bring," the boy informed us. He had stripes buzzed into the sides of his hair, and I was shocked to realize that their hair was unsinged. I don't know why, with these demon children bursting into flames right in front of me, their bad haircuts remaining intact was the magic that fully amazed me, but that's how it works, I think. The big thing is so ridiculous that you absorb only the smaller miracles.

# Four

"I'VE GOT KOOL-AID," CARL SAID, TRYING TO SOUND CHEERY.

The kids smiled, but I shook my head. "No Kool-Aid," I told him. I didn't want these kids drugged, didn't want things to start off any worse than they already had.

Bessie frowned. "You said you'd give us whatever we wanted," she said. Her face reddened a little, and I was already dealing with some trauma, I think.

"We'll get you some sodas at a gas station," I said, and Carl simply nodded; maybe he was as tired as I was.

"That's good," Roland said. "Sun Drop, okay?"

"Okay," I told him.

"Your hand is really messed up," Roland said.

I finally looked down at it, had forgotten about the pain. It was just a dull throbbing sensation traveling all the way up my arm. There were tooth marks all over my hand, purple and deep, blood bubbling out of the wounds. The worst were on my index and middle fingers. I could barely bend them now.

"I scratched up your face some, too," Bessie offered sheepishly.

"Sorry about your knee," I told her, and she just waved me off.

"I've got a first aid kit in the van," Carl said. "You get the kids dressed and I'll come back with it."

I led the children past their grandparents. Mr. Cunningham's steak was now burning and charred on the grill. The kids acted like the grandparents weren't even there.

In the bathroom, I dried them off with some already damp towels. I was a person without much experience around kids, had always avoided them in the past. Bessie and Roland tore off the burned scraps of clothing, got naked so fast I barely had time to be weirded out. I was like, *These are naked kids,* and I tried to be mature about it. Eventually, they got into their clothes: cheap souvenir T-shirts of the Smoky Mountains and baggy shorts, slippery flip-flops on their feet.

I looked at my face in the mirror. The worst was around my right eye, which was puffed up and had pretty jagged scratches running diagonally across the side of my face, the top layer of skin stripped away. I looked like a gladiator in some old, bad movie. I found a nearly empty tube of Neosporin in the medicine cabinet and rubbed it all over my face like a beauty treatment.

"You have any other clothes?" Bessie asked me, and I remembered that I was soaking wet, my shoes squeaky with pool water.

"I do not," I told them, and just then Carl appeared with the first aid kit. He was also holding a muumuu, swirling greens and yellows and maybe purple in there.

"What is that?" I asked him.

"I got it out of Mrs. Cunningham's closet," he replied. "I thought you might need to change."

"I'll just wear my wet clothes," I said.

"Don't be dumb, okay?" he said. "Put it on."

"It's a muumuu," I said.

"Gran-Gran calls them tea dresses," Bessie offered. I liked Bessie okay right then, even though she'd tried to bite my fingers off.

They all left the bathroom and I changed into the muumuu, which was comfortable and not as billowy as I'd expected, not that it mattered how pretty I looked when my face was mangled and my hand was busted. I gathered up my wet clothes and wrapped them up in a towel. Then I unlocked the door and Carl came in with the first aid kit.

"I bandaged up the girl's knee. Now, just to let you know, this is a pretty rudimentary kit," he said, so he grabbed some hydrogen peroxide from the medicine cabinet and used the kit's cotton balls to clean the wounds, which hurt like hell, turning foamy and tinged with pink. Once he was sure they were clean enough, he took some gauze and patted it gently onto my skin.

"You should have waited for me," he told me, and I was pissed off because it was hard to argue with him considering how badly I'd fucked things up.

"I wanted them to like me," I said. "I wanted to be alone with them."

"It's going to take time," he said. "If it works at all. They have been through some awful stuff. They are damaged goods—"

"Jesus, keep your voice down, Carl," I said. "They're right outside."

"Well, I'm just saying. Be careful with them. Our goal is to keep them out of danger for the next few months, to prevent any disaster. It's all damage control, Lillian, okay?"

"I'll be careful," I said. Carl wrapped white tape around the gauze and my hand looked like a flipper.

"That's the best that I can do right now. We'll need to make sure it doesn't get infected, but you don't need stitches or anything. Nothing is broken."

"Rabies?" I asked; if it was a stupid question, I hoped he'd think I was joking.

"No," he said. Then he considered it for a second, looked toward the door, where the kids were waiting. "I don't think so."

When we opened the door, the kids were just standing there like zombies. They were ten years old, but they looked younger, stunted in some meaningful way. I hadn't actually given much thought to how I was going to take care of them. Originally, I had thought I'd just stand next to them for the whole summer and gently direct them toward good decisions. I thought I'd just sit in a beanbag chair and they'd read magazines next to me.

Now it was clear how much this job would require. I was going to have to bend and twist these children into something that could live in that crazy-rich estate back in Franklin. It was going to be like teaching a wild raccoon to wear a little suit and play the piano. I was going to be bleeding and bruised every day, and that would still be preferable to catching on fire, the fillings in my teeth melting while I held on to these little kids.

And as they stared at me, I knew how much of myself I was going to unfairly place in them. They were me, unloved and fucked over, and I was going to make sure that they got what they needed. They would scratch and kick me, and I was going to scratch and kick anyone who tried to touch them. I didn't love them; I was a selfish person and I didn't understand people all that well, not enough to really feel an emotion as complicated as love. But I felt tenderness for them, which felt, to my little heart, like a kind of progress.

"Are you ready?" I asked the kids, and they nodded.

"Two slides?" Bessie asked me, and it took me a second to remember what she was talking about.

"I lied about the slides," I admitted, and she nodded like she had expected lies. They looked at each other for a second, and then Bessie shrugged, and they walked just a few steps ahead of me and Carl to the van, which would bring them home.

WHEN WE TURNED ONTO THE LONG DRIVEWAY THAT LED TO the estate, I crawled over the seats and into the back of the van, where Roland and Bessie slept on the air mattress, their bodies quivering, riding that thin line between dreams and real life. I wondered what the hell their dreams must have been, what kind of mess was inside their heads. I was afraid of getting bitten again, or set on fire, or even just having the children look up at me and frown, pissed that I was not their mom. So I kind of made a soft hissing sound, like I was trying to help someone who was having trouble peeing. That didn't work, so I gently nudged Roland, who seemed maybe a little less prone to violence, and he stirred. And the minute his body temperature shifted by even a degree, his posture slightly altered, Bessie snapped awake, and they both took a few seconds to figure out where they were, what their lives were. And then they looked at me. They didn't smile, but they seemed okay with me being there, hovering over them.

"We're home," I said, and I hoped it sounded believable, inviting.

"What home?" Bessie asked.

"Your home," I replied.

"What is this place?" Bessie asked as the two children looked out the window at the estate.

"Do you not remember? This was your home—" I looked back at Carl for confirmation. "Didn't they live here?" I asked. Carl caught my gaze in the rearview mirror and simply nodded.

"I've never seen this place before in my whole entire life," Bessie said, like a robot.

They had been four or five, I think, when they moved out with their mother. When did children's memories begin? I tried to remember my own life. I could remember things from when I was two. Not good things, but I remembered them. I thought Bessie might be messing with me.

"You lived here," I said, "in this—"

"Hey, Lillian," Carl said, "maybe just let this go."

"You don't remember?" I asked the children.

Bessie and Roland shook their heads. "It's huge," Roland finally said. "That's where we're gonna live?"

"Well," I said, "kind of. Behind that house is our house."

"Probably a crappy house," Bessie said.

"No, it's pretty sweet," I said, and I meant it.

"We're here," Carl said, the engine idling, like if the kids made one wrong move he'd throw it back into drive and speed them to the nearest hospital or military testing facility.

It was just Madison on the porch. She had two teddy bears, but she was holding them like weapons. That's not fair. She was holding them like shields, as if they might temporarily protect her from danger.

"Who is that?" Bessie asked, clearly interested, hypnotized by Madison's beauty.

"That's Madison," I said.

The utterance of the name made both Bessie and Roland stiffen, their bodies crackling. They knew that name. No doubt they'd heard their mother say it, or yell it, or hiss it.

Carl got out of the van and came to the back, opening the doors, the light spilling in. The children seemed wary, started to back away from Carl, and then they were next to me. I wasn't touching them, just letting them know that I was with them, would stick by them. Bessie looked at me; she knew she had no choice. She grabbed Roland's hand and they kind of crawled out of the van. I sat there for just a second, a little afraid. Carl was already walking to the porch, his fingers wiggling like he was about to rope a calf. Then I hopped out, my muumuu riding up, and there was Madison, walking to the kids.

"Hello, Bessie," Madison said. "Hello, Roland." The kids just stared at her, but Madison wasn't deterred. "These are for you." She handed each child a teddy bear, and the kids, slightly stunned, took them. They'd been given stuffed animals in the van, and so it seemed like some strange ritual, this never-ending parade of plush. I watched Roland rub his face against the soft fur, while Bessie gripped the bear's arm like a mom would a small child's in a crowded mall.

"Are you our mom?" Bessie asked.

Madison looked at me, her eyebrows raised. What was her problem? I wondered. Wasn't she their mom now? Like, legally? And for a second, I was like, *Have I adopted these children? Am I their mom?*

"I could never replace your mother," Madison finally said. "I'm your stepmother."

"I've read stories about stepmothers," Bessie said. "Fairy tales."

"But this is real life," Madison said, still smiling. And I thought, *Was* it real life? Was it real life to these kids?

"Where's our dad?" Roland asked, still rubbing his face against that damn teddy bear, his nose so red now.

"He's coming," Madison said, and I saw her face darken for a half second, nothing the kids would notice. "He's just so emotional about finally seeing you again that he needs a second to get himself together."

I wondered if this had all been orchestrated by Madison, step by step, a way to slowly bring these children into this new life. Or, I wondered, was Jasper Roberts just a bum, hiding in his billiards room, terrified of these things that he'd made and thought he'd discarded?

Madison finally seemed to register that I was there, and my presence seemed to confuse her. She regarded me carefully and then said, as if she couldn't help herself, "What are you wearing?"

I looked at Mrs. Cunningham's muumuu. It was so comfortable. Wearing it, I felt like a gust of wind in the spring, just enough motion to detonate every dandelion puffball in my way. "It's kind of like a dress—" I began to say, but Carl broke in.

"We had a slight mishap at the Cunninghams'," he admitted, and I could see how much it pained him to admit the tiniest mistake.

"And what happened to your hand?" she asked. "Goodness, your face."

I didn't have the strength to explain. I just let Carl say, "That was part of the mishap as well."

"I see," Madison said. Then she smiled. "Well, the dress

actually looks kind of nice on you," she said to me, which I already knew.

"She's our nanny," Roland said.

"Or governess," Madison said, kind of correcting him. Or perhaps correcting me.

"What are we going to do here?" Bessie finally asked, as if she'd been thinking about this the entire time.

"Anything you like," Madison said. "Rest, relax, get settled. This is your home now. We want you to be happy."

"Happy?" Bessie said, like she hadn't quite heard that word, didn't know what it meant, or had only read it in a book and never heard it spoken aloud.

"Of course, sweetie," Madison said, but before she could say anything else, there was Jasper Roberts, wearing a linen suit, looking like a preacher about to say the Lord's Prayer before the start of the Daytona 500.

"Children," he said, but his voice cracked just a little. "I've missed you."

"Daddy?" Roland asked, but Bessie grabbed his hand to keep him from moving, from saying another word. Maybe they had been faking in the van. Or maybe this single moment, the appearance of their father, brought it all back, but I could see that they knew it now. They knew this place, their life before their life.

"My sweet children," Jasper said. He was crying a little, and I couldn't quite place why he was crying, what it meant.

"Sir," Carl said, but then Bessie and Roland started to catch on fire. I could feel this little twinge in the air, and I committed it to memory. And then their skin rashed and strawberried. And then these blooms of flame started to appear on their arms, on their hands. It wasn't the explosion of a star, like at the Cunninghams', but they were definitely on fire.

"Back up!" Carl said, jumping between the children and Jasper and Madison. Smoke started coming off the children, their cheap clothes now singed.

"Ohhhh!" Madison said, and everyone was just standing there, not doing anything, while these children increased the intensity of the fire that was inside them. That's what it seemed like, like the fire was inside them, children made of fire. And I knew it would get worse if something didn't happen to stop it. Madison and Jasper seemed stunned, and Carl's only concern was keeping Jasper from getting burned.

I took off my muumuu, which was so easy to remove, by the way, and then I used it to cover my hands and gently lower the children to a squatting position on the ground. "Hey, Bessie. Bessie? Calm down now, okay?" She was rigid, and so was Roland, but the fire was just rolling across them, yellow and red, like what you'd draw with a limited supply of crayons.

"Can you turn it off?" I asked, almost whispering, but they weren't listening. So then I started smothering the flames with the muumuu, which caused it to smolder and spark. I patted the children all over their arms, their backs, on top of their little heads. I went pat-pat-pat-pat-pat and kept whispering, "It's okay, it's okay, it's okay."

I could feel the heat, but I just kept lightly tapping them, and the fire seemed to finally die out. As if they had been holding their breath the entire time, Bessie and Roland each took in a deep gulp of air and then sighed, suddenly sleepy. I leaned against them and they kind of slumped onto me. And Carl finally ran over and scooped them both up, one in each arm, and put them back in the van, gently closing the doors.

I stood up, confused. I realized that I was in my bra and panties, but either people were being really polite or it didn't matter because we'd just fucking watched some fire children do their thing. Carl and I had already seen it, knew it was real, so we both snapped out of it quicker than the Robertses.

"My god," Madison finally said. She hugged Jasper, as if she only now believed him and was sorry for doubting him. I looked down and realized that the teddy bears were lying on the driveway, their fur burned black.

"Sir," Carl said, "you tried, and I respect you for that, but it's time to think about real solutions to this situation. I have a few options."

"What?" I said. "That was an accident. They don't know what's going on. Look at the size of this house. Madison? Right? Wouldn't you be freaked out?"

"They caught on fire," Madison said.

"I'm sorry," Jasper said. "I don't know what I thought was going to happen."

"Sir?" Carl said, waiting for the word. He was jingling the key to the van.

I felt like the only sane person, and I was in my underwear, holding a ruined muumuu that I'd stolen from a sleeping old lady. "This isn't fair to them," I continued. "You have to give them a chance. I can help them, okay? I can figure this out. It's not that big of a deal, honestly; like, I can already see how to handle it."

"Lillian, please," Carl said.

"She's right, though," Madison finally said. "Jasper, she's right. We have to give them time to acclimate to this, to get used to us."

"I don't want any harm to come to you or Timothy," he

said, and then, as if remembering the kids in the van, "or to those children."

"You got that house ready for them, right, the slave quarters—oh shit—sorry, the guesthouse. Okay? You've made a place in your home for them. I can help them."

"Sir, she has no training—"

"*CPR,* Carl, okay? CPR and . . . other stuff," I said.

"We let them stay," Jasper said. "They're staying. They're my children. My son and my daughter."

"This is right," Madison whispered to him, rubbing his back. Jasper was sweating, the linen not doing a damn thing for him. "Family values, okay? Personal responsibility? A better future for our children?" She was saying these things like she was reading them off of huge billboards along the road. Or like she was coming up with campaign slogans.

"They're staying, Carl," Jasper said with some finality. He became senatorial for that moment, standing up straight. Not quite presidential, but maybe vice-presidential.

"Yes, sir," Carl replied, so formal, returning to the back of the van and throwing the doors open. I ran in front of him, kind of nudging him aside. And the kids were sitting there, half-lidded, as if a little drunk.

"We keep getting your clothes messed up," Roland said. He was really staring at my body, but things were too weird to worry about that right now.

"I don't care. I don't care at all," I told them.

"We heard you," Bessie said. "We heard . . . all that."

"Oh," I said, not really remembering what had been said.

"We're staying?" Bessie said, and it sounded like she really wanted the answer to be yes.

"Yeah," I told her.

"And you're staying with us, right?" she said.

"I am. I will," I said.

"So . . . we're home?" Roland said, so fucking confused. Both children looked at me, their huge eyes fixed on me.

"We're home," I said. I knew it wasn't my home. And it wasn't their home. But we would steal it. We had a whole summer to take this house and make it ours. And who could stop us? Jesus, we had fire.

# Five

WHEN I TOOK THE CHILDREN TO THE GUESTHOUSE, ROLAND said, "This looks like TV," and I asked, "You mean like a television show? Like a kids' show?"

"We don't have television," Bessie said. "Mom won't let us watch television."

"But we can watch it now?" Roland asked, like it was just dawning on him.

"Oh, yes," I said. I imagined that we'd watch a lot of television, or I had before I'd actually met the kids. Now I felt like Bugs Bunny would hit Daffy Duck with a hammer and Bessie and Roland would burst into flames. "Well, with some regulations," I continued. "Only a little bit a day."

The kids still wouldn't go in. The door was open, but it was like they were vampires and had to be invited in. Or maybe the house was so pristine, so colorful, that they were afraid of destroying it immediately with what was inside them.

"Are you worried about something?" I asked.

"No," Bessie said, irritated. "We're just thinking."

"About what?" I asked. Their mother, I figured. Their father, maybe.

"None of your business," she said. Their mother, I figured.

I wanted to learn more about her, from people who had actually been raised by her instead of Madison's vague asides. But I also didn't want to know a single thing about her, because it would make me compare myself to her every time the children set their bedsheets on fire.

Finally, Bessie and Roland stepped into the house. "Oh, wow," Roland said, testing the sponginess of the flooring. "This is cool."

"Isn't it?" I said, letting my feet softly sink into the material.

"And look at all those cereals, Bessie," Roland said, pointing to a pyramid of individual boxes of sugary cereals, and I understood his excitement, having lived a childhood where the cereal was off-brand, giant plastic bags that were twenty percent pulverized corn or wheat. But Bessie was walking up to a tall bookcase, filled with every Nancy Drew and Hardy Boys book in existence, lots of Judy Blume and Mark Twain and all manner of fairy tales.

"These are for us?" she asked.

"Yeah," I told her. "I can read you any book you want."

"We can read," Bessie said, her face reddening at the idea that I might have thought that she couldn't. "We read all the time."

"That's all we do is read," Roland said. "But Pop-Pop and Gran-Gran didn't have any books for kids. It was so boring."

"What did they have?" I asked.

"Books about World War Two," Bessie answered. "Two different books about Hitler. Wait, four books about Hitler. And other books about Nazis. And books about Stalin. Patton. People like that."

"That sounds awful," I told her.

"It sucked," Bessie said.

"Well, you can read all these books now," I told her.

"I read a lot of these already," Bessie said, inspecting the spines, "but some look pretty good."

"That's great. And we can get more. We can go to the library and get whatever you want."

"Okay," she said, nodding her approval. She looked at me. "And you can read us a book at night. If you want to, we'll let you read us a book before we go to bed."

"That's great," I said, and I could feel our lives normalizing, a kind of routine forming.

"Do you want to put on some clothes?" she asked me, and I realized that I was still in my underwear.

"Shit—I mean, shoot—yes, I do want to put on some clothes," I told her, but I was afraid to leave them alone. As if she read my mind, Bessie said, "You can go change. We're okay. We're really okay right now." I nodded, and then I was running up to the second floor, counting the seconds, afraid that if I was gone longer than a few minutes, I'd come back to find them digging a tunnel to freedom. I pulled on some jeans, slipped into a T-shirt, and then ran back downstairs in less than forty-five seconds, and they were still there, Bessie making a stack of books that she wanted to read and Roland sitting on the counter, wrist-deep in a little box of Apple Jacks. Bessie opened up one of the new books and smelled the pages. Roland smiled at me and his mouth looked unspeakable, all these little bits of cereal like glitter in his teeth.

This was how you did it, how you raised children. You built them a house that was impervious to danger and then you gave them every single thing that they could ever want, no matter how impossible. You read to them at night. Why couldn't people figure this out?

And then I realized they were still in their smoky clothes from the fire in the driveway, and I felt like a slob and an idiot, and I had no idea how I'd keep them alive. This was the wave of childcare, I supposed, real highs and lows. My mom had once told me that being a mother was made up of "regret and then forgetting about that regret sometimes." But I wouldn't be my mother. How many times had I told myself that, and how unnecessary had it always been? There was no regret for me and these fire kids. Not yet.

I whistled to get their attention, and both kids slowly turned in my direction. "Let's get you dressed," I said, "and then we need to talk about some stuff."

"Sad stuff?" Roland said. They were the same age, but Roland seemed younger, having the benefit of growing up with a sister who would bite the shit out of people's hands in order to protect him.

"No," I said, slightly confused. "Not sad stuff. Just normal everyday stuff. We're going to be together all the time. We just need to talk about stuff."

"Okay," Roland said. I realized that the cereal box he was wearing as a glove was no longer Apple Jacks and was now Cocoa Krispies.

"Go easy on the cereal, okay, Roland?" I kind of asked and kind of demanded. I'd need to get better about that, be more sure of myself.

Roland shoved one last handful of cereal into his mouth, the pieces scattering across the counter and onto the floor. Then he stopped, chewed what he had in his mouth, and hopped off the counter and ran over to me. Bessie stood and we all went into their room, which was, I guess, balloon themed. There were framed posters of hot air balloons, crazy colors like flags to countries that existed in made-up worlds. The knobs on the posters of their beds were designed to look like red balloons.

"This is a lot of color," Bessie said. "It's kind of too much."

"It is a bit too much," I said. "But you'll get used to it." Bessie looked at me like, *Duh.* They were children who caught on fire. Their mother had died. They understood how to adjust to weird stuff.

There were a lot of choices as far as clothing went, and they both picked these black-and-gold Vanderbilt T-shirts and black cotton shorts. I wrapped up their old clothes and tossed them in the trash. How many clothes would these kids go through? Was it better to just let them run around the house naked?

"Okay, so let's talk," I said, and the kids sat on their beds. I sat on the floor and pulled my knees up to my chin, unsure how to proceed. I'd had so much time to prepare for this moment, but I'd spent it playing basketball and eating bacon sandwiches in bed. There had been a folder from some private doctor who'd examined the children, but it was so boring and nothing was actually resolved, so I'd just kind of skimmed it. I wished Carl were here, because he always had a plan, and then I hated myself for it.

"So the fire stuff," I said, and both kids had that look on their faces like, *This shit again, ho-hum.*

"You guys catch on fire," I said. "And so, you know, that's a problem. I know it's not your fault, but it's something we have to deal with. So maybe we can try to figure it out."

"There's no cure for it," Bessie said, and I asked, "Who told you that?"

"We just know," Roland said. "Our mom said we'll always be like this."

"Well, okay," I continued, a little annoyed with their dead mom for being so negative about it, "but what do you know about it? How does it work?"

"It just happens sometimes," Bessie said. "It's like sneezing. You know? It's just this tingly feeling that comes and goes."

"But is it when you're upset? Or does it ever happen when you're just bored?" I wished I had a notebook, a lab coat, something to make this more official. Like I was doing intake, or a school project.

"If we get upset, or if we get freaked out, or if something bad happens," Roland said, "then we catch on fire."

"Or if we have a bad dream," Bessie offered. "Like, a really bad dream."

"Wait, it happens when you're sleeping, even?" I asked, and felt the floor beneath me give way a little, the realization that this might be worse than I thought. Both kids nodded. "But only, like, really bad dreams," Roland said, as if this would comfort me.

"But mostly when you get upset?" I asked, and they nodded again. I didn't know if this was progress, but they were listening to me. They weren't on fire. We were together, in this house, and everyone outside of this house was waiting for us to figure this out.

"So we just stay calm," I told them. "We read books and we swim in the pool and we go for walks and we just stay calm."

"We'll still catch on fire," Bessie said, and she looked so sad.

"But not as much, right? Not like today? You're not always catching on fire?" I asked.

"No, not much. Not all that much. More since Mom died," Bessie offered.

"What would your mom do to keep you guys from catching on fire?" I asked.

"Push us into the shower," Bessie said, seeming to think of this as an injustice, squeaky shoes and damp underwear.

"She made us get up real early, every morning, no matter what," Roland said. "She said it was better when we were a little tired. And she made us do tons of chores. And lessons. All these lessons with pencil and paper. And she would fill up the tub with ice cubes and cold water and we'd have to get in it."

"She kept the house real cold," Bessie said, "even in the winter. But—" She looked away, embarrassed.

"But what?" I asked.

"But I don't think that it really helped," she finally said, the whole time looking at Roland like they held a secret. "It doesn't matter if we're hot or cold when things are okay. It doesn't matter if we're around a fire, like on the stove, but Mom thought it would make us think about fire and then it would happen. But it's not like that. Not really. It doesn't matter except when we start to catch on fire."

"And can you stop yourself?" I asked.

"Sometimes," Bessie admitted. "If Mom was around, she'd see it happening and get so freaked out and try to make us stop, but that would make it worse. But if Roland and I are by ourselves, and we feel it happening, sometimes we just make our minds go blank, and it stops. Sometimes."

"Okay," I said, like I'd cracked some spy code and was going to win a million dollars. "So we'll watch for it and then try to help you calm down."

"What's all that?" Roland asked, pointing to the sprinkler system, which brought me back to reality.

"That's in case of a fire," I told him. "For emergencies."

"Mom got rid of smoke alarms," Roland said. "They went off too much."

"Well," I said, thinking, "the sprinklers are there to keep us safe."

"The fire doesn't hurt us," Bessie said.

Well, I realized, it was to keep me safe. It was to keep the house safe. It was to keep the house where Madison and Jasper and Timothy lived safe. I thought of a little smoke, the sprinklers going off, everything soaking wet, all the electronics and books ruined. I thought about that happening once or twice a day.

"Maybe I can get Carl to turn them off," I offered, and the kids seemed happy with this possibility.

And then, as if by magic or perhaps the possibility of constant, invasive surveillance, Carl's voice echoed through the house. "Hello?" he asked. He was downstairs, and I imagined him holding a fire extinguisher like the hero in a bad movie.

"That's Carl," I said, and the kids nodded.

"He's a real square," Bessie said, and I wanted to hug her so tightly.

"Who is he?" Roland asked. "Is he your boyfriend?"

"God, no," I said, almost laughing. "He's like my manager. Or, no, maybe we're like coworkers with way different responsibilities. Or—"

"Lillian?" Carl now shouted. I had kind of forgotten that he was there.

"Yeah?" I shouted back.

"Everything okay?" he asked.

"Everything is fine," I said.

"Could you come downstairs?" he asked.

"Us too?" Roland shouted.

"No!" Carl shouted, but then he corrected himself. "You guys just stay up there for a second while I talk to Lillian."

"Do you want us to come with you?" Bessie asked. I had a hard time looking at her and not seeing waves of flame erupting from her skin. I simply shook my head. "I'm okay," I said. As I walked out of the room, I peeked my head back in and said, "If you feel it coming, run to the shower and turn it on, okay?" The kids nodded, and I felt like this was a kind of test, to let them out of my sight, to feel them above me, to hear them breathing.

Downstairs, Carl was on his knees, sweeping up cereal crumbs with a dainty little broom and dustpan. He looked up at me. "Seems like they're settling in," he said, and I felt a little judged.

"They haven't caught on fire again," I told him, a little proud of myself.

"We'll see how long that lasts," he replied.

"You heard Jasper, right?" I asked him. "This is happening. You're not getting rid of them."

"So?" Carl asked.

"So help me, okay?"

"I will help you, Lillian," he said. "I'll help you make the right decisions."

"For instance," I said, ignoring the little ways he dug into me, "we have to turn off the sprinkler system."

"It was two grand to install that system," Carl replied, like it was his fucking money, like Timothy's stuffed animal budget wasn't four times that amount.

"How much did all these electronics cost?" I asked. "How

about the books, the clothes, the bedsheets? Those kids caught on fire twice in a single day, right? This house will be like a constant rainstorm if you keep the sprinkler system on."

"So I turn off the system," he said, "and then what happens when they catch on fire again?"

"Carl, please. Carl? Please. *I* will put them out."

"Twenty-four hours a day? What about when you're asleep?"

"Twenty-four/seven. I'm a light sleeper. I have a plan, okay?"

"All right," Carl said. I think maybe he now had a sense of how powerful I was. The children were mine, and that gave me something that he didn't have. "All right, I'll shut it off. But that's our secret. Senator Roberts needs to think that there are true safety measures in place."

"I'm not going to tell Jasper. Holy shit, do you think I would tell Jasper?"

Carl looked at me with some measure of sincerity. His posture changed, just the slightest slackening. "Lillian, honestly? I don't know what you will or won't do. But my livelihood is now connected to yours. So we work together. Agreed?"

"That's great, Carl," I said, kind of meaning it and kind of making fun of him. "I'd like that."

"Now, the reason I came over here was to say that Mrs. Roberts thinks that perhaps having a family dinner might be too overwhelming for the children, not only Roland and Bessie but also Timothy."

"Okay," I said. So this was how it would work, a line demarcating us and them. I wondered if Jasper would ever see the kids again. I wondered if Madison and I would still hang out, and I figured that we still would, but in different ways.

"You'll be okay making them dinner here?" Carl asked.

"Sure. No problem," but I wasn't quite sure of the mechanics of it. I was used to microwaving something and eating it over the trash can. And, over the last week or so, I'd gotten used to Mary making the most amazing meals that I couldn't stop eating. I would miss Mary so much, now that I was fully banished to this guesthouse. I wanted the children to meet her.

"All right, then," he said. He turned but then suddenly turned back. "Do you see that phone?" he asked, pointing to the wall-mounted handset next to the refrigerator. I nodded. "If you ever need me, no matter what time it is or what it's about, pick up that phone and push one-one-one-one. Okay?"

"One-one-one-one," I repeated. "And you'll come to me?"

"I will," he said. This seemed to pain him to admit.

"Good night, Carl," I said.

"Good night, Lillian," he replied, and then he turned into a shadow and was gone.

When I went to the stairs, I saw Bessie and Roland sitting on the top step, not one bit ashamed of eavesdropping, which I loved.

"How did I do?" I asked them.

"You got him to turn off the sprinklers," Roland said. "That's awesome."

"I did it," I said. "I told you I would, and then I did."

"Okay," Bessie said, as if she'd made a decision that she'd been considering ever since she first saw me.

"Do you want pizza?" I asked, and they both nodded enthusiastically, so we went down to the kitchen and I got the oven on and a frozen pizza shoved in there. I cut up some apples, their skin red and waxy like in a fairy tale, and the kids just destroyed the slices, so I cut up two more. I ate a banana. I looked again in the fridge and realized there was no beer, and I almost picked up the phone and dialed 1111, but decided to be responsible. I'd steal some from the mansion tomorrow, or maybe some of Jasper's fancy bourbon, which I believed I'd earned with my work here today. My hand was kind of throbbing, which made me feel a little less proud of myself, and so I took some aspirin, and then the pizza was ready.

Before I let them eat, I said, "I'm happy to be with you."

They just looked at me, dumbfounded. "Can we eat?" Bessie asked.

"I said," I repeated, "that I am happy to be with you."

"That's real nice," Roland said, and he picked up the pizza slice and ate it in three bites, even though it was still pretty damn hot.

After dinner, I washed the plates while the kids picked out a book for me to read to them.

"Can we skip bath time?" Roland asked.

"And do we need to brush our teeth?" Bessie asked.

"You kids were in that chlorinated water this afternoon," I told them. "And, you know, you caught on fire, so it's probably good to get a shower. And you have to brush your teeth."

"Aw, man," Roland said, but I stood firm and the kids seemed to respect me for this, or else they were biding their time before they ran me over.

I stood outside the bathroom while they took turns hopping in the shower. They were ten. I didn't know what the boundaries were at ten, but they seemed too old for me to be dealing with their naked bodies, unless, of course, it was fire related. That was my plan, to let them control themselves until they couldn't control themselves. It's how I would have wanted to be treated if I were a demon child.

I sat on the floor in between the kids' two beds, Bessie

and Roland all fresh in their pajamas, their hair, what a horror show, wet and slicked down into something tame.

Bessie handed me the book, *Penny Nichols and the Black Imp.* "What is this?" I asked. The cover was red and faded, just a hardback book with the silhouette of a girl's profile. I looked at the title again. What in the hell was a black imp? I checked the copyright, which was from the thirties. Was it racist?

"Maybe a different book, guys? There's, like, a million down there. Maybe, like, *Superfudge* or something?"

"This is kind of like Nancy Drew, but weirder," Bessie informed me.

"Have you read this already?" I asked.

Bessie nodded, but Roland said, "I haven't."

"What's the black imp?" I asked.

"It's part of the mystery," she told me.

I scanned the opening page and the first line had a "slightly decrepit roadster" pulling up to a house. One of the characters used the word *shan't.*

"It's just this statue," she finally said, seeing my hesitation. "It's this clay statue. It's not about Satan or anything."

"Fine," I said. "Whatever you want." So I read to them about a girl detective named Penelope Nichols, who was weird enough that it was interesting. It was fun. I liked reading out loud, I realized. I did voices even, though the kids didn't make any sign of appreciation. I read and read, and my voice got soft, and the kids got sleepy, and after a while it was time for bed.

"Good night, kiddos," I said, talking like Penny Nichols.

"Where are you going?" Roland asked.

"To my room," I said, confused. "To my private room. For privacy."

"Can you sleep with us tonight?" Roland asked.

"No," I said. "I can't do that."

"Why not?" Bessie asked, suddenly invested.

"There's no room," I said.

"We can push the beds together," Bessie said, but I told her that the beds didn't really work like that. I thought of sleeping in the crack between the beds, sinking down, and it frightened me, honestly.

"We'll all sleep in your room," Bessie said. "We looked in there. It's a huge bed."

"No," I said.

"Just for tonight?" Roland said.

I thought of them being shoved into this Bozo house with me, their kind-of nanny, their mom dead, their dad in that linen suit, Madison like the good witch in every fairy tale. I thought of them catching on fire in this room, all alone.

"Fine," I said. "Until we get settled. Come on."

The kids shouted and then ran into my bedroom, where they dove under the covers. I turned on the fan. It was nine o'clock. I usually stayed up well past midnight, reading magazines and eating whatever Mary had left over in the fridge. But this, I guess, was what Madison was paying me to do.

"C'mon," I said, like Moses parting the sea, "move aside so I can get in there." They did, and I crawled into bed. They didn't cuddle against me, but they kind of bunched up so they were almost touching me.

"Good night," I said, thinking maybe I could slide out of bed after they had fallen asleep, and then I could do whatever I wanted downstairs.

And then I thought of the entire day, Bessie biting my hand, falling into the pool, watching them catch on fire, watching them catch on fire again, waiting for them to maybe catch on fire again. I was tired, I realized. I touched the places on my face where Bessie had scratched me. I felt like I couldn't breathe; the children were so close, burning up all the available air. I kind of gasped a little, and Bessie asked, "Are you okay?" and I said, "Go to sleep," and then I just closed my eyes and tried to imagine a world where everything worked out.

And then I really was asleep, dead asleep, for maybe ten minutes, and then I heard them talking.

"Is she asleep?" Roland asked.

"I think so," Bessie said. I kept my breathing steady, my eyes closed.

"What do you think?" Roland asked.

"She's okay," Bessie said, "I guess."

"What about Dad?" Roland asked.

"What a jerk," Bessie said, "just like Mom said."

"I kind of like it here," Roland said.

There was a moment of silence and then Bessie replied, "It might be okay. For a little while."

"She's nice," Roland said.

"Maybe," Bessie said. "She's weird."

"So what do we do?" he asked.

"We just wait and see," Bessie said.

"And if it's bad?" Roland said. "Like at Gran-Gran and Pop-Pop's?"

"We'll just burn it all down," Bessie said. "Everything. Everyone. We'll set it on fire."

"Okay," Roland said.

"Good night, Roland," Bessie said.

"Good night, Bessie," Roland said.

They settled into positions of sleep, their bodies relaxing.

It was so dark in the room. I could hear them breathing. And then, maybe a minute later, Bessie said, "Good night, Lillian."

I lay there in the dark, the kids next to me. "Good night, Bessie," I finally said.

And then we were all asleep, inside that house, our new home.

# Six

WE SPENT THE NEXT THREE DAYS IN THE POOL WHILE I WORKED
out what to do with the kids. This is not an exaggeration.
Right when they woke up, their bodies pleasantly warm as they
huddled against me in the bed, I would pick them up, cover
them with sunscreen, just a shockingly ridiculous amount even
though I couldn't imagine that the sun would hurt them, and
we would run to the pool and cannonball into the water. We
played Marco Polo for hours, our fingertips so wrinkled that
it seemed like permanent damage had been done. I'd take a
break around lunchtime and make bologna sandwiches and the
kids would eat them at the edge of the pool, the bread soggy,
their hands smeared with mustard until they simply dunked
them into the water. When they got tired of swimming, we
lounged around under umbrellas and napped. Our eyes burned
from the chlorine, but what else could we do?

And everyone left us alone. No Madison. No Jasper. Not
even Carl hovering at the edges. I didn't see any gardeners
or maids in our area. We were a world unto ourselves, even
though I knew it was temporary. Eventually we would have to
figure something out, a way to integrate the children into the
real world. I imagined a time when they sat at that huge dining

room table in the mansion, eating eggs Benedict or whatever the fuck while their father read the paper and told them scores from the Braves game the day before. I imagined them walking the aisles of the library in town, picking out books, books that we could confidently check out without worrying about them catching on fire, dear lord, the rescinding of our library card. I imagined them inside the mansion, then leaving for school, then coming back home. I imagined them sleeping in a bed that wasn't mine. Where was I during all this? Far away, right? Like, if I got the kids to this level of normalcy, they wouldn't need me anymore. And I wasn't sure if I was happy or sad about it. And then I felt stupid, getting worried about my eventual success as a nanny, because I was dealing with children who burst into flames, so it would probably never actually happen. I was already imagining a world where I hadn't fucked up, where I'd saved the day. How would I make it to that world?

While the kids swam, I took a break and sat at a table with a little notebook and wrote down possibilities. My list looked like this:

Asbestos?

Race car clothes?

Damp towels?

Zen meditation?

Spray bottles / garden hoses?

Live in the pool (build a roof over it?)?

Fire extinguishers (safe for kids' skin?)?

Medication (sleeping pills? anti-anxiety?)?

Therapy (discreet)?

No spicy foods?

Spontaneous human combustion research (Time-Life
*Mysteries of the Unknown*)?

And on and on and on. If someone found this notebook,
they'd have to assume that I was insane, that I was planning to
set someone on fire and then, just as quickly, extinguish them.
But it felt scientific, the way I was proceeding. I had the children. They caught on fire. I had to keep them from catching
on fire. And, also, people did not catch on fire for no reason. Or
at least they didn't catch on fire without dying or having horrible burns. So I was imagining a solution to a problem that,
technically, didn't exist. All I could think to do was give them
more soggy bologna sandwiches and just keep doing that until
they turned eighteen, until we all just dried up and faded away.

"Look," Bessie called out, and I looked at her, only to see her
pointing toward the mansion. I turned. "Up there," she said. In
one of the windows on the second floor, Timothy was watching
us. He was, for crying out loud, looking at us through his own
little pair of opera glasses, like he was in a grand theater house
in London. He was motionless, watching the children, and it
unnerved me to such a degree that I finally looked away, just in
time to see Bessie flipping Timothy the bird, her face twisted
into meanness.

"Hey, don't get agitated!" I shouted, and then immediately
felt like a nag, like my anxiety was going to ruin them. I had
to be cool. I was the cool one, or at least I'd promised them
that I was.

When I looked back, Timothy had disappeared from the
window. "Maybe don't flip him off, okay?" I said to Bessie.
"That's your brother."

"Half brother, right?" Bessie said, like this was the same as a great-great-great-great-grand-uncle.

"You have to be nice to him," I said.

"No way he knows what the middle finger means," she said, and Roland said, "It means *fuck you!*"

"No," Bessie said, annoyed, "it means *up yours.*"

"Come on, guys," I said. "Do you want a juice box?"

"We're bored," Roland said.

"How can you be bored in this giant pool?" I asked. "It's, like, three times the size of your grandparents' pool."

"We want to do something fun," Bessie said.

"Like what?" I asked.

"Hide-and-seek?" Roland offered.

"I don't know if that's such a hot idea," I said, thinking of the children tucking themselves away in the most flammable parts of the house, all bunched up, waiting and waiting and waiting for something to happen.

"Can we go get ice cream?" Bessie asked.

"We have ice cream in the freezer," I told her.

"No, I want ice cream at a store. I want to watch them scoop it out and serve it to me."

"We're still getting settled," I said. "We should stay on the estate."

"Can we go inside the mansion?" Roland asked.

"Not yet," I said.

"This sucks," Bessie said. "It sucks."

She was right. It sucked so bad. It fucking sucked. I wanted to gather them in my arms and say, "Children, this fucking sucks. I hate it. I think I'd better be heading back home. Good luck." I imagined stealing Carl's Miata and hitting the road. I imagined Madison trying to raise these kids, and I enjoyed the slight twinge I felt at her discomfort. If anyone else had tried to hurt Madison, I would have murdered them, but I felt like I'd earned the right to imagine little aggressions against her.

I couldn't help feeling like I was failing everyone. But then other times I thought maybe this was what everyone wanted from me, to simply keep the children occupied until something else could be worked out. But that would be a failure to me, to these kids. I had to find a way to integrate them into this new life, to make them just the slightest bit less feral, have them walk through a crowded mall and try on clothes without burning the whole thing down. And maybe, selfishly, I thought that if I could do these things, I'd become an expert. If some rich family in Argentina discovered that they had fire children, I'd hop on a plane and sort it out for them. I'd give lectures. Maybe write a book about the whole experience. And, Jesus, right now the book that I would write was so goddamn boring. *Once upon a time, I babysat fire children and made them stay in a pool for three months. The end.* I had to write a better story for them, for me, for everyone.

"What are you writing?" Carl asked from behind me, and I jumped. "Oh fuck," I said, and the kids giggled loudly, even though they hated Carl. How had he appeared without my knowing it? I felt like maybe Carl was the kind of guy who put a lot of effort into being invisible until just the right moment. I bet he practiced walking without making noise.

"What is this?" he said, gesturing to the notebook. He looked at one of the entries, squinting as if he couldn't believe I'd taken the time to write it down. "Zen meditation? Are you serious?"

"This is private," I said, closing the notebook before he could read anything else, though he'd probably read it all.

"If it's about those kids, it's my business," he said, and when he saw that I did not like people telling me what to do, how to behave, he softened and said, "I've actually made my own list."

"I bet it's just things like, *send kids to boarding school, send kids to military school, send kids to sanitarium in Switzerland, freeze kids in carbonite,*" I replied.

"Those are definitely on the list," he said. "But let's talk."

"We can hear you," Bessie shouted.

"It's not a secret," he said, his voice rising just a little.

"Then let me come sit with you guys," she said.

"No," Carl replied, so effortless. It was easy for him to do this, to deny any and every little thing that a person wanted. I used to be good at that. I used to refuse people even when it didn't benefit me, when it actively inconvenienced me. I didn't know if this was progress or not.

"We have to come up with a plan," I told him.

"I agree," he said. "Something that will help the children and allow Senator Roberts and Mrs. Roberts a measure of security."

"Well, first, what about therapy? Discreetly done, of course, 'cause I know you're big on keeping it all a big secret."

"That's not going to happen," he said flatly.

"Discreet? Did you hear me say *discreet*? Carl, their mom died. They've been living with crazy people for two months. They need to talk to someone."

"They can talk to you," he replied.

"I have no training," I said.

"Well," he replied, "it's nice to hear you admit it."

I just stared at him, angry.

"Senator Roberts does not believe in therapy," he continued, "and he will not allow his children to see a psychiatrist. He is uneasy with the entire concept of psychoanalysis."

"I wonder why that might be, Carl."

"It's not going to happen. So move on."

"So, okay," I began, starting over. The tone of my voice was unnatural to me, like I was trying to get a bank loan. "The way I figure it, this is being generated inside of them, right? The fire? They combust when they get agitated."

"That seems to be the case," he replied, listening to me, hearing me out.

"So we have to find ways to address the problem both within and without . . . is that the right way to say it? Inside of their bodies and outside of their bodies."

"Just say what you want to do, Lillian," he said, taking a deep breath.

"So the outside stuff is just, like, putting out the fire when they catch on fire."

"Fire extinguishers," Carl said, nodding.

"You ever used a fire extinguisher? They're a fucking mess. The chemicals can't be safe to breathe in. I think if we can get attuned to how they behave, how their bodies work, we don't need fire extinguishers. We just need, like, damp towels."

"Lillian, dear lord, is this what you've been working on for three days? Damp towels?"

"Okay, yes, when you say it like that, it sounds really shitty and stupid. But, yeah, we have these damp towels or cloths. We keep them cold. We can carry them around in a little cooler or something."

"Oh my god," Carl said.

"And when the kids start to get weird, catch on fire, we just pat them down, keep them cool. It keeps the fire from breaking out."

"Do you have any other ideas? Please say you have other ideas."

"Well, Jesus, Mr. Ph.D. in fire management, I do have other ideas. So, like, when race car drivers are in their cars, you know, like, during races, they wear these clothes that keep them from catching on fire, right? Even if it's just for a few seconds or a minute. It lets them get help."

"It's called Nomex," Carl said, a know-it-all. "Firefighters use it, too."

"Okay, then we get that stuff. We make them wear socks and shirts and underwear made out of that stuff."

"But those fibers are to keep the fire away from people," Carl said. "The kids are the fire. We're not keeping the fire away from the kids. We're trying to keep the fire away from everyone else. From other things that might catch on fire."

"Wouldn't it work the same way? If it's flame . . . what do you call it?"

"Flame resistant," Carl replied.

"Right, if it's flame resistant, then it still does the same job. The kids catch on fire, and the material keeps it contained to them."

"I guess that's right," Carl said, like I'd solved a very simple math problem but it was still kind of impressive.

"It buys us time. It protects us. It protects the house. Right?"

"I guess so," he said. And then, like it had just occurred to him, he continued, "I have a buddy. He's a stuntman in Hollywood. They have this kind of gel, a water-based gel, that they use for fire stunts. You rub it on your skin and the fire won't hurt you. It would do the same thing. The kids catch on fire, and this gel would contain it just long enough for us to put them out."

"Okay, cool. Buy, like, a hundred gallons of that gel. Buy firefighter clothes. But that's only half of the problem."

"What else?" he asked.

"We have to keep them from catching on fire in the first place. We have to make it so that when they find themselves in situations where they usually catch on fire, they don't catch on fire."

"Zen meditation," he said, actually snapping his fingers, like it all made sense now, like maybe I wasn't as insane as he'd thought.

"Something like that," I said. "One of my mom's boyfriends did yoga, and, god, it was so stupid-looking and irritating because we all had to be quiet while he did it, but he was the calmest motherfucker I've ever met in my life. Nothing my mom did would even faze him for a second. She ended up leaving him because he was too calm. She said—"

"That's fine, Lillian," Carl said, cutting me off.

"Anyway, we do yoga every morning. We teach them, I don't know, like a mantra or something so they can calm themselves down."

"Why not just give them a ton of medication, lithium or something? Keep them at an enforced level?"

"Do you think Jasper wants us drugging his kids?"

"I don't think we have to tell Jasper that we're drugging his kids," Carl replied.

"We're not drugging children, okay?" I said. "We do deep breathing exercises. We stay calm."

"Cognitive behavioral therapy," he said.

"Well, get me some books on that," I told him. "Get me that weird fire gel from Hollywood and get me books on cognitive behavioral therapy. Yoga tapes."

"Okay," he said, and he sounded actually kind of satisfied. "Okay, this is what we'll do."

"What is?" Bessie said. She and Roland were standing right beside us. Even Carl jumped when he heard her.

"You're supposed to be in the pool," I told them.

"Tell me about that stuntman gel," Roland asked Carl.

"No pills," Bessie said. "No pills. If you tried to make us take something, it would make me so angry. I would catch the couch on fire."

"No pills," I said, nodding.

"Okay," Bessie said, and her gaze was so far off, staring into a deep cave, like she still wasn't sure that she could trust me, which kind of hurt my feelings. Then I realized that my brainstorming notebook had listed sleeping pills as an option.

"The real reason that I came to see you," Carl said, "is that Mrs. Roberts wants to have a family dinner. Senator Roberts will be home this weekend. She wants the children to come to the house. She wants to try to make this work."

"Can we have pizza?" Roland asked. "Or chicken nuggets?"

"That's not up to me, Roland," Carl said.

"So we get to go over there?" I asked, not quite believing it.

"In four days," he said. "As long as there aren't any incidents in the meantime."

"It's not our fault, okay?" Bessie said, indignant.

"We were born this way!" Roland shouted.

"I'd better get going," Carl said, standing up. "Good luck, Lillian."

"Bye, Carl," I said, and, then, out of the corner of my eye, I saw Roland peeing directly into the pool.

"Roland!" I shouted.

"The chemicals," he said, flustered. "The pool stays clean."

"Look at that jerk," Bessie said, and I thought she meant her brother, but then I saw that she was looking back at the house, and there was Timothy again, holding a stuffed animal, looking at us through those opera glasses. And behind him was Madison, beautiful even from this distance. I waved, and Madison waved back. I gave her a thumbs-up. I wanted to tell her about Nomex, about yoga, but she was so far away, all the way in that giant mansion. I missed her.

"Okay, kiddos," I told them. "Back in the pool." They groaned, but then cannonballed into the water, splashing my legs.

"Come in with us," Bessie said, but I shook my head. I got up and walked to a lounge chair, reclined. In my sunglasses, I felt like a movie star. I couldn't see myself, which helped the fantasy. "I'm going to lounge for a bit," I said.

"Aw," Roland said. "That's no fun."

"Watch us," Bessie said, her hand slapping the surface of the water, like she was punishing some stupid baby.

"I am watching," I said. With my sunglasses, they couldn't really tell where I was looking. I just needed a second, this little space where they were not my entire world. I needed the smallest break. Who would deny me this? I mean, besides these two kids. I looked up at the clouds. They all looked like things, but I was too tired to give them names.

I wondered what Madison was doing. It was hard not to feel like she had tricked me. I had barely seen her. I remembered those first days, before the kids, when it was just the two of us. She bought me a wardrobe. We played basketball. I thought we'd be together. I mean, I knew I'd be here, with the kids, but in my mind, Madison was sitting next to me, laughing. I thought we'd be eating those dainty, gross tea sandwiches while the kids played hopscotch or some shit.

"Watch us," Bessie said again, louder.

"I am watching you," I said. "You look beautiful."

"Aww," Roland said, knowing that I was lying.

I felt the sun on my face, listened to the sound of the kids in the pool. It was peaceful. It was boring as shit, but it was peaceful. I closed my eyes for a second. The summer seemed to stretch out for miles, forever.

When I woke up, my whole body startling into consciousness, I looked in the pool and the kids were gone. How long had I been asleep? A minute? Eight years? Anything between these two periods of time seemed possible. My neck was killing me. "Bessie?" I said, quiet, so no one would hear me. It defeated the purpose, but I was trying to be cool, so cool. "Roland?" I said. Nothing. The pool was calm, empty. I looked around. The kids were gone. I instinctively looked toward the windows in the mansion. There was no sign of Timothy, no witness to my irresponsibility. And then I thought, *What if the kids are in the mansion? What if they sneaked into it? What if they've got Timothy in a headlock?* I felt sick to my stomach.

I stood up and started walking around the pool, checking behind the lounge chairs, making sure they weren't hiding from me to teach me a lesson. I looked into the pool, all the way to the bottom, but it was empty. I ran back to the guesthouse, opened the door, and shouted for them, but there was no response. I checked every room: no sign of them. I looked at the phone, thought for a split second about calling Carl, but I could not imagine the judgment inherent in that interaction. I'd never live it down. It would be noted in the permanent record on me that Carl kept inside his brain.

I slipped into the mansion undetected and went to the kitchen, where Mary was making pasta, folding the dough into these intricate little purses.

"Mary, have you seen the kids?" I asked her, so casual, like I already knew the answer and was only testing her.

"Not in here," Mary said, not even looking up at me. "You lose them?"

"Maybe," I said, unable to lie to Mary. She smiled a little, her hands moving so effortlessly. "Better find them," she replied.

"I guess so," I said. "Don't tell Madison about this?"

"No," Mary said, the word so certain, so strong, that I wanted to kiss her. I knew we weren't in this together. But it made me happy to be protected by her, even if just for a few seconds.

And now the world seemed to become large and overwhelming. I'd spent so much time inside this estate, which, yes, was fucking huge, but it had seemed manageable, safe. I looked around, I am not joking, to see if the kids had sprinkled bread crumbs to make their path visible to me. They had not. Goddamn, these children. Not a single crumb of bread. And now some witch was eating them. Or they were burning down the witch's house. Whatever they were doing, I knew who would get blamed.

I kept walking, not calling out for them, trying to locate them by some kind of ESP, like I would find them just by holding them in my mind until they simply appeared in front of me, definitely not on fire. I kept looking toward the horizon, searching for smoke.

And now that I was a one-woman search party, it finally hit me that I was responsible for these children, me and me alone. This was a big fucking responsibility. Why had Madison and Jasper entrusted me with such a job? The magnitude, the lives of two children, holy shit. It's strange that this didn't sink in when the kids were actually on fire. Fire had seemed manageable. Disappearing without a trace, that seemed more problematic, more serious. Or at least, I knew which situation would result in my getting blamed more than the other. One was genetics. One was negligence. I wasn't prepared for this. If someone stole a package of steaks from the Save-A-Lot, who cared? I didn't. I most certainly did not. This was different. How had it taken me this long to realize it?

And, then, like a second bolt of lightning, it struck me with dead certainty what would happen if the children disappeared, if they died, if they simply inconvenienced everyone around us. I would be blamed. And I would be sent back home. And just like all those years ago, when I'd been kicked out of Iron Mountain, everyone would sit there blaming me, wondering why I thought I was anything other than what I was. Madison? That would be the end of our relationship. She had asked me to do this one thing for her . . . well, this second thing for her. If I couldn't do it, if I failed her, why would she need me? I would lose her again. I had never let her down before. I felt my heart stutter in my chest. I couldn't let this happen.

"Kids!" I shouted now. "Bessie? Roland?" I walked into the woods at the edge of the estate. "Bessie! Roland! Come back! Get back here right now!" I shouted. I didn't care who heard. Maybe one of the gardeners would come running, help me look for them. But, no, it was just me. It was always going to be just me, walking into the dark woods, looking for these kids.

I kept following the trail that someone had blazed through the forest, though it was slightly overgrown and thorns kept sticking to my bathing suit. I wished I had something other than flip-flops on. "Bessie! I am not joking. Bessie? Come back," I said, but there was no response. I could be going in the exact wrong direction, but what else could I do? I just kept walking, every once in a while saying their names so they knew that I was coming for them. What I'd do with them when I found them, I tried to keep that out of my voice.

After about twenty minutes, I finally saw the woods open up, and there were the kids, right where the light came in. They were standing there in their swimsuits, and it looked like they were taking and retaking this one tentative step. They were so close to running away. Just beyond the woods was a road. But they were paralyzed, right at the moment when they had to decide. And I caught up to them. I was right on them. My hands were on them, touching their weird little bodies.

"You scared the absolute shit out of me," I told them, and I realized that I hadn't been breathing, that I'd been holding the air in my lungs until I had them in my grasp.

"Sorry," Bessie said, not looking at me.

"What the fuck were you doing?" I asked. "Why did you leave me?"

"You weren't watching us," Bessie said, so petulant, just like a child. "So we left. And then we kept walking."

"We tried to get a car to stop for us," Roland said, "but there have only been, like, two cars and they didn't even slow down."

"Why are you running away?" I asked them.

"It would be easier, right?" Bessie said. "If we just disappeared, everyone would be happy."

"I wouldn't be happy," I told her, meaning it. "I would be so sad."

"Really?" Roland asked, surprised.

"Yes—Jesus Christ—yes, I would be sad."

"Okay," Roland said, satisfied.

"And would you be happy?" I asked them.

"No," Bessie said. "Not really. I was just standing here, and I couldn't move because I didn't know where I could go. Not back to Mom. No way would we go back to Gran-Gran and Pop-Pop's house. Where else is there? We don't have anyone, Lillian. We don't have anyone."

"You have me, okay?" I said, and I guess I meant it. Regardless, it was a fact. They had me. They had me.

And all this time I'd been worried about what would happen to me if I fucked it up. I'd lose this life. I'd lose Madison. But I hadn't thought about the kids. If I failed them, where would they go? Somewhere bad, that was for sure. Somewhere worse than this life. Carl was ready to send them there. For all I knew, Jasper and Madison would be ready to send them there if I slipped up just a little bit. I remembered that feeling, driving down to the valley, no longer welcome at Iron Mountain. It had felt like my life was over. And it kind of was. I wouldn't let that happen to these kids. They were wild, like me. They deserved better, like me. I wouldn't fuck up. I resolved myself to this future. I would not fuck up. No fucking way.

And just then a car slowed, pulled over, rolled down its window. A dude in a Hawaiian shirt peered over at us.

"You need a ride?" he asked.

"No," Bessie said suddenly, her face red.

"You sure?" he asked. I had him figured out. He was not a threat. He was a doofus. Still, we were not meant to be seen. We were not for public consumption.

"We're on a hike," I told him.

"In your bathing suits?" he asked, curious.

"Hit the road," I said, making myself bitchy. It felt good.

"Well . . . bye," he said, driving off. We watched the car head down the road, disappear.

"Can we go back to the house?" Bessie finally asked me.

"Okay," I said. "Let's go." And the two of them took my hands, and we made our way back to the house that was ours but wasn't quite ours.

"Have you guys heard of yoga?" I asked them, and both kids groaned, because nothing that was called yoga was probably much fun.

"Just read to us?" Bessie asked. They were ten years old, but sometimes they seemed so much younger, undernourished, wild.

"Okay," I said. "Let's just read. I'll read you a story."

We listened to the sounds of the woods, and we noticed how, once we made it back home, those sounds had changed, gotten quieter. Or maybe they had gone inside us. Whatever it was, we were back. And we would not leave again.

THE NEXT MORNING, I AWOKE TO ROLAND'S FINGERS IN MY mouth, Bessie's feet pressed hard against my stomach. The possible inappropriateness of the situation, of sleeping with these two kids, gave me momentary pause, and then I thought, fuck it, nobody else was going to hold on to them. Their lives, up to this moment, could not have been less weird than sleeping with a grown woman who was nearly a stranger to them. I spit out Roland's fingers, and he twitched a little. I pushed my belly out, and Bessie felt the resistance and stirred. "Wake up, kiddos," I said, stretching my arms over my head.

"Do we have to go swimming again?" Bessie asked, and she seemed shocked that she had become bored with a swimming pool, glimmering chlorinated water.

"No. We've got a new routine," I said, trying to think of the routine. "We're doing some exercises."

"Right now?" Roland whined.

"Yes, right now," I told him.

"Can't we have breakfast first?" Bessie asked.

"I think, hm, I think we do exercises first. You don't want to exercise on a full stomach. That's bad for you, I think." I was making this shit up as I went along. I didn't have the yoga tapes from Carl yet, so I tried to remember my mom's ex-boyfriend. I couldn't recall the poses, though I did remember that his butt was often in the air in ways that made me embarrassed for him. He had a ponytail, which was distracting.

"What kind of exercises?" Bessie asked.

"Breathing exercises," I said.

"That doesn't sound much like exercising," Roland conceded, and I said, "Just sit on the floor."

They sat on the floor, their legs tucked underneath them. "Sit cross-legged, okay?" I said, demonstrating. I was not flexible, lived a life that required me to be tense at all times in case someone tried to fuck me over, and I found the simple act of making my spine erect, making my pelvis and thighs do regular stuff, was a little more difficult than I'd expected. I hoped that the kids didn't notice, but they were easily making their bodies into pretzels, like I could have twisted them into any shape and they could have held it.

"Now what?" Bessie said.

"Close your eyes," I said.

"No way," Bessie replied, and I again felt tenderness for her because I also understood how ridiculous my request was. When I was ten, I wouldn't have closed my eyes for all the money in the world.

"We're all going to close our eyes," I said.

"So you'll close your eyes, too?" Bessie asked, as if she hadn't expected it.

"Yes," I said, trying to maintain calm, to not be irritated.

"So you won't know if my eyes are closed or not?" she said.

"I guess not," I said. "I just have to trust you."

"You can trust me," Bessie said, and I knew that this was a test. So I just closed my eyes.

"Now," I said, feeling their hot little bodies, their sour breath, the tremors running all over them, "take a deep breath."

Roland sucked in air like he was trying to drink the world's biggest milkshake. He coughed a little.

"Just an easy, slow breath, and then you hold it," I said. I tried it myself. The air went inside me, more than you'd think, and I just held it. It sat there, mixed with whatever was in my body that made me who I was. And I don't know if the kids were doing it right or not, but I wasn't going to open my eyes. I held it, and it felt like the world was spinning just a little less quickly than it had been before.

"Now exhale," I said, and I could hear the relief in their lungs as they blew the air out of their bodies in one long, ragged exhalation.

"Are we done?" Bessie asked. I opened my eyes and saw that they both had their eyes closed.

"No," I said. "We're going to do it again."

"How many times?" Roland asked.

I had no clue.

"Fifty times?" I said, and Bessie immediately protested.

"No way," she said. "No way fifty times; come on, Lillian."

"Okay, okay," I said. "Twenty times."

"Fine," Bessie replied. And so that's what we did. We breathed. We held our breath. We breathed again. And I had never thought about it this way, had always assumed that whatever was inside me that made me toxic could not be diluted, but each subsequent breath made me a little more calm. And I lost track of time. I had no idea how many breaths we'd done. But I didn't care. I just kept breathing, and the temperature of the room stayed the same. And, finally, when it seemed enough, I said, "Okay, then."

"That's it?" Roland asked. "We're done? We can eat breakfast?"

"How did it feel?" I asked them.

"Silly," Bessie said. "At first. But it's okay. It wasn't so bad."

"So we'll do that every day," I said.

"Every day?" they both whined.

"Yes," I said. "And if you feel yourself getting worked up, you breathe like that. Okay?"

"I don't think that's going to work," Bessie admitted.

"We'll see," I said, and we went downstairs to eat Pop-Tarts and drink huge glasses of milk.

After breakfast, I got out these little workbooks from one of the closets, all wrapped in plastic from some educational company for weirdos who believed the end of the world was coming and wouldn't let their kids go to a normal school. Or maybe that's harsh. Maybe it was for parents who couldn't let their kids out of the house or else they'd catch on fire. Or, maybe, just parents who thought they could give their kids something good and true. Who knows? The workbooks were high quality, though, at least that.

I found a math workbook for fourth grade. What grade was ten years old? I had no idea. I tried to think back to my own life. Was it third? Fifth? I truly had no idea. The fourth grade one would be fine, I decided. I ripped out some pages, basic multiplication, and slapped them on the counter. The kids looked at them like they were written in Chinese.

"School?" Roland moaned. "No way."

"I just want to see what you know," I told them. "You'll be going to school in the fall."

"Mom never made us go to school," Bessie said. "She says school is for sheep. She says it's for people without creativity."

"Well, that's actually kind of true, but creative kids like you and me find ways to make it work."

"Why can't you just teach us?" Roland asked. "Or Madison?"

"We don't have the proper training," I told them. "Look, that's a long time from now. Right now, we're just going to practice. We're going to learn and have fun, okay?"

"I hate this," Bessie said.

"It's pretty basic stuff. Like, see, what's four times three?"

"Seven?" Roland offered.

"No," I said, and then quickly, "close, though."

"I hate this," Bessie said again.

"C'mon, Bessie. Four times three?"

"I have no idea," she replied, her face red with embarrassment.

"Okay, it's just four three times. So what's four plus four plus four?"

"I don't know," she said.

"It's twelve," I said. "Four plus four plus four is twelve. Four times three is twelve."

"I know that," Bessie said, her voice rising. "I know addition. I know." I could see her getting angry now, not just embarrassed. I could see her body getting red. She took the pencil and started to write a giant 12 on the page, but the pencil lead snapped off before she could even complete the first number.

"Breathe," I said, softly, calmly. "Okay, Bessie? Breathe deep."

"We never do math," Bessie said. "We don't do math, so we don't know math."

"Don't talk," I said. "Just breathe." I looked over at Roland. His mouth was wide open. He had drawn a frowny face on the worksheet. But he wasn't red. He wasn't angry.

"Roland," I said, so quiet, so calm, like I was euthanizing a cat, "go get me a towel, okay? From the bathroom. Roland?" Roland just stood there, frozen with fear. "A towel? A towel? Roland? In the bathroom? A towel? Roland? Can you get that for me? In the bathroom? A towel?"

"Okay," Roland finally said, and he ran off.

Bessie's face was all scrunched up. "I knew that Mom wasn't teaching us enough," she said. "She says math doesn't matter. But I knew this would happen. I knew this would happen, and everyone would think I was stupid. We tried to figure it out ourselves, but it didn't make sense. I tried, okay?"

"I can teach you, Bessie," I said, but she was really red now. I picked her up, felt how hot she was, and I set her on the floor. "Don't talk, just breathe. Can you breathe?"

Bessie started breathing, deep breaths. "It's not working!" she yelled.

Roland came back with a towel and I ran to the sink and soaked it, then wrung it out as much as I could. When I turned around, there were little flames starting to form on Bessie's arms, at her ankles. I took the towel and rubbed it on her arms and legs, and each time, there would be this steam coming off her.

"Bessie, please. Just breathe, okay? See, the towel is helping."

"Just throw me in the shower," Bessie said.

"No," I said. "We can do this." I rubbed the towel over her, then wrapped it around her body like a cocoon. Roland ran off, but I was too focused on Bessie to do anything about it.

"I'm right here, okay?" I said to her, whispering in her ear. Her body was so fucking warm, like the worst fever. The towel was smoking. "Just breathe. And then it will go away. And then we won't do the math worksheet. We'll have ice cream. And in a few days, we'll go to the mansion for our family dinner, and we'll eat whatever you want. And pretty soon, we'll go into town. We'll buy some toys. We'll get new books. We'll buy clothes that you like. We'll get a real sundae at a real ice cream shop."

"With sprinkles and a cherry. And hot fudge," she said. The towel was on fire, it was burning. I took it off Bessie and threw it on the floor, where it smoked. I stomped on it until the fire went out, which didn't take long. And then, like magic, Bessie wasn't on fire, like it had transferred from her to the towel.

"Okay," she said, looking at me. "Okay, then."

She sat on the floor, exhausted. I cradled her. "Where's Roland?" she asked.

"Roland?" I shouted. A few seconds later, Roland, fully dressed and absolutely soaking wet, walked into the living room, water pooling around him. "I jumped in the shower," he said.

"That's fine," I said.

"She's not on fire," Roland said, pointing at Bessie.

"Not right now," I replied.

Roland came and sat down next to us.

"I'm going to take care of you guys," I said.

"Are you a good person?" Bessie asked, which was such a strange question, the kind of question a kid asks because they haven't lived long enough to know how easy that question is to answer.

I paused, giving it mock thought. "Not really," I said. "I'm not a bad person, but I could be a lot better. Sorry. But here I am. And here you guys are."

"You'll leave, though," Bessie said.

"Someday," I said. "When you don't need me."

"I knew it," Bessie said.

"Not for a long time," I said. Was three months a long time to a kid? It was a long time to me.

Bessie and Roland looked at each other. They were doing that twin thing where they talked without talking.

"I'll stay as long as you want me to, okay?" I finally said. "I'll stay."

They didn't seem to hear me. We just sat there, and I prayed that Carl would not come to the house right at this moment. How would I explain it? I'd have to knock him out with a lamp, drag him to his car, and make him think that he'd dreamed the whole thing.

"Our mom—" Bessie said.

"I know," I said. "I know I'm not your mom. Nobody will be as good as your mom was—"

"She killed herself," she said. "Because of us."

I tried to remember if Madison had ever told me that their

mother had killed herself. Why hadn't she told me? Did she know? Was it a secret? If I ever saw Madison again, I'd ask her.

"Not because of you guys," I said. "C'mon now, Bessie."

"She said it was too hard. She said that things were going to change, that we'd have to start going to regular school, that she couldn't do it anymore. She said that our dad wanted us to be normal. She said that it would never happen."

"I'm sorry, Bessie," I said. Roland curled up, and I put my arm around him.

"She took all these pills," she said. "We watched her take all these pills. And then she died."

"Oh my god," I said. "I'm sorry."

Bessie looked like she was entirely empty of emotion, like there was nothing inside her. She looked over at Roland, who nodded.

"She told us to take the pills, too," she finally said.

"What?" I said, though I understood perfectly fine. What else could you do but pretend that you didn't know that was possible in this world?

"She had these two little plates with pills on them for me and Roland. And she said to take them. And she had these huge glasses of orange juice. She was crying and said that this would make all of us feel better."

"But we didn't take them," Roland said, his voice scratchy.

"I told Roland not to take them. We just put them in our pockets and pretended, and Mom didn't even notice. We drank all this orange juice, and it was so much that we had to pee. But then Mom made us go into the bedroom and we all got into the bed. And she said we had to go to sleep, even though it was daytime. And Roland was on one side of her and I was on the other. And I couldn't see him. Mom was between us. And

I put my hand on Mom's chest, and I felt her heartbeat, and it was fine."

"I'm sorry, Bessie," I said, because I wanted to have just a little bit of time, a moment before I had to hear the rest, because I wasn't ready to hear it.

"And it took forever, but then Mom fell asleep. And I had my hand on her chest. And it took forever. It took so long. And I had to pee so bad, so I just peed in the bed."

"And I peed the bed, too," Roland offered.

"And then she was really asleep. And I told Roland that we needed to get up. So we got up, and Mom was still asleep. And I knew that she was dead, because I felt her heartbeat. And then we changed our clothes because they were wet. I made us peanut butter and crackers, and we ate them. We took all the pills out of our pockets, and we flushed them down the toilet. And then we went outside. We went into the front yard. And then we both caught on fire. It was really big, the fire. It was more fire than we've ever made, our whole bodies. And the grass around us caught on fire. And then a tree caught on fire next to us. And somebody, people who lived, like, a mile away, saw the smoke, and they called 911. And that's how they found us. And that's how they found Mom."

And then she was quiet. And Roland was quiet. We were all breathing, in and out, deep breaths. Our hearts were so steady, so strong. If there were a button that would end the world, and that button were right in front of me, I would have smashed it so hard at that moment. I often thought about a button like that, and when I did, I always knew that I'd push it.

"That's awful," I said. "And that wasn't your fault. Your mom was going through something, and she didn't mean to hurt you guys. She just couldn't think clearly."

"Sometimes I think we should have just taken those pills," Bessie said, and I was about to cry, but these kids, who had been so fucked over by life, were not crying, and it felt like such a wimpy thing to do if they were holding it together.

"Then I wouldn't have met you," I said. "That would suck for me. I'd have been so angry."

"You'd have been pissed off," Roland offered.

"So pissed off," I said. "You guys are so cool, and I'd be sitting at home, all by myself, no friends, and I'd never know you guys had ever existed."

"You'd be so fucking pissed off," Bessie said, and it seemed to sound exactly right to her.

"So fucking pissed off," I agreed.

"I do want to learn math," Bessie said, and I almost laughed because, Jesus, what the fuck was she talking about right now? My muscles were so tight I thought I was dying, but I said, "I'll teach you math. We'll go slow."

"But not today," Bessie said.

"Not today," I said. And after a few minutes, I took the towel and threw it into the garbage can.

THAT NIGHT, WHILE THE KIDS WERE TAKING BATHS, THE phone rang. I hustled over to it, eager for any news from the outside world, wondering if something awful had happened. But it was just Carl.

"Oh," I said. "It's just you."

"I'm calling you on behalf of Mrs. Roberts," he said.

"Why doesn't she just call me?" I asked. "Or come over?"

"Can I give you the message," he asked, "or are you going to keep asking questions?"

"What does she want?" I finally replied.

"She would like to see you, tonight, at eleven P.M.," he said, and I could hear it in his voice, how miserable this was for him.

"Oh," I said. "I can't leave the kids, though, right?" I asked.

"I'm going to watch the children while you're meeting with Mrs. Roberts," he replied.

"You?" I said, almost laughing. "If they wake up and find you in the house instead of me, they will burn it to the ground."

"Do they ever wake up at night?" he asked.

"Well, no," I answered, perhaps realizing this for the first time, "they don't. They sleep like rocks."

"Okay, then," he said.

"Don't snoop around my stuff," I told him, and he didn't respond.

"Where do I go?" I asked.

"She'll meet you at the front door of the mansion," he said.

"What do I wear?" I asked. "Are we doing something?" I was starting to feel a little dizzy, not sure what to do. I wasn't sure that I could go back into that house again without passing out.

Carl took a deep, steadying breath. He was trying not to yell at me. "Just normal clothes," he said, and then hung up the phone.

I couldn't shake the feeling that I needed to tell the kids what I was up to. I felt like if they were going out while I was asleep, and Carl was on the sofa downstairs, I'd want to know. But I needed something for myself after so many hours with the children wrapped around me, the constant pressure. Madison was a secret, and I was going to keep it from them.

And it wasn't that hard to disentangle myself from them once they'd fallen asleep. I had been keeping children's hours since they'd arrived, finding it too much trouble to get out of bed. Once, actually, I think I fell asleep before they did.

I put on some cool jeans and a T-shirt, sneakers. I had to look good enough that if Madison wanted to see some alternative band in Nashville, I wouldn't have to come back to change, to tell Carl what we were up to.

At 10:55, Carl was at the door, holding a *Sports Illustrated* and a book of crossword puzzles.

"Hey, Carl," I said, smiling. "They're asleep."

"Have fun," he said, brushing past me. I wondered if he was jealous, if Senator Roberts ever played poker with him, let him drink some of his expensive scotch.

I walked under the stars, strolling across the manicured lawn, and then around to the front porch, where Madison was sitting in a rocking chair, waiting for me. She was wearing a huge T-shirt that came down past her knees and a pair of tights, no shoes. She had a bucket of iced-down beers, some chips and salsa. "Hey," she said, once I stood next to her.

"Hey," I replied.

"Sorry for the secrecy," she said.

"It's okay," I told her, and then I tried to think about what the secret was. Did the senator not know we were meeting? What was going on, exactly? "I mean, it's been a weird few days."

"Super weird," she said, nodding. "But . . . but you're okay?"

I nodded. "I'm okay," I said, though I liked being asked. No one had asked yet, and I realized how much I'd needed it.

"Thank you, Lillian," she finally said.

"You're welcome," I told her, and then I sat in the rocking chair next to her. She handed me one of the beers, and I drank it in a few gulps, not even trying to pace myself. I didn't know how much time I had before I'd have to go back to the kids. I was going to take what I could get.

Madison took a beer and sipped it slowly, staring out into the darkness. "They caught on fire," she said.

"They did," I answered.

"It was something to see," she admitted. "It was . . . well, it was so scary."

"It doesn't hurt them," I said, just as I realized that Madison wasn't worried about the kids.

"I mean, I knew that's what they did, of course," she continued. I realized this was what she needed me for. Someone to tell her that what she saw was real. "But I wasn't prepared for how . . . bright, I guess? How bright it was."

"It's intense," I admitted.

"And have they caught on fire since?" she asked.

"Nope," I lied. I didn't hesitate. "No fire. Not even a spark."

"Well . . . that's good," she replied. "That's what we hoped. I knew you could do it."

"How did you know?" I asked.

"I just knew," she said. "I just knew that if anyone could do it, it would be you."

In the years since high school, sometimes Madison would invite me to come visit her, to reunite, but in my next letter, I'd talk about everything but the invitation, hoping it would just drop. And it always would. Madison never tried too hard. And I had always wanted to say yes, but I couldn't bring myself to go to her. Because I worried that if I went, just once, and it didn't work out, if she realized that I wasn't who she thought I was, I'd never hear from her again. If I stayed where I was and she stayed where she was, we'd still have the year at Iron Mountain, when things had been perfect for a little while. And now here I was, sitting close to her, the world so silent that it was like no one else existed.

"Have you told them about me?" she finally asked, her voice so soft.

"The kids?" I said, and I could feel the disappointment in my stomach, to remember the reality of the situation. "Have I told them about you?"

"Yeah, like, have you talked me up? Have you told them that I'm good? That I'm cool? That I'm kind? That they can trust me?"

I was still trying to get the kids to believe all those things about me. I hadn't had time yet to bring anyone else into the discussion. But Madison looked so hopeful, and it was strange to see her this way, worried about what someone else thought of her.

"Of course," I said. "I told them that you're a great person, that you'll be a great stepmother to them."

"And they believe you?" she asked.

"I think so," I said. I could tell this didn't satisfy Madison, so I said, "By the end of the summer, I promise that they'll love you."

"Okay," she finally replied. "Find out what they like, and I'll buy a bunch of it and give it to them."

"Bribery?" I said, smiling.

"What's the point of having money if you can't use it to make people like you?" she said. She reached into the bucket and produced another beer, popped the top, and handed it to me.

"How much time do we have?" I asked her.

"How much time?" she replied, confused.

"Until I need to go back to the kids."

She thought about this, looking at me. "How much time do you need?" she asked, but I didn't even answer. Nothing that I said would be enough.

# Seven

"WE WANT TO SHOOT!" ROLAND SAID, BUT I WOULDN'T LET them. Not yet. We were building something, and we had to start with the most basic things. I was learning, with these children, you had to build some kind of foundation or life would get tricky very quickly.

"Okay, we're going to dribble," I told them, holding my basketball. I don't know why I hadn't thought of this before. It was the thing that I loved most in the world. Maybe raising children was just giving them the things you loved most in the world and hoping that they loved them, too.

And, okay, I understood that whatever I did was going to be stupid. The kids had confessed to me only two days earlier that their mom had tried to kill them. Of course, yes, Jesus, they needed to be in therapy. But it had been made clear to me that therapy was not an option. What else could I do? I had to believe that these children, who could not be burned, who were immune to hellfire for crying out loud, were simply tougher than most people. If their bodies were invulnerable to fire, what was inside them? Maybe they could keep themselves alive. Maybe I could keep them happy. And all I had, right at this moment, was basketball.

"We want to shoot!" Roland said again, looking at the basket, but I put my hand on his basketball—such a weird broken-wing form he had—and pushed the ball gently back toward him. My hand was still aching from Bessie's crazy teeth, but I could bend the fingers without much pain, and the swelling was gone.

"Do you know what dribbling is?" I asked them. They looked at each other. They did not like questions, I knew, but how else would I know?

"Like this?" Bessie finally said, slapping at the ball to make it hit the ground and come back to her. She caught it awkwardly, with both hands, like a fish had jumped out of the water and into her arms.

"Like that," I said. "That's all it is. You bounce the ball and it comes back to you."

"And this is fun?" Bessie said. "Dribbling is fun?"

"It's the most fun thing," I said. "You've got the ball, right? It's your ball. And you bounce it and it's not in your hand anymore. But before you can even worry, if you do it right, it bounces right back to you. And so you bounce it again. And it comes right back. And you do that, over and over, for hours every day, and after a while, you don't worry about it anymore. You know that ball is your ball and that you will never lose that ball. You know that it will always come back to you, that you can always touch it."

"That does sound nice," Bessie offered.

I felt like a coach in an inspirational movie, like the music would be really stirring, and you'd see the players' expressions as they started to get it, and it wouldn't be long before they were hoisting me up on their shoulders, fucking confetti just raining down on us.

And then Roland bounced the ball right off his goddamn toe, and it rolled all the way across the court.

"That's a good try," I said.

"I don't want to go get it," he said, but I told him, "You have to go get it," and he walked this Charlie Brown walk, head down, like a rain cloud was following him, until he picked up the ball and brought it back.

"So let's dribble," I said, and I watched them standing there, their bodies robotic and rigid, while they bounced the ball. Bessie actually seemed to get it. She was up to ten, then fifteen bounces before she mistimed the rhythm and had to catch the ball so it wouldn't bounce away.

"You're good," I said to Bessie, and she smiled.

"What about me?" Roland said, running off to chase down the ball he'd bounced off his toe again.

"You're pretty good, too," I said.

"I thought I was," Roland admitted.

We took a Gatorade break because eye-hand-coordination stuff is tricky with kids; it's so easy to get tired and just keep fucking up constantly. We ate bananas with peanut butter, each of us taking a turn licking the peanut butter off a butter knife.

"So you're good at this?" Bessie asked.

"I used to be. I used to be amazing," I said. Sometimes basketball was the only thing I was honest about or felt like I knew inherently.

"But you're short," she said. "Aren't basketball players real tall?"

"Some are," I said. "They have it easy. But I'm good even though I'm short."

"Can you, um, slam . . . slam-dunk it?" Roland asked.

These kids were like aliens, like they'd been given a really incomplete book about humans and were trying to remember every detail.

"No," I admitted. "But you don't have to slam-dunk to be good." I didn't tell them that I'd probably pay a million dollars just to dunk a basketball once in a real game. I would never admit this to anyone, but it was true.

"And you think this will keep us from catching on fire?" Bessie asked.

"I hope so," I said. "It always made me happy, kept me from wanting to kill people."

"You want to kill people?" Roland asked, confused, and I realized that I was talking to children. I'd already just assumed that they were my best friends or something insane.

"Sometimes," I admitted, no way to walk it back.

"Us too," Bessie said. And I knew who she meant. I knew she was thinking about Jasper.

We tried dribbling while walking around, which is harder than it seems. Doing two things at once for the first time, no matter how simple it looks, requires your body to adjust, to find the instinctual rhythm that makes it work. And the kids, Jesus, they were not good.

So we took a break, jumped in the pool. We ate bologna sandwiches, all that mustard, and we ate cheddar-and-sour-cream chips that turned our fingers orange. I realized that someday soon, I'd need to stop feeding these kids so much junk food and we'd have to start eating cottage cheese and figs and, I don't know, low-fat cookies. Wait, do healthy people like fat or hate fat? I'd always just eaten junk. Which I guess is why my body was always just a little too soft. I wasn't super heavy, because my anger burned calories like crazy, or so I imagined, but I was soft, always this give to my skin. I thought about Madison's body, and I wondered what it would be like to have that, if it required more effort than I imagined. But if I knew that a body like Madison's was possible for me, I guessed it would be worth the inconvenience to keep it.

After lunch, we went back and dribbled up and down the court. And Bessie, honestly, was good at it, or was figuring it out quickly. Roland was fine, good enough for a ten-year-old who had never touched a real basketball in his life, but Bessie started to move like the ball was on a string, finding that rhythm. At one point she started running, leaving Roland behind, which made him shout at her to slow down and wait for him, but she was gone. And she got a little too far ahead of herself, and the ball fell behind her for a second. And then I watched her reach behind her back, flick her wrist with the slightest motion, and send the ball bouncing toward her other hand, still moving, and she just kept going. I shouted out in approval. "You went behind the back," I said to her, and she looked so proud.

"It's fun," she said.

"My hand hurts," Roland whined when he caught up to us, but Bessie just stood there, thumping the ball against the court, again and again and again.

"Watch this," I said, and I picked up my ball and spun it on my finger, like a Globetrotter.

"Oh wow," Roland said, impressed, and I felt silly, but not enough to stop showing off. I tried to remember the last time I'd done something and received an *oh wow* from another human being. Years, probably. Maybe longer. I hadn't even gotten an *oh wow* when I gave in and did weird stuff in bed for guys I didn't care about.

"Hey," Bessie said, her face darkening. "Somebody's coming."

I figured it was a gardener or, at worst, Carl, but then I realized that it was Madison. She was holding a tray with a pitcher on it. Timothy was behind her, holding some plush weasel with a hunter's cap.

"Hello," Madison said. "We saw you playing and thought we'd come visit."

I wondered why she had decided to come see the kids. I wondered why, if the family dinner that weekend was so important, she undercut it by coming out now. Maybe this was just how she operated, always an envoy to test things before Jasper had to deal with them. Maybe her entire life was stepping out in front of everyone else because she knew that she was immortal, that nothing would hurt her. And I knew, even then, that this was mean, that Madison obviously had her own frailties. Her father was a fucking asshole, I knew that. Her brothers had never respected her. She had not become the president of the United States of America. I tried to feel tenderness for her, and it came easily enough.

"Timothy," Madison said to her son, "this is your brother, Roland, and your sister, Bessie."

"Half sister," Bessie said.

"That's true," Madison offered, "but I think it's easier for Timothy to think of you as his brother and sister."

"Okay," Bessie said, shrugging, though I could tell that she wanted this distinction to be made clear.

"Hi," Roland said to Timothy, who hid behind his mother. Eventually, though, he replied, "Hello," and things seemed okay.

She offered us lemonade and we each took a glass and it was so cold and so sweet. The kids gulped it like they were dying of thirst, the lemonade leaking down the fronts of their shirts.

"You're teaching them how to play basketball?" Madison asked me, and I couldn't tell whether she thought this was a good or a bad idea.

"Trying to," I said. "They're getting it."

"And things have been . . . good today?" she asked, and of course I knew what she meant. She meant, *Have these children, who are now my wards, caught on fire and burned something beyond repair? Are they demons? Will they hurt me? Will they keep Jasper from becoming secretary of state?*

I didn't know exactly how to answer all that. There was so much to cover. So I just nodded. "Things are fine," I said, as if that helped.

"Great," Madison said, and like she had torn the wrapping off a gift, she smiled and moved on to whatever was next. She was wearing this Lycra thing, like something a speed skater would wear, kind of risqué, honestly, or maybe only I thought that. "Have you been exercising?" I asked her.

"I was doing aerobics in the workout room," she said. "And then Timothy told me that you were out here, so I thought we'd come over and say hello."

"Hey, Timothy," I said, and the boy waved, the kind of wave that could easily have been dismissive but had just enough movement to be okay.

"Lillian is really good at basketball," Roland offered.

"She is," Madison acknowledged, and it gave me a slight thrill to hear it.

"Are you good at basketball?" Bessie asked her.

"I am," she said, not the slightest hesitation.

"Better than Lillian?" Roland asked.

"Different skill set," she said, and, even for me, an adult, this was not a satisfactory answer.

"You should play each other," Bessie said, and I shook my head.

"Madison has stuff to do," I told the kids.

"No," she offered. "I don't mind."

"Well, we have lessons, right?" I asked the kids. I don't know why I didn't want to play her. Well, shit, no, I knew why. I didn't want to lose in front of the kids. I didn't want them to love her more than they loved me.

"No lessons," the twins whined.

Madison took the ball out of my hands and started dribbling. "It'll be fun," she said. "Come on."

I tried to think of a time when I hadn't done what Madison had asked me to do. That time did not exist.

"Okay," I said. "A quick game, I guess."

"Timothy," Madison said, "sit on the bleachers there with Roland and Bessie." Timothy looked like he'd been asked to sit on a hill of fire ants, but he did what he was told. Bessie and Roland sat scrunched together on the edge of the bleachers, amazed to see this sport, this game of basketball, performed right in front of them, like it had been invented only fifteen minutes earlier.

"Do you need to warm up?" I asked her, and she shook her head.

"I'm good," she said. "We'll play to ten." She passed the ball to me and set herself for whatever would follow. She was giving me enough room to shoot, almost daring me to take the shot, just to get a sense of my range. Or maybe, I thought as I started dribbling, she wanted me to drive, so she would tower over me, ruling the interior. I faked a drive, but Madison didn't even seem concerned, simply postured up again and waited. I threw up a shot, perfect from the moment it left my hand, and it fell effortlessly through the hoop.

"Hell yes!" Roland shouted.

"Watch your language around Timothy," I said, and Madison nodded her approval, of both the admonishment and the shot.

She had chased down the ball and passed it back to me. 1–0. This time, she played me a little closer, those long arms, her hand just a few inches from my face, her fingers almost wiggling. I stepped back, took the shot, and it went through the hoop again, nothing but net.

"Yay," Roland said.

"Nice shot," Madison said, and I didn't reply. My heart was racing. I loved playing. Even at the YMCA, when I played girls a lot younger than me but not nearly as good, when I played men who let me join, no matter what the stakes were, I would feel my heart hammering in my chest. Like I couldn't believe I was getting to do this, like it might be the last time. And I loved the way it felt.

This time, Madison was right on me, and I dribbled to get away from her, but she moved laterally with ease, sticking to me. I faked a drive, put up a shot, and Madison, not even really jumping up, managed to get the tip of her finger on it, which sent the ball off its course. It hit the side of the rim and bounced away. In two steps, Madison had it, and she reset. I got low, bending my knees, my arms spread out. She drove by me, smacking my shoulder hard enough to spin me just a little, and put up a floater that bounced around the rim before falling in.

"Yay," Timothy said, a little squeak, and Roland and Bessie turned and frowned at the kid.

"Good one," I said.

"Lucky," she admitted. "You're good."

"So are you," I replied.

"We're still good," she said.

"We are," I agreed.

And then she drove right past me, like a fucking gazelle, and rose up so high that for just a second I thought she might dunk. She hit the layup, and this time all three kids on the bench went "OOOOHHHH," and I got red and a little angry. And now, only in that single moment when I checked the ball for Madison and she stared at me, did I know that we were actually playing. That this was a game. And that one of us would lose, and one of us would win. And I wanted to win. I truly wanted to win.

And it went on like this, trading baskets, me hitting my jumpers from outside but not able to get much going inside, while Madison used her size to force me to post up while she kept banking in these turnaround jump shots. No one ever led by more than two points. The kids were really into it. Timothy scooted closer to the siblings, assured that they would not eat him, or, god forbid, smudge dirt on his slacks.

It was tied, 9–9, and I had just pulled down a rebound when Madison's jumper clanked off the rim. "Goddamn," she muttered under her breath. We were really sweating now, Madison because she had just recently killed herself doing aerobics and me because I hadn't really exercised since I'd moved to the estate. My arms felt like rubber, but I dribbled between my legs, looking for something. Madison was right there, waiting for me.

"C'mon, Lillian," Bessie said, and there was way more intensity in her voice than I wanted there to be. I looked over at the kids. "Breathe now," I said, afraid they were going to burst into flames, and just saying this made Madison look worried for a second, checking on Timothy. And if I'd driven to the basket right then, I would have hit an easy layup, but I let her recover. I drove and then did my little step-back move, and the moment I put up the shot I knew it was off, so I started running toward the basket. And when Madison felt that pressure from me, that movement, she turned and ran to the basket, too. And, like I knew it would, the ball hit the rim and nearly got a playground bounce before it skittered away. I was about to reach it when I felt something hard slam into my face, and all these stars blasted into my head, this stinging pain.

"Oh, fuck!" I said, holding my left eye, and I heard Madison say, "Oh, shit, sorry."

I just stood there, pressing the palm of my hand hard against my eye, like I could jam the pain back inside me. But that wasn't working. When the pain finally turned into something throbbing and manageable, I looked over at Madison, who was holding the ball. "What happened?" I asked.

"She hit you in the face," Bessie said, "with her elbow."

"It was an accident, of course," Madison said. "Shit, I'm sorry, Lillian."

"Does it look bad?" I asked, and Madison immediately started to nod.

"It looks pretty bad, yes," she replied.

"That's not fair," Roland said, but I waved him off.

"It was an accident," I said, nodding to Madison. But I remembered how she played in high school, where things looked effortless until the pressure increased. Then she got weird with her elbows, could get dirty if it meant she'd win.

"It's the height thing," she said, now bouncing the ball. "You're right at my elbow."

"It's fine," I said, touching the edges around my eye, wincing. I didn't want to kill her, not really, but I wanted to beat her so bad.

"You can have the ball back," she said, "if you want to call a foul."

Ooh, maybe I did want to kill her, actually, but what could I do? The kids were watching. This was a game. "No, you got the rebound. It's good."

I scuffed my high-tops on the court, digging in, knowing she'd be backing me up to the rim, wearing me down, seeing what she could do to me. She was at the three line, and she kind of shrugged and then started dribbling. And then, like a rifle shot, she fired a perfect jumper, way outside her usual range, and it went right in. And that was that. Madison had won. I had lost. I was good, but she was better.

"Yay, Mommy," Timothy said, and this time Roland and Bessie didn't look angry. They looked sad. Defeated. Like they had hoped for something different and now felt embarrassed for having thought it might happen. I knew that look. I knew that feeling. And it hurt me to know that I'd made them feel that way.

"We should get some ice on that," Madison said to me.

"We have some at the house," I said. "I'll get it."

"It'll still look pretty bad," she said. "Again, I'm sorry."

"It's no problem. It's basketball. Good shot, by the way."

"I can't believe I hit it," she replied.

"I can," I said. I turned to Bessie and Roland. "Okay, kiddos," I said. "Let's get a snack."

"Your eye is really messed up," Roland said.

"It'll be okay," I told him.

"Timothy," Madison said, "say goodbye to Bessie and Roland."

"Goodbye," he said, and the twins grunted and waved.

"See you in a couple days for dinner," Madison said. "And then maybe one night we can have a night with just the two of us. Have a drink and sit on the porch."

"That would be nice," I said, gritting my teeth, my head still cloudy.

We watched the two of them walk off, leaving us behind, and then Bessie went over to the basketball and started dribbling.

She looked at me. "How did you do that thing where you dribble between your legs?"

"Practice," I said. "Just kind of using both hands to put the ball in the right place, bending your knees."

"Can I do that?" she said. "Can you teach me?"

"Sure," I said.

She looked up at the hoop like it was a mountain, like the air was thinner up there. She weighed the ball, shifting it between her hands, and then threw up a pretty ugly shot. It took part in three distinct movements, but I was amazed that she got it up to the hoop, just over the front of it. It bounced up in the air, and then it bounced and bounced and bounced, and I was just praying, *Pleasepleasepleasepleaseplease,* and then the ball fell through the hoop, the luckiest shot I'd seen in a long time. It was true happiness I felt, that I felt for Bessie, because I knew what it felt like to make that shot, to get what you asked for, and how rare that was in life.

"Oh my god, Bessie!" Roland shouted. "That was amazing!"

"Was it good, Lillian?" she asked me.

"It was amazing," I said.

"I think I like basketball," she said, not smiling, a little angry, like she was accepting some kind of ancient curse.

"I don't like it so much," Roland admitted, "but it's okay."

"Let's go back home," I said. "We have lessons."

The kids groaned, but I could tell that they weren't that upset, that they'd let me take care of them, that I'd make them do stuff they hated, but they'd let it happen. Because who else did they have but me?

# Eight

THE NEXT DAY, STILL NO FIRES, DEEP BREATHING, A LITTLE yoga from a tape that Carl had left on our doorstep, we sat in the living room, class in session. They had their notebooks open, pencils ready, and I felt like a small animal about to be run over by a tractor, or like a meteor was about to hit Earth and I was the only person who knew and I was trying to be real cool about it so no one panicked. I had assumed that if I had been a good student, it wouldn't be that hard to be a good teacher. But teaching required preparation. You had to learn it first, and then you taught it. I didn't have that kind of time. At night, the children slept in my arms, bashing me with their limbs while they dreamed of manageable terrors. When would I study? They were always with me. So I was winging it.

The night before, my eye had swollen completely shut from Madison's errant elbow, the skin angry and purple. And I rued the fact that the other side of my face, where Bessie had clawed me in the pool, was just starting to heal and scab over. The kids kept asking if they could touch the new bruise, if I wanted to put more ice on it, like I hadn't spent the last few hours holding a bag of ice to my face. They seemed intrigued by my pain, the way I seemed to bear it without complaining. I think they appreciated this about me, that I wouldn't cry. I had battle scars, and their skin could not be marked, not even by fire.

That morning, when I looked in the mirror, it was gruesome, radiating nearly to my hairline. During our breathing exercises I would occasionally steal a glance at the kids, and they were openly staring at the injury, the whole time taking cleansing breaths of air into their lungs.

We were doing Tennessee history, since I wanted their learning to be connected to their lives, to feel like we weren't rigidly adhering to whatever "the man" said we needed to learn. But now, I kind of missed "the man." He was always so confident, even when—especially when—he was fucking things up left and right.

"So," I said, tapping the cool little chalkboard, like something from a one-room schoolhouse on the prairie, "let's think of famous Tennesseans and then we can go to the library and find out more about them." I want to say that, yes, the Internet existed. Madison had it in the mansion. But I didn't really know anything about it. The one time I'd been on it, at the house of a guy who sometimes invited me over to smoke weed, I'd waited for, like, thirty minutes to print off Wu-Tang Clan lyrics. I honestly had no idea what else the Internet might be used for.

So what we had was the library, and I used that, a trip out in public, as a way to get them to focus. "Who are famous people from Tennessee?" I asked them. They just shrugged.

"You don't know anyone famous who was born in Tennessee?" I asked again, then I tried to think if *I* knew anyone famous from Tennessee. I knew the professional wrestler Jimmy Valiant was from a town near my own, because some guy at the Save-A-Lot talked about it all the time. But he didn't seem famous enough.

"Our dad, I guess," Roland offered.

I blanched, visibly. "Somebody else," I said.

"We don't know," Bessie said, again frustrated to have to admit what she didn't know. I watched her stop, take deep breaths. I was proud of her. She looked at her notebook, thinking. "Ooh," she suddenly exclaimed. "I know!"

"Who?" Roland asked, genuinely curious.

"Dolly Parton!" she said.

"Holy shit," I said. "Oops, okay, sorry, but, yeah, that's perfect. Dolly Parton is perfect."

"Mom played some of her records for us," Roland admitted. "*Jolene.*"

"*Nine to Five,*" Bessie said.

I thought it over. Dollywood. "Islands in the Stream." That body. She was the best thing that had ever come out of Tennessee. Jesus Christ, it wasn't even close. Bessie had got it on the first try.

"She's the greatest," I said. "So let's write that down. We'll see if we can find a biography of her at the library."

"Who else?" Roland said, now excited, like it was a game.

"Well," I said, "Daniel Boone, maybe? No, wait, Davy Crockett."

"With the coonskin cap?" Bessie asked. "Our mom had a record about him, too."

"That's him. I think he's from Tennessee. We'll look it up." There was a row of encyclopedias, so I grabbed the third volume (*Ceara* through *Deluc*) and looked it up. "Okay, yes, he was born in Greene County, Tennessee," I told them. "Add that to the list."

"Who else?" Roland asked, a black hole, wanting everything. But I was confident now. I was rolling.

"Oh, I think, um, Alvin York?" I offered. I knew he had a hospital or something named after him near Nashville. There was a movie one of my mom's boyfriends made us watch that starred Jimmy Stewart or Gary Cooper, someone handsome like a dad should be. "He was in one of the world wars, maybe World War Two. He killed, like, a lot of Germans. I think that's right. He killed a ridiculous amount all by himself."

"Ooh, I'll do my report on him," Roland said.

"Okay, that's perfect," I told them. "Bessie, you'll write a report on Dolly Parton, I'll do some research on Davy Crockett, and, Roland, you'll do Sergeant York. Is that cool?"

"Super cool," Bessie said. It was weird to realize that, for all the ways that they'd been neglected, they were intelligent, so quick to figure things out. You only had to tell them once, and then they knew what to do.

"So can we go to the library?" Roland asked.

"And get ice cream?" Bessie asked.

"Well, let me check with Carl," I said, and both kids groaned, fell dramatically across the sofa.

I went over to the phone and dialed his number. He answered before the first ring had ended.

"Yes?" he said.

"It's Lillian," I said.

"Yes, I know. What's going on?"

"Oh, not much. Just wanted to hear the sound of your voice," I said, just to fuck with him.

"Lillian, what do you need?"

"Are you busy?" I asked.

"Obviously this isn't an emergency, so I'm going to hang—"

"We need to go into town," I finally told him. "To the library."

"I don't think that's a great idea," he replied.

"So we'll never leave the estate?" I asked. "We can't live like this, okay?"

"Jesus," he said, his voice rising and then, with crazy self-control, lowering before he finished the sentence, "they haven't even been there a week. You act like it's the Iran hostage crisis or something."

"Well, to them it is," I replied, keeping my voice low so the kids wouldn't hear. "The more we keep them cooped up in here, the more they feel like freaks, like we're hiding them."

"I don't think this is a good idea," he said.

"I'll be with them the whole time," I told him.

"If they go," he said, "*if* they go, then we'll both be with them."

"That's fine," I said.

"Let me talk to Senator Roberts," he finally said.

"Isn't he busy?" I asked.

"He is," he said. "He's incredibly busy, and he's not going to be happy to be disturbed."

"Then just ask Madison," I told him, and he paused for a long time. "You know I'm right," I continued. "You know it, Carl."

"Fine," he said. "I'll call you back."

I turned to the kids. "Maybe!" I said, but I said it in this really hyperpositive way, like the power of my good cheer would make it happen.

"Yes!" they shouted. "We're going to the library!"

"Maybe!" I said, this time with my teeth showing too much, like I was being held at gunpoint but couldn't let anyone know.

Ten minutes later, while the kids were kind of shimmying

around the room, like maybe moonwalking poorly, the phone rang and it was Carl.

"Okay," he said. "We can go. I'm coming over there. I have something that I want to try."

"Come on over," I said, so excited. With the chance to leave the place, I finally realized how long I'd been at the estate, how stir-crazy I'd become. I'd still have the kids with me, and they still might catch on fire, but if they did, there'd be so much open space for me to run away and hide from the consequences.

"We're going to the library!" I said, and the kids did their weird shimmy dance, and I wondered if that's what they'd been taught was dancing.

When Carl showed up, we were all dressed and ready, the kids' awful hair slicked down and styled like they were in a Duran Duran cover band. I had tried to put makeup on the bruise, but it made it look worse somehow, almost like I was faking an injury, so I rubbed it off, which hurt like hell.

"Dear lord," Carl said when he looked at me. "What happened to you?" He immediately looked at the kids. "What happened to her?" He suspected them entirely.

"Madison hit her!" Roland said.

"Basketball," I told him. "It's fine."

"Mrs. Roberts plays to win," Carl admitted, as if my face getting smashed made perfect sense to him now.

"Did you put ice on it?" he asked, and I just made a face.

Carl was holding this giant black bucket.

"What's that?" I asked, changing the subject, and Bessie shouted, "It's ice cream!"

"No—" Carl replied, his face so pained, like these feral kids actively caused him real and lasting trauma. "It's not ice cream. Why would you think it was ice cream?"

"It's in a big bucket," Roland offered.

"I kind of promised them that we could have ice cream," I told him.

"Well, it's not ice cream. Sorry."

"What is it then?" I asked.

"It's stunt gel," he said. "Remember? What we talked about?"

"Oh," I said, remembering. "That's a big bucket."

"I had to buy it in bulk," he said. "I have six more buckets, five gallons each, in the garage. So it'd better work." He pried open the bucket and we all looked inside like it might hold the soul of an ancient king. But it wasn't exciting. It was just a big bucket of gel. It looked, honestly, like semen. It looked like a big bucket of, I don't know, drool. The point is, it looked gross. And we were supposed to slather the kids in it.

Carl rubbed a little on his index finger and then clicked open a lighter, the flame nearly an inch high. He held his finger right over the flame, then directly in the flame, for about three seconds. "Nothing," he said. "It's good."

"It smells funny," Bessie said, holding her nose. It actually smelled kind of like eucalyptus, but it was overpowering, so much so that it seemed unsafe.

"Okay," Carl said. "So I talked to my buddy, and he said we just apply it directly to their skin—and, yes, he says that it's safe—and that should do it. And we just reapply it throughout the day, I guess."

"You guess?" I said. "You don't know?"

"Well," he said, "I couldn't tell him the real reason for why we were getting it, could I? And stuntmen don't just walk around all day with it on. They do it for a specific scene, a single shot. But, yes, it's mostly just water and tea tree oil with some scientific stuff added to it. It's safe, I think."

"Why are we talking about this?" Bessie asked, slowly backing away from the bucket.

"It's for you guys," I said, "to help keep you from catching." At this point, I didn't want to say *fire* around them if I could avoid it. I just called it *catching*.

"Why can't we just keep doing the breathing stuff?" she asked.

"This is an extra level of security," Carl said, and I so badly wanted Carl, that square, to shut up. He wasn't helping. "It's kind of a plan B, okay?"

"I don't want to put that on," she said.

"What about the fireman stuff?" I asked Carl.

"The Nomex?" he replied. "I'm still waiting for it."

"Why is it taking so long?" I asked.

"First of all, it's only been a few days, okay, Lillian? And how easy do you think it is to obtain it? Like, do you think I can just find child sizes of Nomex clothing at Walmart? Like, for tiny firefighters? I'm having to get it altered. It's complicated. I'm being pushed to my limits in terms of thinking creatively about our situation."

He looked a little frazzled, actually, his hair not perfectly combed, and so I put up my hands. "Fine," I said. "I'm sorry. Thank you for all that you're doing."

"Thank you," he replied.

"Okay, kiddos," I said. "Let's just try it, okay? It's like a science experiment. This will be our science lesson for today."

"You first," Bessie said.

"Of—of course," I said, angry at the reversal but acting like I'd already thought of it, "of course I'll go first." I looked at Carl, and he blushed a little. Then he dipped his hand into the bucket and took a sharp breath. "Cold," he grunted. The gel was weird and viscous, and he started to apply it to my bare arm. It was so cold, just so weirdly cold that it kind of felt good. He rubbed up and down my arm, coating it. Then he did the other.

"Do you want to do your legs?" he asked, and I shook my head. "That's good for me," I told him. He held up the lighter and flicked the flame back into existence. "Don't flinch or anything," he said. "It doesn't hurt." He held the flame directly under my arm, and there was this weird moment where I was certain that my skin was burning, that I was on fire, but I just gritted my teeth and realized that, no, I was fine. I wasn't burning. And even for a few seconds, it felt amazing, like nothing could ever hurt me. Was this what the children felt when they were burning? I had no idea, but I wished it would last forever.

Once Carl turned off the lighter, I looked at the kids, showing them that I was fine. "See, it's awesome. God, it's really neat. And it's cooling. It feels good in this hot weather."

Roland put out his arms. "It's like slime," he said, excited. "It's so gross."

Carl kind of grinned, just a little, and then dipped his hands into the bucket. He did Roland, and I did Bessie, their arms and legs. "It's so cold!" Roland shouted. When we were finished, we stared at them, appraising how strange they looked, like a ghost had run right through them and left them traumatized.

"It's not . . . it's not great," Carl admitted.

"Maybe it'll dry a little?" I said. "It'll get a little less . . . shimmery?"

"I don't think so," he said. "But let's go. Let's just get it over with."

I SAT IN THE BACK OF THE VAN WITH THE KIDS, TOWELS ON the upholstery to protect it from the gel, while Carl drove us to the public library. Even though they'd been chattering about getting off the estate, the kids were eerily silent on the drive, like they'd been drugged, their faces pressed against the windows.

When we pulled into the parking lot, Bessie said, "What if they don't have the book that we want?"

"They'll have it," I said.

"Maybe you should go in and check them out for us," she said, leaning back in her seat.

"That's fine with me," Carl said. "Tell me the books that you want, and I'll get them."

"No," I said. "That defeats the whole purpose of coming."

"I don't want to go in there," Bessie said. "Everyone is going to stare at us."

"No one is going to stare at you, Bessie," I told her.

"They will. They'll think we're weirdos."

"Honestly, Bessie? People don't care about anyone but themselves. They don't notice anything. They are never looking at what's interesting. They're always looking at themselves."

"Are you sure?" she asked.

"I promise," I told her, hoping that I was right.

"C'mon," Carl said. "Let's move."

We walked into the library, air conditioner humming, not much activity on a weekday morning. The librarian, an old man with thick glasses and a really lovely smile that showed crooked teeth, waved to us. Bessie frowned, suspicious, but Roland said, "Hi!" A few seconds later, we passed an old lady with a stack of books in her arms. "Hi!" Roland said, and she nodded. There was a toddler in the kids' area with her mother, and Roland said, "Hi!" and the toddler looked confused, but the mother replied with her own greeting.

Carl said, "Roland, you don't have to say hi to everyone, okay?"

"Don't make it weird, Carl," I said. "It's fine, Roland. Say hi to anyone you want."

"I will," Roland said, looking over his shoulder at Carl and making a face.

We walked over to a computer and did a quick search. Carl went with Roland to one section of the library, and Bessie and I walked over to another stack. "I feel funny," Bessie said. "This stuff feels funny on my skin. I don't like it."

"I kind of like it," I said, looking at my arms.

"Let's just go," she said, but I directed her to the aisle of books and we searched the call numbers until we found it: *Dolly: My Life and Other Unfinished Business*. Dolly looked like a good witch, like someone who just absolutely fucked up evil queens with her kindness.

"This looks good," Bessie said, flipping through the pages, calming herself. But as soon as she looked up at me, the anxiety returned. "Can we please go now?" she asked.

"Okay, okay," I said. "Let's find Carl and your brother."

As soon as I said it, Carl was there with his hand firmly attached to Roland's shoulder. Roland was holding two books on Sergeant York. "I think we're good," Carl said.

"Okay," I said. "Let's go check them out."

"Wait," Carl said. "Do you have a library card?"

"What?" I asked. "No. I don't have one. I don't even live here."

"Well, I don't have one," Carl said. "I don't have a library card."

"Carl, why don't you have a library card?" I asked him.

"Because," he said, staying calm, "I do not like to borrow things. I like to have them. I like to keep them. So I don't use the library. I just buy what I want."

"Well, go get a card. Go sign up for one."

"You need a proof of address," he said, "like a piece of mail."

"Do you have that?" I asked.

"Do I have a piece of mail with my address on it? On my person?" he replied. "Are you serious?"

"Well, why didn't you think about this before we drove here?" I asked.

"Stop fighting," Roland said. "Just ask the librarian if we can borrow them."

"We need a card," I said, and now it felt like we were stuck behind enemy lines with sensitive documents. It felt like a movie. Why was I doing this? Why didn't we just put the books away and come back another time? Why didn't we act like normal people instead of huddling up in the stacks, our bodies shiny with fire gel?

"I knew we shouldn't have come," Bessie said. It was weird to watch her, a kid who bit strangers, who seemed so angry, turn into this person, someone who was scared of the world. I wanted her to catch on fire, to jump out a window. That, I thought, I could handle. I could mitigate damage. I could not make people feel better.

"Do you want the book?" I asked Bessie.

"Yeah," she said, looking at the Dolly Parton book. "I mean, she seems like a cool lady."

I grabbed a book off the shelf, something about a monastery in Germany. "Give me that Dolly Parton book."

Carl said, "Lillian, we'll just come back. Madison definitely has a library card. She's on the board for the library."

"Here," I said, handing Carl the Dolly Parton book. "Put this in your pants."

"No way," he said, but I punched his arm as hard as I could. "Just do it," I told him.

Carl put the book down the front of his pants, and I hissed, "The back of your pants, man. Come on." Then I turned to Roland. "Pick one of these two books," I said, "and put the other one back," and Roland, god bless him, simply turned and threw one of the books into the aisle, so hard and so beautifully, the book skittering across the floor and then bumping against the wall.

"Put this one in your pants," I said, and he put it behind him, tucking it into his waistband and pulling his shirt over it.

"Lillian," Carl said, "this is not—"

"Come on," I said. I handed Bessie the monastery book. "Hold this and act normal, okay? Nothing to see here. No one cares. No one cares about us."

And I pushed them all, one-two-three, out of the aisle and we walked toward the exit.

"Find what you needed?" the librarian asked us, and I nodded. "We took a lot of notes," I said. "Good research."

As we passed through the doors, the alarm went off, and I looked surprised. Both children froze, and Carl looked like he was going to vomit. I kind of nudged Carl and Roland farther outside the door, onto the stairs.

"Oh my," I said, and the librarian stood up slowly, shaking his head.

"No problem," he said, but before he could get up, I looked

down at Bessie and took the book out of her hands. I walked back to the librarian, and he sat back down, relieved to not have to move.

"She's always grabbing things," I said, and the man laughed.

"No harm done," he said, and then he seemed to notice my bruise but was unfazed, to his credit. It made me love him.

"No harm," I said, "of course not," and then I walked outside, where the three of them were waiting for me.

"Let's just keep going, super cool," I said. "Nothing to see here."

When we got to the van and packed ourselves inside it, Carl and Roland removed the books from their pants. I took the book from Carl and handed it to Bessie.

"Thank you," Bessie said. "You stole it for me."

"We're borrowing it, okay?" I said. "Just in a roundabout way."

For a second, there was that weird flicker in her eyes, that wickedness that I loved, that I wanted to live inside. A wicked child was the most beautiful thing in the world.

"Nobody cares," she said.

"Nope," I replied.

"Nobody cares about us," she said, almost laughing.

Carl started the van, and we pulled out of the parking lot.

"We looked like a normal family in there," Roland said, and this made Carl breathe sharply through his nose.

"I guess so," I told Roland.

"Can we still have ice cream?" Bessie asked.

"Carl?" I asked.

"We can have ice cream," he said. "That's fine with me."

The kids read their books, and they leaned against me, and

even though I actually did not like to be touched, I just let it happen. I allowed it. It was fine.

**AFTER THE ICE CREAM—SO MANY SPRINKLES—STILL DELIRIOUS** from the simple act of walking into an open space, of not being inside our house, we happily went right back to that house and waited for the next day, when we'd have our family dinner.

That morning, we found ourselves easily taking up the routine. Roland was a master of yoga, and I eventually just kind of let him take it over, because my body simply wouldn't hold the positions. "This is easy," he said, doing this weird kind of crow pose, his entire body supported by his two noodle arms. "Why is this supposed to be hard?" We did some basic math, using Oreo cookies as props. We took notes for our biographies of Parton and York. We shot baskets, and I showed Bessie the proper form, the smoothness of it, the way the ball was just an extension of your arm. It took her a lot of effort, but she was hitting about twenty percent of her shots. And her dribbling, holy shit.

Sometimes, when the kids were invested in something, when they didn't look entirely blasted by how shitty their lives had been, I'd try to truly look at them. Of course, they both had those bright green eyes, like you'd see on the cover of a bad fantasy novel where the hero can turn into some kind of bird of prey. But they were not attractive children, the rest of their faces soft and undefined. They looked ratty. I hadn't even tried to fix their cult haircuts. I feared that fixing them would only make the kids more plain. They had round little bellies, way past the point when you'd expect a kid to lose it. Their teeth were just crooked enough that you could tell they hadn't been handled with care. And yet. And yet.

When Bessie managed to get the layup to bank perfectly off the backboard, her eyes got crazy; she started vibrating. When Roland watched you do anything, even open a can of peaches, he looked like he was cheering you on at mile marker nineteen of your marathon. When Roland put his fingers in my mouth in the middle of the night, when Bessie kicked me in the liver and made me startle awake, I did not hate them. No matter what happened after this, when the kids moved in to the mansion with Jasper and Madison and Timothy, no one would ever think that they were really a part of that immaculate family. They would always, kind of, belong to me. I had never wanted kids, because I had never wanted a man to give me a kid. The thought of it, gross; the expectation of it. But if a hole in the sky opened up and two weird children fell to Earth, smashing into the ground like meteroites, then that was something I could care for. If it gleamed like it was radiating danger, I'd hold it. I would.

"Are we gonna dress up for tonight?" Bessie suddenly asked me, breaking me out of my daydream.

"Do you want to dress up?" I asked.

"I just bet Madison and Timothy are gonna be dressed up. I don't want them to look better than us," she replied.

"Can I wear a tie?" Roland asked.

"I guess," I said, and he cheered and ran off, his only wish granted.

"Can you fix our hair?" Bessie asked. "Make it like Madison's?"

"I can't do that," I admitted. I had to be at least somewhat honest with her. "Madison is lucky," I told her. "She's just made that way."

"Can you make our hair look normal?" she asked.

"It's in a bad place," I said, and she nodded, like she knew. "There's not much you can do but let it grow out and then get it into the right shape."

"Could you cut it shorter?" she asked.

"I could," I guessed. I had learned how to cut one of my mother's boyfriends' hair. He'd get drunk and then try to talk me through the steps to make it neat. He knew what he liked, and I could eventually get it there. He let me shave him, too, which was terrifying, how badly I wanted to cut him, even though he was one of the nicer ones.

"I hate him," she said, meaning her father. "But I want him to think we're good."

"You are good," I said. "Your father knows that."

"No, he doesn't," Bessie said.

"He does, Bessie," I said.

She wouldn't say anything, and I just watched her grinding her teeth.

"What would you do to him?" I asked.

"What do you mean?" she replied, her eyebrow cocked.

"If he were here right now, what would you do?" I asked her, curious.

"I'd bite him," she said.

"Like you bit me?" I asked, laughing.

"No. I didn't know who you were then," she said. "I'm sorry about that. Him, I would really bite him. I'd bite his nose."

"You have really sharp teeth," I said. "That would definitely hurt him."

"I'd bite him so hard that he'd cry, and he'd beg me to stop," she said. I could see her body warming up, turning patchy. I didn't care. We were outside. We had infinite clothes. We were practicing.

"And what would you do if he begged you to stop?"

"I'd stop," she said, as if it surprised her. Her whole body temperature changed, like the sun had gone down without warning.

"That sounds okay to me," I told her. "That's fine."

"Do you hate your dad?" she suddenly asked, like she didn't want to think about her own dad anymore.

"I don't have a dad," I replied, and she accepted this without question.

"Do you hate your mom?" she asked.

"Yeah," I said.

"Would you bite her?" she asked.

"It wouldn't hurt her," I said.

"Was she bad to you?"

"Yeah, she was. Not horrible. She just, like, didn't care about me. She didn't like to think about me. It made her upset to know I was there."

"Our mom," Bessie said, "she gets upset if she isn't thinking about us. All she does is think about us. And if for even a second she thinks that we're not thinking about her, she gets so sad."

"I think maybe parents can be pretty bad at this stuff," I told her.

"Do you want to be a parent?" she asked.

"No," I said. "Not really."

"Why not?"

"Because I wouldn't be good at it, either. I'd be so bad at it."

"I don't think so," she told me.

And I could feel it washing over me, wanting to take these kids. I'm not joking when I say that I never liked people, because people scared me. Because anytime I said what was inside me, they had no idea what I was talking about. They made me want to smash a window just to have a reason to walk away from them. Because I kept fucking up, because it seemed so hard not to fuck up, I lived a life where I had less than what I desired. So instead of wanting more, sometimes I just made myself want even less. Sometimes I made myself believe that I wanted nothing, not even food or air. And if I wanted nothing, I'd just turn into a ghost. And that would be the end of it.

And there were these two kids, and they burst into flames. And I had known them for less than a week; I didn't know them at all. And I wanted to burst into flames, too. I thought, *How wonderful would it be to have everyone stand at a respectful distance?* The kids were making me feel things, and they were complicated, because these kids were complicated, were so damaged. And I wanted to take them. But I knew that I wouldn't. And I knew that I couldn't give them the hope that I would.

"Bessie?" I finally said. "Your dad seems like he fucked up, okay? But I think he wants to be a good person. And Madison is my friend. And I know that she is a good person. And Timothy, whatever, he's just too little right now, but he'll end up being fine. This is your family, okay? And I don't know if you understand this, but your family is so rich. They are richer than anyone I've ever known in my entire life. They are richer than all the people I've ever known put together. This will be good for you. Whatever you want, they will try to give it to you. And that might not seem like such a big deal now, but you'll be happy for it someday. When you really want something, you'll be able to take it. If you stay with them. If you give Madison and your dad a chance."

"I understand," she said, but her eyes were so intense. I couldn't look at her. I was talking to this spot on the ground.

"How much longer is summer?" she then asked.

"A long time," I told her. "A really long time."

THAT NIGHT, WE WALKED OUT OF OUR GUESTHOUSE AND made our way to the mansion. Roland had some khakis on and a white dress shirt with a blue tie that had taken me seven tries to knot correctly, the mechanics all weird on a little kid. I'd clipped his hair pretty easily. Boys are easy with hair, you just keep it neat and nobody cares beyond that. I don't know that I'd ever heard a straight man compliment another straight man's hair in my entire life. Bessie had on a black floral summer dress, kind of grungy actually, quite cool. Roland looked like an intern at a bank, but Bessie looked like a girl at her mom's third wedding. I'd buzzed the sides of her hair, left it floppy on top, and it didn't make her pretty, but it accentuated her eyes, the wildness of her face. They both looked like wild kids in disguise, undercover, but that was good enough. All that Jasper probably wanted was an attempt at normalcy. That's all Madison wanted, I was sure. She'd never want them to lose their actual weirdness. The fire, yes, okay, she wanted that gone, but what was underneath that. She'd appreciate it. I knew she would.

I had brushed on a thin layer of the stunt gel, though it was hard to get the amount right. I was worried about the mess it would make, the kids' clothing, the chairs in the dining room, but whatever. I knew that the moment they saw Jasper, I'd be relieved that I'd put the goop on them.

Madison, always Madison, like a spokesperson for the rest of the world, all the good things contained in it, welcomed us at the back door. "Oh," Madison said, looking at the children, "you two look wonderful. So grown-up!"

She then looked at me, my fucked-up face with bruises and scratches. "Oh god," she said, not able to hide her surprise. She hadn't seen me since she'd put that elbow in my face. "You know, I have makeup that would . . . I don't know, Lillian. That's bad."

"It's fine," I said.

"Lillian's tough," Roland said proudly.

"She's the toughest person I know," Madison replied. "But I wish she didn't have to be so tough all the time."

I thought, *Then maybe you didn't have to become a psycho in a one-on-one game in front of children,* but I let it go. I breathed deeply.

And then, five seconds later, there was Jasper. "Hello, children," he said, and this time he seemed more put together, more charming. No seersucker, thank god. Seersucker was for fucking dolts. He smiled at them. "I know this is hard for you guys," he continued, the shyness adding to the charm, the way he looked at them like he was counting on their votes. "But I've been really looking forward to this. And I won't ask for a hug right now, but sometime, when you're ready, I've been thinking about giving you guys a hug and telling you that I'm happy that you're here."

The kids just nodded, maybe a little embarrassed. Madison touched Jasper and smiled at him, nodded her approval.

"Who's hungry?" Madison asked.

"I'm hungry," I said, answering for all of us, and we walked into the dining room.

Timothy was already there, his hands clasped together on the table like he was ready to pray or like he was your boss and was really sorry but he was going to have to fire you. The more I saw of Timothy, his formality and robotic qualities, the more I liked him.

One time, I'd asked Madison about Timothy's—how do you phrase it politely?—eccentricities, and she'd nodded, like, yes, yes, she knew.

"He's not good with other kids, honestly," she'd said. "He's weird, I know it. But, fuck, I wasn't the most normal kid, Lil. I was a beautiful child, truly. I know that's vain to say, but I was. But I was a kid, so I could be ugly in my thoughts. It made me happy sometimes, to not be pretty on the inside. And my mom, god, she hated it; she was this prim and proper woman, and she was real pretty, and it was like she'd never had a dark thought in her life. I think I scared her, like maybe it was something inside her that had unwittingly made me like this. Every little thing that wasn't from a lady's handbook, every sharp edge, she tried to sand it down. She had this running commentary, all the things that I was doing, which I wasn't aware of doing because I was a kid, and she made me feel like shit. She was used to my brothers, these dopey fucking boys who tortured the dog and broke shit and were a hundred times worse than me, but they were boys, and that was okay. No, she focused only on me. 'Madison, people are going to get so tired of these little tics of yours,' she'd tell me.

"And so I doubled down. I tried to break her as she tried to break me. We fought a lot, over the pettiest things. She tried to keep me from playing basketball. And, whatever, I know she loves me. And I love her. At least she cared in some messed-up way, unlike my dad, who didn't even seem to know that I existed until I got older and could be of use to him. But she hurt me. She hurt me at the moment when I didn't need to be hurt. So when Timothy became this strange little toddler who was, like, fascinated by pocket squares, I said I would never try to curb it. I knew that the world would do that eventually anyway. So I let him be weird. I like it. It makes me happy."

And I guess I was beginning to understand. I was used to it. It seemed like maybe he was a performance artist, a compelling mimic, and this was just how he fucked with people. What I'm saying is that all children seemed cool to me at this point.

Mary came out with her arms full of plates. The adults each got a Caesar salad with grilled chicken on top, and Timothy had a plate of homemade chicken fingers and mac and cheese. And Bessie and Roland got what they had explicitly requested: Tyson frozen chicken nuggets.

"Oh, wow," Roland said. "Thanks."

"Mary made sure to get what you wanted," Madison said, and Bessie, embarrassed now that what she wanted was something nobody else would ever dream of wanting, looked down at her plate and said, "Thank you, Miss Mary."

"It's nothing," Mary said. "There is no point in making children eat what they don't want. A fool's errand."

"Could I have some of that salad, too?" Bessie asked, and Mary simply nodded and then returned with a small plate and a huge bottle of Heinz ketchup for the nuggets. "Welcome back to your home, children," she said, and, man, there was some weird judgment in there, but she pulled it off like a badass. Who was gonna stop her?

"This is nice," Madison said. "Jasper, do you want to say the blessing?"

Jasper nodded. Bessie and Roland looked dumbfounded. Madison and Timothy and Jasper all closed their eyes and clasped their hands, but me and the kids just stared at one another. Obviously we knew what prayer was—or did the kids know what it was? Did they know who God was? Did they think that their mother had made them out of clay? I had no idea. But I was not going to make them pray if they didn't want to. We'd listen, politely.

And Jasper talked about gratitude, about infinite wisdom, about families made whole again. He talked about sacrifice and appreciation of those sacrifices. It was hard to tell who he thought was making the sacrifices. Him? Could he be that stupid? He was one in a series of Roberts men who had been given everything they had ever wanted before they even had to ask for it. Was the sacrifice simply not taking the things that other people were entitled to? Were the kids the sacrifices he was making? Maybe I wasn't giving him the benefit of the doubt. But if he said the word *sacrifice* one more time, I was going to punch him in the face. He finally moved on, talking about forgiveness and the desire for new beginnings. Bored, Roland grabbed one of the nuggets and ate it in one bite.

"Amen," Jasper finally said, and when he opened his eyes and looked up, he stared right at me, before I could even pretend that I'd been participating, and so it looked like I had been staring at him the entire time. But he held my gaze and smiled. "Let's eat," he said.

And it was fine. It was awkward, but it felt like the size of the mansion, how fancy everything was, would make any normal situation more awkward. It wasn't bad. The kids weren't on fire. That was my new measuring stick for what was good and what was bad. Eating a Caesar salad and making boring small talk was not bad, not when the alternative was pulling down a set of thousand-dollar curtains because they were ablaze.

"What is your job like?" Bessie finally asked her father, and you could see how happy it made him that she had tried, and yet it also seemed to confuse him because he wasn't exactly sure how to respond.

"Well," he began, genuinely considering how to answer, "everyone in the state of Tennessee entrusts me with looking after their interests. For instance, I work with other senators to make sure that the things our citizens need are taken care of. I make sure that jobs come to this state, so people can work and support their families. And I make sure that the country, the whole country, is moving toward a better future."

"You take care of people," Bessie said.

"Sort of," he replied. "I try to."

"Okay," she said.

"Your family," Jasper said to her, "for generations and generations, have made their home in Tennessee. It's a wonderful state. And I make sure that it stays that way, or when it needs help, I try to get that help so it can stay great."

"Pop-Pop said that politics is mostly moving money around and making sure that some of it sticks to you," Roland said.

"That does sound like Richard," Jasper replied. "But that's not the way that I've tried to do my job."

"'Cause you don't need more money," Bessie said.

"No," Jasper said, "I don't."

"We're studying Tennessee with Lillian," Roland told the table.

"Is that right?" Jasper said, smiling.

"We're doing biographies on great Tennesseans," I told him, like I was still interviewing for the job, or maybe like I was hoping for a letter of recommendation later.

"Like who?" Madison asked.

"Sergeant York," Roland said. "Oh, man, he killed like twenty-five Germans."

"He was a great man," Jasper replied. "A good Democrat, a lifelong Democrat. He said, 'I'm a Democrat first, last, and all the time.' There's a statue of him at the state capitol. Wonderful statue. Maybe Lillian can take you there sometime to see it."

"Okay," I said.

"What about you, Bessie?" Madison asked.

"Dolly Parton," she announced.

"Hmm," Jasper said, considering the name. "She's an entertainer, though, isn't she?"

Bessie looked confused and turned to me. "She's an artist," I said.

"Well, I suppose," Jasper said. "I can think of several real Tennessee icons that might make for a better report."

"It's not really a report," I admitted. "We're just researching our interests." I reached over to Bessie and touched her arm, feeling for her temperature, but the gel made it hard to accurately gauge.

"And Dolly Parton is a humanitarian, Jasper," Madison added. "She's done a lot for the state and for the children of the state."

"She's an actress," he said, like this was evidence of something. He was smiling, maybe playing, but Bessie seemed embarrassed now, like she'd made a mistake, and I got angry.

"She's the greatest Tennessean in the state's entire history," I said flatly, definitively.

"Oh, Lillian," Jasper said, chuckling.

"She wrote 'I Will Always Love You,'" I said, dumbfounded that this didn't end the debate.

"Lillian," Jasper said, his charm turning serious, so haughty, "do you know that there have been three Tennesseans who have served as the president of the United States?"

"I know," I told him. As a kid, I had memorized every single U.S. president, and could recite them in chronological or alphabetical order. I could do it right now, if I wanted to. "But none of them were born in Tennessee."

"Is that right?" Madison said. "Is that right, Jasper?"

Jasper's face got a little red. "Well, I mean . . . technically that's correct—" he said, but I cut in, "And Johnson was impeached. And Jackson, c'mon, he was kind of a monster."

"That's not entirely—" Jasper sputtered.

"Dolly Parton," I said, now looking at Bessie, waiting until she looked right at me, "she is way better than Andrew Jackson." Bessie smiled, her crooked teeth showing, and I smiled back, like we'd played a practical joke on her idiot dad.

Jasper looked like he was dying. He was holding his fork like he wanted to stab me with it. And I knew, right at this moment, that Jasper would find a way to remove me from this house, when it was prudent, when I'd done what he needed me to do. Jasper, like most men I'd ever known, did not like to be gently corrected in public. And I should have been more careful, but I wasn't savvy. I didn't see the point.

"Could we go to Dollywood?" Bessie asked, and Jasper was now stone-cold dead. It was beautiful.

As if conjured by a spell, a charm created to intervene whenever the senator had been utterly humiliated, Carl appeared in the dining room.

"Sir?" he said to Jasper. "I'm sorry to interrupt this family dinner, but you have a phone call."

"Well," Jasper said, trying to return to his usual nature, "can it wait until after dessert?"

"It's rather urgent, sir," Carl replied. "And I believe that perhaps Mrs. Roberts might also want to be privy to the information."

Madison locked eyes with Jasper, and it was interesting to watch them work, the way they seemed to be two halves of a singular unit, the way they both stood at the same time. Madison kissed Timothy, who acted like maybe his parents were called away for urgent business all the time, and then followed her husband out of the room.

"What's going on?" I asked Carl, but he shook his head and walked behind the two of them.

"That was weird," Roland said.

"Do we have to wait for them to eat dessert?" Bessie asked.

I got up and went into the kitchen, where Mary was already plating four slices of chocolate cake. "I'm coming," she said. "You didn't need to get up, of course."

"Looks good," I said, and she nodded.

"I know," she replied.

I went back into the dining room with the kids, like I was the most embarrassing guest at a wedding. I tried to think of something to say, but then Mary was putting the cake in front of us, and that seemed to remove the need for conversation. We ate, and then, when we were finished, the four of us just sat there. "Can we go?" Bessie asked.

"I don't think so," I said, like I was a child and needed an adult to excuse me from the table. "We can't just leave Timothy here."

"We can bring him to the guesthouse," Roland offered.

"Do you want to see the guesthouse?" I asked Timothy, who merely shrugged, like a puppeteer had a slight tremor and the strings connecting him to Timothy had moved ever so slightly.

And I liked the idea of taking Timothy hostage, of forcing Madison or Jasper to come get him.

"Let's go," I said, and I helped Timothy out of his seat and we all walked across the manicured lawn to our house, all lit up and happy and deranged.

"What do you want to look at?" Roland asked Timothy, who again just shrugged. Bessie ignored the boy and pulled a book off the shelf and pretended to read it. I knew she didn't want the boy in our house, since he already had so much.

Roland showed Timothy an Etch A Sketch, and they each handled one of the knobs, working together to make a mess on the screen.

I sat next to Bessie and watched the boys play fine enough, though they didn't really talk. Every once in a while Roland would grab the toy and shake the shit out of it, which seemed to both frighten and delight Timothy in equal measure. And then they went back to it, Roland watching Timothy more than the screen.

"So, that wasn't so bad, right?" I asked Bessie.

"I guess," she said.

"I like this dress," I told her.

"You don't wear dresses," she said. I just had on my jeans and a nice enough top.

"No," I said, "not really."

"Do you think Madison likes us?" she asked. I knew how she was feeling, the need to have Madison look at you, direct that sunlight your way.

"Oh, yes," I said. "She's stoked to have you guys here."

"I liked the food," she offered.

"Mary is the best."

"She's scary," Bessie said.

"Cool people are scary sometimes," I told her.

"You're not scary," she said, and I didn't know what to say to that.

And then Timothy and Roland tired of the toy and came over to the sofa. Timothy was looking at Bessie, trying to make sense of her. When Bessie finally couldn't ignore him any longer, she looked at him, glaring. "What?" she asked.

"You catch on fire?" he asked, curious.

Bessie looked at me, and I shrugged. I wasn't sure what we were or weren't supposed to tell Timothy. But I guess he knew. Or had overheard. Or could simply sense it; the kid was that spooky that I'd believe this possibility.

"Yeah," Bessie said, and Roland nodded.

"Can I see?" Timothy asked.

"It doesn't work like that," Bessie said.

Timothy touched Bessie's hand like he thought it might be hot. Bessie let him.

And then someone was knocking on the door, and Madison and Carl appeared in the doorway. Timothy pulled his hand away from Bessie and immediately started walking toward the door. Madison came in. "Look at this!" she said. "Are you having fun?" she asked Timothy, who actually nodded, or what for him was a nod.

"Well," she said, "we'd better get back to the house."

"Where's Dad?" Roland asked.

"Well, he's been called away on some important business," she said, as much to me as to the kids. "Very important. But he'll see you again soon."

Madison took Timothy's hand and they stepped outside, but Carl hovered in the doorway, which I took as a sign for me to come talk to him.

"What's going on?" I asked. "Is it about the kids?"

"The secretary of state just died," he whispered to me. "Just dropped dead in his kitchen."

"Wasn't he dying?" I asked.

"Well, he was dying, but he was a powerful man. He was going to die very slowly. This was unexpected."

"So what now?"

"So Senator Roberts has been offered the post."

"Oh, shit," I said. "Really?"

"There's a process that starts in earnest now," Carl replied, "but they've already been doing a lot of preparation. It looks promising."

I thought about Madison, one step closer to what she wanted. I thought about Jasper, but there wasn't much feeling there.

"And so what does it mean?" I asked. "Like, for the kids?"

"Let's just see how this plays out," he said.

"But are the kids being considered?" I asked. "How all this affects them?"

"Honestly, Lillian?" Carl replied. "Not really. Not much. So just keep taking care of them. Do what you need to do to maintain order."

"You don't want them to fuck this up?" I asked.

"I do not want them to fuck this up," he repeated.

"Okay, fine," I said.

"Good night," he said to me. "Good night, kids," he said to the twins, who didn't respond.

He left, and I went back to the kids.

"Is Dad dying?" Bessie asked.

"What?" I replied. "No. No way."

"All right," Bessie said, suspicious. Hopeful? I couldn't tell.

"He was supposed to give us a hug after dinner," Roland said.

"I don't want him to hug me," Bessie said.

"You guys look really cool," I said, changing the subject. "I'm going to take a picture of you."

I found the camera, the one Madison had asked me to use to document their lives, like maybe she needed pictures in order to quickly make a happy photo album for visitors to see. The kids were slumped on the sofa, tired.

"You don't have to smile," I said. "Just stay the way that you are."

Roland's head was resting on Bessie's shoulder. Their arms weren't quite as shimmery as they had been earlier in the night. I took the picture, then took one more.

"We want you to be in the picture," Roland said.

"I can't," I told them. "It's just you two."

"Can we go to bed?" Bessie asked. "Can you read us a story?"

"Hell yeah," I told them. "Hell yeah."

# Nine

**THE NEXT THREE WEEKS FELT LIKE THE WORLD WAS SPINNING** slightly faster than usual, all this weird activity swirling around us, no one telling us anything, but my life with Bessie and Roland didn't really change. Of course, we saw in the newspaper, front page, how Jasper had been nominated, and everyone said this was a savvy decision on the part of the president. Everyone seemed to love Jasper, and perhaps it's because I didn't like him, but it seemed like what they loved about him was that he was inoffensive and gentlemanly, that he looked like he knew what he was doing. Good for him, I guess. If you were rich, and you were a dude, it really felt like if you just followed a certain number of steps, you could do pretty much whatever you wanted. I thought about Jane, abandoned, dead, and I wondered how any kind of vetting didn't think that mattered. I thought of Bessie and Roland on the front lawn, on fire. How did that not matter? But maybe it really didn't matter. Jasper was a good senator; he made rich people and poor people equally happy, which must have been some kind of magic trick.

Madison and Timothy had flown to D.C. with Jasper, to simply be visible. Carl was on the property, but of course he was preoccupied with other stuff, barely seemed to care what I did with the kids. We played basketball, swam in the pool, read books, did our yoga. It was peaceful, honestly, like the end of the world had happened and we'd missed it. So much intensity had been directed toward these kids, and now that everyone was getting what they wanted, it was like we became invisible. They hadn't caught on fire in a long time; at least it seemed like a long time to me. And when you are weird, when your surroundings become quiet, you think maybe you aren't quite so fucked up. You think, *Why was it so hard before?*

One morning, we'd been testing the starch level in potatoes, and Bessie said, "Is anybody in the mansion?"

"No," I said. "Well, I mean, the staff is there."

"Can we go over there?" she asked, and I was like, why not? Who the fuck cares? Or, no, who the fuck was going to stop us?

Just to be safe, they put on their Nomex long underwear, which had finally arrived, this scratchy white material that made them look like they were living in a science fiction movie. They kind of loved it, except for how sweaty it made them. I wasn't sure if memories of the mansion, long forgotten, might surface and cause them to catch.

So we walked over and of course the doors were locked. And we just banged on the rear entrance until Mary, so pissed to be disturbed, opened the door.

"What do you want?" she asked.

"We want to explore," Roland said.

"Fine," she replied, and waved us in like she was letting the plague spread through the house, like she didn't care if she lived or died.

"Thank you, Miss Mary," the kids said, and she replied, "Come by later. I have bread pudding. With whiskey sauce."

"Yay!" the kids shouted.

But once they were inside, free, they grew quieter, more respectful, like they were in some old European cathedral, like the place was lousy with important dead people.

"Do you remember it?" I asked, but they both shook their heads.

"I bet your rooms were upstairs," I said, and we walked up the staircase. I told them how horses had been hidden in the attic during the Civil War, but they didn't care any more than I had cared.

We walked down the hallway, peeking our heads into each room. We saw Timothy's room, all those stuffed animals, and the kids' eyes got real wide. They walked in carefully, fully expecting it to be booby-trapped, and then they stared at the piles of plush. Bessie punched her fist into one of the piles and retrieved a zebra with Technicolor stripes. "I'm taking this," she said, a kind of tax, and I was like, A-okay with me, so Roland grabbed an owl with a monocle and bow tie.

We walked around some more, and then they stopped in the doorway of one of the rooms. "This was it," Bessie said. "This was our room." I had no idea how she could tell. Now it was an exercise room with a NordicTrack and some weight machines, and all the walls were covered in mirrors. "It was right across from that bathroom," Bessie said, remembering. "And we had bunk beds, and I slept on top."

"And there was this toy box right under the window," Roland continued.

"It was white and had flowers painted on it," Bessie said. "And we each had our own desk."

"Where is all that stuff?" Roland asked me, and I just shrugged.

"Maybe it moved with you and your mom when y'all left the mansion," I offered.

"We didn't take anything with us," Bessie replied. "Mom wouldn't let us."

"So where is it?" Roland asked.

"I guess we can ask Madison," I said. "Do you want that stuff?"

"No," Bessie admitted. "I just want to know if he kept it."

They seemed tired now, and so we went downstairs to the kitchen and Mary let us have bread pudding, which really had a kick of whiskey to it, but I let the kids have it anyway. We sat there, the three of us eating this sweet thing, Mary watching us, tolerating us. When I finished my bowl, without thinking, I dipped my finger in the glaze that had accumulated and Roland licked it right off my finger, ravenous. "Quite a sight," Mary finally said, and I felt like maybe she was sincere, that we were something to behold.

ONE MORNING, CARL SHOWED UP AT THE DOOR. "WE NEED TO take the kids to the doctor," he said, and I knew that he had practiced how he would say this and had decided that a direct statement, like it wasn't up for debate, was the best way to proceed. I imagined him saying it to his reflection in the mirror.

"Why?" I asked.

And, like he had also prepared for this outcome, like he just fucking knew this was coming, he rolled his eyes. "Lillian? Why do you think the kids might need to see a doctor?"

"Because they catch on fire?" I offered.

"Yes, because they catch on fire," he replied.

"But why now?" I asked. "That's what I don't get."

"Just a precautionary measure," he said. "Just to make sure

everything's the same. Not better. But not worse. Do you understand?"

"Because of the secretary of state thing?" I guessed.

"Yes," he replied; he was tired. It was a little easier working with him when he was tired.

"I wish you'd told me earlier," I said. "I have to put that gel on them, and it takes a while."

"No," he said. "We need them in a natural state. For the exam."

I didn't know if there was a way to say the word *exam* without it sounding creepy, but if there was, Carl had not found it. "Carl, is this a real doctor?" I asked.

"It's complicated," he said, which is absolutely not what you want to hear when you ask if the person you're going to see is a licensed physician.

But I also knew it was pointless to fight him, that this came from Jasper, or Madison more likely. It was going to happen. At least the kids could have more ice cream afterward.

"I am going to be there the entire time, okay? Both of us, actually," I told him.

"Of course," he said.

Once we were dressed and ready, Carl pulled up in a green Honda Civic, a surprisingly ugly car, considering how nondescript it was. It looked like the kind of car that a man who sold calendars door-to-door would drive.

"Whose car is this?" I asked Carl.

"It's mine," he said.

"I thought you had the Miata," I told him.

"I have two cars," he said.

"Why do you have this car?" I asked.

"Because sometimes you don't want to show up in a red

sports car," he told me. "Sometimes you need to show up in a Honda Civic. And tell me again what kind of car you drive?"

"That's not important," I said. "C'mon, kiddos."

The interior was pristine, like it had just come off the lot. It was so impressive that I smiled at Carl, nodding my approval.

"Can we listen to music?" Roland asked.

"Absolutely not," Carl replied, checking his rearview mirror. And we were off.

WE WERE HEADED TO A LITTLE TOWN NORTH OF NASHVILLE called Springfield. We drove past acres of tobacco on country roads until we pulled up to a two-story house with a white picket fence, the state flag of Tennessee flying from a pole set in the middle of the front yard.

"So," I said, "just somebody's house? Not a doctor's office?"

"You'll see," Carl said, already stepping out of the car. As I collected the kids, who were bored and hot, I saw an ancient man appear on the porch, wearing a huge red bow tie, a blue oxford shirt, khakis, and red suspenders. He had on little round glasses. He looked like Orville Redenbacher, the popcorn guy. He looked insane in that way of people who put great effort into choosing ridiculous clothing. I prayed this was not the doctor.

"I'm the doctor!" he said, waving to the children.

"Oh god," I said, and Carl surreptitiously jabbed me in the side.

"Hello, Carl," he said.

"Dr. Cannon," Carl replied.

"Well, come on," Dr. Cannon said to the children, walking down the steps of the front porch. "Let's have a look at you." The children seemed baffled by this man, his enthusiasm. But they weren't afraid. They walked toward him.

"Come on to my office," he told them, and we all followed him around the house to a small white building, a single room, set in the backyard. He unlocked the door and walked in. "This belonged to my grandfather, if you can believe that," he told us. "Eighteen ninety-six. Every town of a notable size would have a good country doctor, of course. Now, this hasn't been in use for many, many years, but ever since I retired from practicing medicine, I like to sit in here. I like to sit in here and think."

The wooden floors were painted gray and the walls were white. It felt so tiny in there, with all of us packed in. There were really old-looking medical instruments that I hoped would not be used today. There was a rickety wooden examining table upholstered in black leather. There were oil lamps and old bottles with labels for various quack pills. It looked like something you'd find in a living museum, a historical village. It looked like something a crazy person would have in their backyard.

"This is really wonderful, Dr. Cannon," Carl said.

"So you're a retired physician?" I asked him.

"Oh, yes. Practiced medicine for fifty years. Now, you know, I was the family doctor for the Roberts family when Senator Roberts, that is, Jasper's father, was alive. I was considered the best doctor in Nashville, in the whole state of Tennessee."

"Okay," I said, not sure what else to say.

"I very much value my relationship with the Roberts family," he said. "And they, of course, value my discretion."

This all sounded creepy, like it had to be about venereal diseases, so I just kept saying "Okay" and hoping for the best.

"But these children!" he said, his voice booming. "How interesting. Now, as I'm sure Carl told you, I'm not only a doctor of medicine."

"He did not tell me," I replied, looking at Carl, who hadn't even taken off his sunglasses yet.

"I am also a doctor of the paranormal, which is its own kind of science, I can assure you. And, wouldn't you know it, I have done quite a bit of research on spontaneous human combustion."

"Is that so?" I said, ready to scream.

"But medicine and the paranormal, while equally important, are two different things. So we keep them separate, or at least I do. Let me check these children out. Hop up, one at a time, on this table."

Roland hopped up. The doctor took his temperature, thank god reaching into a little black bag with modern instruments, and then took his blood pressure and checked his eyes and ears and throat. He did the same for Bessie, who looked right at me the entire time, trying to keep herself calm. But the doctor was careful, mindful of the children. He wasn't invasive. He simply observed them and made notes.

"This is all fine and good," he said. "They're in perfect health, of course. I could tell by looking at them that this would be the case."

"That's wonderful, Dr. Cannon," Carl said.

"Is that it?" I asked.

"Well, from what I understand, what Jasper has told me, you children catch on fire, is that right?"

The kids looked at me, and I gave them a thumbs-up sign and so they nodded in agreement.

"That is fascinating. I wish I could see that, but, no, I understand that's not a good idea. And you are unharmed?"

The kids again nodded.

"It's interesting because in the clear cases of spontaneous

human combustion, well, the afflicted person typically dies from the flames. Or the smoke. One or the other. This is not, I believe, as straightforward as that. And also different from those cases, I understand that you can sense the arrival of the combustion? Would that be correct?"

"Yes," Bessie admitted.

"Where, sweetie?" he asked.

"Where?" Bessie replied, confused.

"In your head? Your stomach? Your heart?"

Bessie looked at Roland, who then nodded, their little silent communication. "It kind of starts in our chest and then moves outward, like to our arms and legs and head."

"Yes, that makes sense. A kind of radiating heat. Interesting, interesting," the doctor said, making some more notes. "This is all very fantastical. I mean, the children combust, but are unharmed. It's most unusual. But we can try to be scientific, to adhere to medical truths."

"That would be perfect," Carl assured the doctor.

"My initial thoughts have to do with ketosis. Do you know what that is?" he asked the children, who shook their heads. I was shaking my head, too, without realizing it. Carl, of course, was nodding. Of course he knew.

"It's just a natural metabolic process that happens in your body. If you don't have enough glucose in your body for energy, your body starts to burn fat. Like a candle, perhaps, if that helps? And so, some people say this is good and some people say that it can be bad. I'm not interested in that, because I think your case might exist outside those worries. But, if you could create a diet that avoided ketosis, then, and this is only a theory, you might prevent the body from so easily creating a kind of internal combustion. Does that make sense?"

"I suppose it does, Dr. Cannon," Carl replied.

"Can we eat ice cream?" Roland asked.

"Well, that is high fat, but there's sugar, so I think that would be okay," Dr. Cannon replied. He tore off a piece of paper and handed it to Carl, who pocketed it.

"It's simple," Dr. Cannon said. "You might already be doing it without knowing it, which of course would mean this entire visit was useless. I'm afraid I can't offer much more than that while maintaining such strict protocols for privacy, without much more testing."

"This is fine," Carl said. "It's greatly appreciated."

"Now, children," he said, redirecting his focus, "if we move beyond medicine and look at the paranormal, we might think about the idea of fire, and how a fire is contained within a human vessel."

"Huh?" Roland said.

"Well, the only fire that I know of that exists within a human body is the Holy Spirit."

"What now?" Bessie said.

"Say what?" I said.

"The Holy Spirit? The unveiled epiphany of God?" he continued, frowning. He looked like he was on *The $10,000 Pyramid* and he couldn't believe his partner hadn't yet guessed the answer. "The Holy Trinity?"

"Oh, okay," Bessie finally said, trying to get on with it. "Like, your soul?"

"No, dear," he said, chuckling. "Not quite."

"Dr. Cannon," Carl said, "we need to get go—"

"So, the Holy Spirit," Dr. Cannon interrupted, moving on, still staring at the children, "resides in your heart. And so, if you children are experiencing these moments where the fire manifests itself externally, well, that could mean quite a few things. Perhaps you are prophets, chosen by God—"

"We really must be going," Carl said.

"Prophets?" Roland said, trying out the word, liking the sound of it.

"You might be envoys for the second coming of Jesus Christ, our lord and savior," the doctor elaborated.

"Carl?" I said.

"Or—and this is quite radically different—it could be a case where the devil, in his multitudinous evil, is warring with the Holy Spirit inside you. That would make you, Bessie and Roland, demons. Or, perhaps, simply possessed by demons. Whatever the case, it is possible that there is an evil inside you, one that must be purged."

"Okay," I said, "no way." I reached for the kids, pulling them off the table.

"But I want to hear more," Roland said.

"Thank you, Dr. Cannon," Carl quickly said, opening the door to the office, leading the children outside. "Ketosis. Very good. We have all we need."

"Say hello to Jasper for me," he said, waving. "He was always such a wonderful patient. I can't remember a time when he was sick."

We hustled the children into the car, and Carl quickly pulled back onto the road. I stared at him, but the sunglasses made it hard for me to really see him. "Who wants the radio?" he asked, turning it on without waiting for a response, which made Roland cheer.

"That was a mistake," he admitted to me, keeping his voice

down. "I don't know that Senator Roberts has been in contact with Dr. Cannon in quite some time. I don't think he knows the full extent of his, uh, condition."

I didn't say a word, just kept staring at him.

"He's one of the most revered doctors in the entire state," Carl continued. "All the governors and country music stars, he was their physician. All kinds of published articles."

"Fascinating," I replied.

"I'm just doing what the Robertses have told me to do," Carl said, looking back to make sure the kids weren't listening. "And, honestly, the real doctors, the specialists who saw the kids right after Jane died, they didn't have much else to tell us. I think one of them even mentioned ketosis. So, no harm done."

"Now the kids think they might be demons," I told him.

"Well, I don't know how much of that they understood." He quickly turned back to the kids. "Double-scoop sundaes, okay?" he said.

I groaned and turned off the radio. I looked back at them. They both seemed bored, but I could see them working through something in their heads, passing it back and forth. "Look," I finally said, "you are not demons, okay? No fucking way. That man was crazy."

"Maybe we're prophets, though," Roland offered.

"No," I said, my voice rising. "You're just normal kids, okay? You catch on fire, but you're normal kids."

"Okay," Bessie replied. "We believe you."

"Okay," I said. For a few miles, we drove in silence, but then Roland started to giggle. I turned back around. Bessie's face looked both pained and relieved at the same time. She looked at me. She started to laugh a little, too. "We're not demons," she said, and I shook my head. And I knew that they were my kids, that I protected them, because they believed me. For right now, in this car, they trusted me. They were not demons.

**THAT NIGHT, BLANKETED IN CHILDREN, I HEARD MADISON** whispering above me. "Lil," she said, and I thought it was a dream because, honestly, I dreamed about Madison a lot.

"Yeah?" I said.

"I'm back," she said, still whispering. "Timothy and I just flew home. Come with me. Let's hang out. Let's talk."

I realized that she was real, and I felt myself waking up. I looked at her. I couldn't make out her features, only her form, in the dim light from the bathroom in the hallway.

"The kids will wake up," I said.

"No, they won't," she said. "Just come on." She sounded like maybe she was drunk, her voice kind of husky.

"Bessie?" I whispered, and the girl shrugged away from me before turning back over and opening her eyes.

"What is it?" she asked. "Are you okay?"

"Madison is here," I said, gesturing to Madison, who waved.

"What do you want?" Bessie asked.

"Lillian," Madison replied. "Just for a little while."

"I'll be back soon," I told her. "Just keep sleeping."

"Okay," Bessie said. "I guess so."

I slipped out of the bed, Roland snoring hard, and followed Madison as she tiptoed from the room. I grabbed a pair of sweatpants on the way out, some sneakers.

"Come outside," she told me. "I made margaritas. To celebrate."

"Celebrate what?" I asked, being petty, being dumb, because we were in very different circles of the blast radius of this good news.

"Jasper!" she said. "You know it's Jasper, silly." We sat on the steps that led to the house and there was that fucking pitcher again, that tray. There was something Stepfordish about everything being served in a pitcher, instead of, I don't know, putting your face in a giant punch bowl and just vacuuming it up. I don't know what I wanted. I guess I wanted Madison to be a little more like me and a little less like the kind of person you had to be to live with this sort of wealth. And yet here I was, living on their estate, my bank account filled with so much money, not having to spend a dime while I strolled the grounds. This was my life, a good part of it, hating other people and then hating myself for not being better than them.

She poured the drinks, and it was so good, cold and strong.

"It worked," she said. "I kind of can't fucking believe that it worked."

"All the vetting?" I asked. "I thought, I don't know, they'd come talk to me."

"No," she said, "I kept them away from everyone. I shamed them. The thing we thought would be so bad, Jane killing herself, the kids abandoned, actually gave us the chance to keep them at a distance, or else they'd look like ghouls, you know?"

"I guess so," I said. I just kept drinking.

"I mean, they definitely wanted to make sure that Jasper hadn't killed Jane or anything like that. And they have some secondhand reports about the kids, about the fire, but it's so unbelievable that they can't really do much with it."

"Oh, good," I said. Being rich, of course, meant it was easier to just keep getting what you wanted. It took less and less effort to keep it.

"And they really just wanted to make sure that Jasper wasn't crooked, that he didn't have financial ties to anything that would look bad. That he hadn't pissed off the wrong people. It was all a lot easier than we thought."

"It happened so quickly," I said.

"Because the guy died!" she said, fucking giddy. "How could we have known? We thought this was going to be drawn out, and, you know, the longer it went on, the more other people would want to butt in. But Jasper's steady. He's really good."

"So what'll happen now?" I asked.

"Well, there's a confirmation hearing. It's mostly a formality. I've coached Jasper anyway. He just has to be so noncommittal that it actually seems like he doesn't know anything. He'll keep saying how much he looks forward to exploring these issues and finding the best way to proceed. It's pretty much a done deal."

"Well, okay," I said. "So then what?"

"Then he's the secretary of state," she replied.

"I don't even know what that is," I admitted.

"Foreign affairs. Big-time stuff. He's, like, right next to the president, advising him. Fourth in line to the presidency, actually."

"Oh, wow, I guess I didn't realize that."

"And, honestly, it's huge for me. It's the kind of visibility that means I can start to advocate for things I want to do. The party is already talking about how to utilize me moving forward."

"Well, cool," I said, and I felt like the biggest nerd in the world, pretending I knew what kissing felt like, what boys wanted.

"We'll have to move to D.C., of course," Madison continued.

"Really?" I asked.

"For sure. There's already people who are looking at real estate for us."

"What about the kids?" I asked. "Do you think they'll be okay with that?"

"Timothy can handle anything," she said, not even really looking at me, her mind racing, like, four or eight years into the future. "The schools in D.C. are a hundred times better than the ones here anyway."

"What about Roland and Bessie?" I asked.

"Well—" she said. "I don't know about them. I just don't know."

"What don't you know?" I asked.

"I don't know if they'll be able to handle the city. It's much more public, a lot more stressful."

"They're never going to see Jasper, are they?" I said, like, of course they wouldn't, and, like, how did I not already know this?

"Not much," she admitted. "Who knows? Maybe that's for the best. Jasper is a better parent in theory, like if you look at his actions and his values from a distance. They'll still have access to what he can *provide* for them, Lillian. That's what really matters."

"So you'll be taking care of them?" I asked.

"I won't even really be able to take care of Timothy," she said. "This is a huge responsibility."

"So do you want me to stay with them?" I asked, my heart beating because I didn't know exactly what I wanted the answer to be.

"No," she said, so chipper, so happy, "you've done so much for them. You've done so much for us. I wouldn't ask you to do that."

"Oh, okay," I replied. "So then, what? You get them, like, a real governess?"

"Well, I haven't had much time to think about this, you understand? Like, there are huge things going on. But I think maybe boarding school would be good for them."

"They're ten years old," I said.

"In Europe," Madison said, "kids go to boarding school when they're eight. That might be really good for them, to go abroad, to experience the world after being cooped up in that house with Jane all this time."

"I think that's a terrible idea," I countered. "I mean, what happens if they catch on fire, right? Don't you think sending them away is going to make that worse?"

"Honestly, it's better if they catch on fire in Europe than in D.C.," she replied. "It's less visible, less verifiable."

"They've just been through a lot," I said.

"We went to Iron Mountain," she replied, "and that wasn't so bad, was it?" And before I could even reply, her face fell, and she stuttered, "Well, I mean, it was a good school, right?"

"You're going to ship them off somewhere?" I said. "That fucking sucks, Madison."

"What else can we do?" Madison replied.

"You can take care of them!" I said.

"Okay, Lillian," she said, taking a deep breath. "I appreciate the fact that you helped me when I needed it. But, truthfully, you have been watching them for, like, hardly any time at all. You think it's just so easy. But you don't have the kind of pressures that Jasper and I have. You can focus entirely on these kids because that's all you have to do. We have to plan for our long-term future."

"This isn't right," I said.

"This is the thing about you sometimes, Lillian," Madison said, and I knew that this was going to be soul-crushing. I knew it was going to hurt. "You act like you're above it all, and you act like the whole world owes you something because you had it rough. And you judge people like crazy. Like, I know you hate Jasper. I know you think he's not nice. But you haven't given him a chance. You just saw that he was rich, and that makes you feel weird, and so you think he's a bad guy. You never really tried at anything. You had this bad thing happen, you got kicked out of school, and you let that sit there forever like it was the worst thing that had ever happened to anyone in the world."

I honestly couldn't tell if Madison remembered the past at all. All those years that I wondered why she never once thanked me for taking the fall for her, I had just assumed that it was because she was so embarrassed. But now it felt like maybe she just didn't remember it, like her version of the past was that I'd gotten caught with some coke and gotten kicked out. And that she had stayed friends with me because she was a good person. And that I had fucked up because I was bound to fuck up.

"Your father paid my mom so that I would get kicked out of Iron Mountain instead of you," I said.

"Okay," she said, like she was humoring me, like she would let me spin this conspiracy theory for as long as I needed to.

"And you let them. You let your dad do that, because you didn't want to get kicked out. And because you thought it didn't matter if I got kicked out, because I didn't really belong there."

"That's really unfair," she said. "I was your friend. I cared about you. And you never thought about what I was going through, what I was dealing with. And, Lillian, even if you'd graduated from Iron Mountain, what would you have done? Do you think you'd have my life? Do you think that would be possible?"

"I don't want your life," I told her. "Your life seems fucked up. It seems sad."

She stood up suddenly, and I thought we were going to fight. I clenched my hands into fists, my face already so messed up that it didn't matter what else happened to it. But Madison just started jogging away from me. She started running. She ran to the basketball court and she flicked on the floodlights, the whole court now illuminated. She started dribbling, running drills, and hitting layups. She set up at the free-throw line and hit turnaround jumpers. And that sound, the ball bouncing on the court, the way the net swished, it just opened me up, made me feel like there wasn't a single emotion in my body. It made me not want to kill her. I was so grateful for that half-second reprieve from wanting everyone to be dead. And I walked over to the court.

For a while, I just watched her shoot. And she ignored me. And if I was in her head, her game didn't show it. She was hitting almost everything, so easily.

"You really are my best friend," she finally said, not looking at me. "And, yes, I know that's pathetic because I haven't seen you since freshman year of high school. But you were. For that little while, you were the best friend I ever had, and I just never met another person like you. But I was so embarrassed by what my dad did—or what I did, whatever—that I kind of thought of you as my friend, but frozen there, in that dorm room. I wrote to you and it made me happy to share my life with someone who fucking cared about me. And I liked hearing from you, knowing that you still thought about me. I wish I'd been a better friend to you. I wish I'd done the right thing and taken the blame. Honestly, I'd still be right here. Nothing was going to keep me from this. But, okay, maybe your life would have been better."

"I was in love with you," I told her.

"I know you were," she admitted. She took a shot and it clanged off the rim and that gave me this tiny measure of hope.

"It was so easy to be in love with you back then. And I liked it, because as long as I was in love with you, I didn't have to love anyone else," I said. "And I've always kind of been in love with you. And I'm still kind of in love with you."

She nodded, and then she looked over at me. She was so beautiful, and I remembered those nights in our dorm when she looked at me and accepted my weirdness. She held on to me like nothing mattered. She was kind to me. Even if it had only been a few months, it was longer than anyone else had.

I waited for her to say something, and she just stared at me, figuring me out. I don't know what I thought would be there, in her eyes. She just shrugged, like what could she do about it? I knew she was sorry. It broke my heart, and I knew that a good part of my life had been spent waiting for it to break so I could get it over with.

I didn't think she was going to say anything, but then she started speaking, not really at me, to the darkness, to the universe, which of course wouldn't be able to hear her. "I know, Lil. I know. I know. I know. But what? What did you think I'd do with that? What kind of life could I have? Us? I think about it, okay? I think about you. But it can't be anything else. The minute it became something else, what would happen? We'd be so unhappy."

"I wouldn't," I said, staring right at her. "I would not be unhappy."

"You have no idea," Madison said.

"Could you just say it?" I asked her. If I heard her admit it, if I heard the words in her own voice, I could remember them, could replay them in my head. Maybe it would be enough.

"I can't," she admitted. "Lillian, I can't."

And that was it. What else could I do?

"Please don't send the kids away," I told her.

"Do you want them? Is that it?" she asked. "Do you think that would make you happy?"

"I just want someone to take care of them," I said.

"Why does it have to be me, though?" she asked. "Why does it have to be Jasper?"

"Because you're their parents now," I told her, and I thought maybe this was a trick question.

"I hate my dad," she said. "I was glad to get away from him. Your mom, holy shit, Lillian."

I knew that nothing I said would change anything.

"I want you to stay with them through the end of the summer," she said. "Here at the estate. And then they'll go abroad. And Jasper will see them, okay? He'll see them on breaks and holidays. They'll have their trust funds. They'll be a part of the family."

I was crying so hard, but I didn't know when it had started, what had been the exact thing. I couldn't say anything.

"I'm sorry, Lillian," Madison said, but I didn't know what she was sorry for. She took another shot, made it easily, and the ball bounced right back into her waiting arms.

**BACK AT THE HOUSE, BESSIE AND ROLAND WERE STILL ASLEEP,** and I crawled into bed. Even though I tried to be as quiet as possible, Bessie woke up. "You're crying," she said, her voice so soft and dreamy.

"It's nothing," I said.

"What happened?" she asked.

"Nothing," I said.

"Are you mad at us?" she asked.

"No," I said. "God, no, never."

Roland turned, reaching for us, and then propped himself up, waking to the room around him. "Is it morning?" he asked.

"Lillian is sad," Bessie told him.

"Why?" he asked. I wanted to shoot into the sky like a comet. I was a grown woman, crying, surrounded by fire children who were not mine. No one looking at this would feel good about it.

"Life is hard," I said. "That's it. C'mon, kiddos. Bed. Let's go to bed."

I settled into the bed, and the kids repositioned themselves around me. I closed my eyes, but I could tell that Bessie was still staring at me, wanted to know what was inside me. And I knew a secret to caring for someone, had learned it just this moment. You took care of people by not letting them know how badly you wanted your life to be different.

"Lillian?" she whispered once Roland started snoring again.

"What?" I asked.

"I wish you'd never leave us," she said.

"I do, too," I told her.

"But I know you will," she said, and, holy shit, this cracked me open. It made me want to die.

"Not yet," I told her, and it sounded so wimpy, and I hated myself.

"Can I tell you something?" she asked.

"Let's talk in the morning," I told her.

"No," she said, "right now. You know the fire?"

"Inside you?" I asked.

"Yeah. It just comes, you know? It just happens."

"I know, kiddo," I said.

"But sometimes it doesn't just come," she said. I could tell this meant something to her. And so I let her say it. "Sometimes I can make it come."

"That's okay," I said. "It's not your fault."

"Watch," she said. She slipped out of the bed. She rolled up her sleeves. "It usually happens when I'm angry. Or when I'm scared. Or when I just don't know what's happening. Or someone hurts me. And that's scary, because I can't stop it. But sometimes, if I think about it really hard and I hold myself together just right, if I want it, it will come."

"Come back to bed, Bessie," I told her.

"Watch," she said. She closed her eyes like she was making a wish for the entire world. It was so dark, I couldn't see her skin, but I could feel the heat, the slight change in temperature, the way it moved in waves. And then, after about fifteen seconds of complete stillness, utter silence, there were these little blue flames on her arms. I wanted to put her out, to reach for her, but I couldn't move. And the flames rolled back and forth across her arms but they never went beyond those parameters, never flared up more than that. And the light from the fire made her face glow. And she was smiling. She was smiling at me.

Then, slowly, the fire rolled down to her hands, and there was this jittery flame and she was holding it. She was holding it in her hands, cupped together. It looked like what love must look like, just barely there, so easy to extinguish.

"You can see it, right?" she asked me, and I said that I could.

And then it was gone. She was breathing so steadily, a perfect machine.

"I don't ever want it to go away," she told me. "I don't know what I'd do if it never came back."

"I understand," I said, and I did understand.

"How else would we protect ourselves?" she asked.

"I don't know," I answered. How did people protect themselves? How did anyone keep this world from ruining them? I wanted to know. I wanted to know so bad.

# Ten

JASPER WAS ON C-SPAN, SMILING, LISTENING THOUGHTFULLY, nodding, so much nodding, like he understood every fucking thing that had ever happened in the entire world. They would cut to different senators who were on the committee and it was like a practical joke because they all looked exactly the same. I had it on mute, so I didn't actually know what was going on, but it wasn't hard to imagine. It wasn't hard to know what would come next. This was just a rerun of the confirmation hearing anyway, the channel filling time until the official Senate vote came in today.

The kids were on the sofa, reading books. They reeked of chlorine from the pool, a smell that I loved. I was pacing through the house, brushing my hair, rubbing moisturizer on my face, clipping my toenails, all these little things to make myself presentable, and, each time, I'd look at myself again in the mirror and feel like not a single thing had changed.

On the coffee table there were these index cards that listed all the former secretaries of state, like, sixty little cards all over the place. I was getting the kids to memorize them, or some of them, because Madison had said that it might be nice if they knew something about the position, as if the kids needed conversational openers to talk to their own father. So we studied the names. I'd never heard of most of them. It was interesting to look at the six secretaries of state who had gone on to be president. I knew this was something Madison and Jasper thought about a lot. But it was more fun for me to look at the three who had unsuccessfully run for president. I made Bessie and Roland memorize these names first, before anyone else.

Madison thought it was better if Roland and Bessie stayed behind, that the craziness of the proceedings, being shuttled from place to place, would be overwhelming for them. And she wasn't wrong. I mean, yeah, they probably shouldn't have gone to one of the biggest cities in America in support of their father, a guy they kind of hated. But I thought of the Smithsonian, a place I had always wanted to see and knew I never would. The Washington Monument. The Lincoln Memorial. I thought about, holy shit, the Tomb of the Unknown Soldier, that eternal flame. I wanted them to see these things. I even showed Madison the wardrobe for the kids: a layer of flame gel, the Nomex long underwear, clothes like you'd wear at Catholic school, so much coverage.

"It's just a risk/reward kind of thing, you know?" she told me. We didn't talk about that night between us, not a word. We didn't act like it hadn't happened. That would have been bullshit. But we acted like if we talked about it, it would only keep happening, the same result, the same pain, and what was the point of that?

"I do want them to watch it all, though," she said. "And read them the newspapers, okay? I want them to appreciate their father. I think it might help, if they see how important he is."

"They know he's important, Madison," I told her. "They don't think *they're* important."

"Well," she said, "you have to make them think otherwise."

"That's all I've been doing, okay?" I said, getting angry.

"Let's not fight," she said, reaching to touch my arm, so calculated, her skin on mine. I let her hand sit there, like a butterfly on my arm, its wings beating just so.

"Sorry," I said. "Okay. You're right. Okay."

"This is how the world works," she told me, and she meant this was how *her* world worked, as if I didn't already know. "Things are bad and crazy and chaotic. But you ride it out and you don't let it hurt you, and then there's this stretch of time that is so calm and perfect. And that's what was always waiting for you."

"Okay," I said, ready to be done with all this.

"That's what you tell them," she said, removing her hand from my arm. "That's what you get them to understand."

AFTER WE HAD LUNCH, THE VOTE CAME IN, NO SURPRISES, and Jasper Roberts, Bessie and Roland's dad, was the new secretary of state of the United States of America. I finally turned on the volume, but it was just more words, nothing that really mattered.

"Your dad did it," I told them.

"Well, okay," Roland said.

Bessie said, "I remember something," and scattered index cards until she held up a name, Elihu B. Washburne. She flipped it over to the back, where there were one or two interesting facts that we'd written. She held it out to me.

"This guy only did it for eleven days," she told me. "Maybe Dad will be like that."

"Maybe," I told her.

And then, on the steps of the Capitol, there was this podium and all these people milling around. I sat on the sofa with the kids. I was looking for Madison, wanted to see what she was wearing. And then there was applause, and I saw all three of them, Jasper, Madison, and Timothy, walking to the podium. I saw Carl behind them, official and serious. Madison was holding Timothy, resting him on her hip. He had a little sports coat with an American flag pin on the lapel. Madison had on this tight maroon dress, like Jackie O or something. Jasper, who the hell cared, had on a boring-ass gray suit, but he looked handsome enough. They looked like a beautiful family, no denying it. They looked so complete, so compact, so perfect. We were here, and they were there, and this all made perfect sense to me.

Jasper started to talk, and it was like when he prayed at dinner that night, just platitudes, like a computer program had written them based on phrases in the Bible and the Constitution mixed together. He talked about responsibility and protecting the country and yet also ensuring its growth and prosperity. He talked about his own military service, which I actually hadn't known about. He talked about diplomacy, but I wasn't watching any of that. I was looking over his shoulder, at Madison, who was beaming. She was stunning, the ease of her posture, how relaxed she was now that she had something she wanted. And resting on her shoulder, there was Timothy, who was making this weird face. He was frowning, like he heard a little sound that no one else could hear. And then, there was this noise, like a firework exploding, and someone gasped. For a second, I thought someone had been shot.

Bessie and Roland stood up, focused on the screen. And all three of us could see it so clearly. It was right there.

Timothy was on fire.

He was completely ablaze, not like the popping and crackling, no little sparks. Real fire. Madison screamed, dropping him on the ground, out of sight of the camera. Her dress was smoking, just these little wisps of smoke rising off of her. Jasper didn't seem to understand what was going on, kept looking ahead as if turning around would be a major sign of weakness, as if someone else would handle it. But now Madison was really screaming, and there was Carl, his jacket off, slapping the ground, where I imagined Timothy was. And finally the camera kind of moved, adjusted so that Jasper was now off-screen, who gave a fuck about him, and there was Timothy, kind of crouched on the ground, burning so perfectly, brilliantly burning. I could hear all these voices, but over the noise there was Jasper's voice, distorted and angry, yelling Madison's name over and over.

"Holy shit," Bessie and Roland said at the same time.

And then, like magic, Timothy wasn't on fire. He was fine. He was actually smiling, not a hair out of place. Carl wrapped him up in the jacket and lifted him into his arms, and some other men in suits and sunglasses kind of blocked everything off, and they all ran toward this long line of identical black cars. And the cars drove off. And that was it. They cut back to the studio, where a man in tweed looked like he'd eaten poison. He made this dry little hissing sound, like we hadn't all just seen this kid on fire, and he said, "A historic day as the Senate confirms the appointment—"

I looked over at the kids just as I felt the temperature of the room subtly shift. And they were rigid, staring at the screen, their eyes so wide. And even with the Nomex clothing, I could see them starting to burn. "Outside!" I shouted, because I knew that fucking breathing exercises were not going to work. I knew what was coming. But the kids weren't moving, and now they were really smoking, and the air smelled like chemicals, so dense and acrid.

"Bessie!" I shouted. "Roland! C'mon, kiddos. Let's go outside."

I started pulling on them, and they finally seemed to snap out of it. They walked with me to the front door and we stepped outside, the weather so clear, so perfect. The sun was high up in the sky. Bessie and Roland walked onto the lawn. And they were laughing. They were laughing hard. And it was difficult to look at them, they were so bright, this white, blinding light. And then they were on fire, too, these vivid red and yellow flames. They stood there, burning. And I was happy. I knew they were okay. I knew that they couldn't be hurt. The grass turned black at their feet, and the air around them turned shimmery. It was beautiful. They were beautiful.

Inside the guesthouse, the phone was ringing, again and again and again, but I didn't move. I looked across the lawn, and Mary was standing on the back porch, watching the children, completely unaffected, as if she were watching some ordinary birds at a feeder. I waved to her, and she waited for a few seconds before she waved back.

The kids ran in circles, the flame trailing off of them and falling to the ground, where the grass caught fire for a second before it smoldered. They burned and burned, like they were eternal. But I knew that it would die down, that it would fade away, back inside them, wherever it hid. I knew that soon they would turn back into the kids I knew so well, their weird bodies and tics. I didn't try to catch them or put them out. I let them burn. I sat on the porch, a perfect day, and watched them burn. Because I knew that when it was over, when the fire disappeared, they would come right back to me.

# Eleven

WE BARELY SLEPT THAT NIGHT, SO REVVED UP, NOTHING WE could do about it. The minute the sun rose, the kids jumped out of bed. The sheets were sticky from the fire gel, beyond saving, and the kids took turns in the shower to wash the rest of it off. I didn't try to stop them. It seemed pointless. Either they'd burn the house down or they wouldn't.

WHEN I'D FINALLY ANSWERED THE PHONE THE DAY BEFORE, Carl, who sounded out of breath, said that they were coming home, driving back to Nashville. He said that Madison was handling damage control, that I wasn't to talk to anyone. He told me to keep the kids inside the house, to cover them in fire gel. "Keep them safe, okay?" he said, and before I could ask about Timothy, he hung up.

Bessie and Roland wanted to see it again, over and over, Timothy on fire, but I unplugged the television, knew that it would only make it worse, that it was already burned onto the insides of our eyelids. Of course, I wondered what was going on outside of our house, what the newspapers would say, but I just pushed it out of my mind. I focused on these two kids.

After they'd finally stopped burning, we'd peeled off the

ruined Nomex and put on a fresh set of clothes. I'd made them sit on the sofa, dumped a bunch of apples on the coffee table, and we'd read three Penny Nichols novels, my voice droning and droning, working our way through the mystery to that moment when it all comes into the light. This was how we'd survive, huddled together, words on the page, the ending of one story just a moment of silence before a new story began. And we made it. The kids were happy. They had added another to their numbers. They didn't want to set the world on fire. They just wanted to be less alone in it.

IT TOOK SOME COAXING, BUT I GOT THEM TO DO THIRTY MINutes of yoga, and while they ate cereal, I ran over to the mansion to get a copy of the newspaper. I could not imagine the angle, how the narrative would be assembled. I wanted to know if Bessie and Roland would be mentioned, to be prepared. I knocked on the back door until Mary opened it for me. "Do you want something to eat?" she asked, and I did kind of want a bacon sandwich, but I ignored that desire and got on with it.

"I wanted to get a copy of the newspaper," I told her. She stared at me, unblinking. I had no idea whether she knew about Timothy. I wanted to say something, but it's a hard thing to introduce into polite conversation.

"Come in," she finally said.

All the lights in the house were off, no activity.

"Kind of spooky in here," I said.

"Everyone else has the week off," she said.

"That's nice, I guess," I said.

"Here's the newspaper," she said, handing me a copy of the *Tennessean*. And there it was, the headline: FIRE MISHAP MARS ROBERTS CONFIRMATION.

"Oh shit," I said, looking at the picture of Jasper, his face both confused and furious, being hustled to the car, Madison right behind him. I looked for Timothy and Carl, but they must have already been inside the car.

"Mmm," Mary said, noncommittal, almost bored.

"Did you see it on TV?" I asked.

"I don't watch television," she replied.

"You saw us yesterday, though," I said. "In the yard? Bessie and Roland."

"I saw it, yes," she replied.

"That's what happened to Timothy," I told her.

"I figured as much," she said. I couldn't tell if it was because of her position in the household, one of servitude, or if her natural demeanor simply wouldn't allow the display of emotion for people who didn't deserve it.

I read the article, which repeated the official statement from Jasper Roberts, which was that a spark had caused Timothy's shirt, which had been heavily starched in anticipation of the press conference, to momentarily catch on fire. The boy had been treated for minor burns, as had Madison, and released from the hospital that same day. It went on to state that Jasper would return to Tennessee so that Timothy could be seen by the family's personal physician. And then, that was it. I flipped through the section, looking for more information, but there was nothing else. There was another article about what the implications were for national security, how Jasper would both continue the work of the previous secretary and build upon that work. I couldn't believe that something so strange could be met with such an easy willingness to disbelieve that it had happened. A starched fucking shirt? Really?

I grabbed the *New York Times,* but there was even less about

Timothy, not even a picture at the press conference, instead an official portrait of Jasper. It was all so formal, all about policy, about governance. Who the fuck cared about that?

"Did you know?" I asked Mary.

She nodded.

"Who told you?" I asked.

"I saw it," she finally said. "In this kitchen. I saw the little girl catch on fire."

"When they were still living here?"

"Yes," she said. "Just before Senator Roberts sent Mrs. Jane and the children away, when they were fighting all the time. The girl, Bessie. She came down and asked for something to eat. And then Senator Roberts came in and said that she couldn't have anything until dinner. And she yelled that she was hungry. And Senator Roberts grabbed her arm and said that he made the rules, that he decided what was best for everyone in the family. She just burst into flames, and Senator Roberts jumped away. He stared at her. The smoke alarm started going off. I took a pitcher of water and poured it on the girl. Still on fire. I filled it up and poured it again. Still on fire. And then another. And she finally stopped burning, no more fire. And the girl looked completely fine, very red but not crying. Then Mrs. Jane shouted from the living room about the smoke alarm, and Senator Roberts said that I had burned a grilled cheese. Now, that I did not care for."

"Yeah, that sucks," I replied.

"He took the girl upstairs. When she came back down, wearing new clothes, her hair still damp, Senator Roberts was nowhere to be found, and she said that she'd like a grilled cheese. So I made her one. I made her two, I think. And that was it. Not long after, they were gone."

"Did Jasper ever talk to you about it?" I asked.

She shook her head. "I received a generous raise, though," she said. "So much money."

"This family," I said, shaking my head.

"No worse than any other family," Mary offered. She shrugged.

"No," I admitted, "maybe not."

"You want to keep the papers?" she asked. I remembered that the kids were back in the guesthouse, waiting for me.

"Save them for Jasper," I told her. "Maybe he'll want them for his scrapbook."

**"WILL TIMOTHY COME LIVE WITH US?" ROLAND ASKED.**

I hadn't fully considered it. "I don't know," I admitted. "Maybe." What would it matter? Another child in the bed, another set of lungs taking in air, holding it, and releasing it. I wondered if Jasper had fathered any children out of wedlock. Should a note be sent to the mothers of those children? A pamphlet? The guesthouse would become a home for wayward children who spontaneously combusted.

It made me happy, after everyone had seemed so convinced that Jane was responsible, that it was Jasper's fucked-up genes that had made this happen. It made sense to me, these privileged families turning inward, becoming incestuous, like old royalty. It was bound to happen. It was all on him. And yet it worried me a little, that if Jasper knew without a doubt that he made these fire children, what would he do to them? How much of himself did he see in them? Too much or too little seemed dangerous to me.

We just waited for them to come home. I had no idea how long it took to drive from D.C. to Franklin, so we tried to go about our day, but whatever I came up with—math flash cards, Silly Putty, animal masks—I'd catch the kids staring off into space. Their skin was splotchy, warm to the touch, but the fire never came to the surface, as if they were holding on to it for when they really needed it. Or maybe they had burned themselves out the day before. I should have been keeping notes, doing scientific research, wearing safety goggles. There was so much that I should have been doing, that I could have been doing, but not a fucking thing made sense to me. I just fed them, made them wash their hands, listened to whatever nonsense they wanted to tell me. I took care of them, you know?

We were outside on the basketball court just as dusk began, the light all red and golden and perfect. Bessie was trying to hit five free throws in a row, and when she did that, she made it six, then seven. She had a nice shot, a little janky, but we could work with it. Whenever she tracked down the ball after a miss, she practiced dribbling between her legs, taking these weird strides, keeping her head up like a general surveying the battlefield. With her hair and her determined scowl, she looked like a punk rocker, like apocalypse basketball. Roland was on the other side of the court, throwing up underhanded free throws and hitting a lot of them, like Rick Barry, though the kid seemed to be putting no thought or effort into it, which, of course, also made me happy.

I called them over for a game of H-O-R-S-E, the three of us lined up single file. Before they had time to blink, Roland was out and Bessie was at H-O-R- and I was pristine. I knew kids, just like adults, wanted to win at everything they ever did, but I thought this was good child rearing, to show them how difficult it is to be good at something, to rejoice when you made small improvements. The kids didn't seem to mind, liked watching me line up the hardest shots and effortlessly knock them down.

"How much longer is summer?" Bessie asked me.

"Still a while to go," I told her.

"What will you do when it's over?" she asked.

"I haven't thought about it," I replied, and it was true that I really hadn't. "I haven't had time to think about it. I've been thinking about you guys."

"Where will you go?" she asked, not letting it go. "Will you stay here?"

"No," I admitted. "I'll probably go back home." I thought about my mom, that room in the attic, and I wanted to cry. But I had money now, though I hadn't checked my bank account since I got here. I could get my own place. A decent apartment, something with windows, where normal people congregated.

"Will you take care of some other kids?" Roland asked.

"Probably not," I said. "I'd probably hate them after being with you guys. They'd be so boring."

"They'd suck," Bessie offered, helping me along. Roland nodded his approval; how could those kids be anything other than sucky?

"Yeah," I said. "I might go back to school. That would be the smart thing to do." I had almost a year and a half of credits from community college and night school, all the fits and starts when I'd told myself that I would pull my life together and then never lasted long enough to save myself. I prayed that they wouldn't ask me what I'd major in, because that felt like a riddle, all the steps I'd have to take to give them an answer.

"Maybe you'll meet somebody," Roland said. "And get married. And have kids."

"I doubt it," I told him.

"Maybe," he said. "You never know, right?"

"I guess not," I said. I didn't want to weigh him down with my life; what would be gained? I turned around, facing the opposite hoop, and threw the ball over my head. It went right in, and the kids cheered. It made me smile. I remembered those games when you would just ride this wave, when it felt like all you had to do was keep your feet under you and you couldn't miss. If you thought about it, tried to figure out why it was happening, it would leave you, and you could feel it when you put up your next shot. It was gone. So you put your head down, ran down the court, stayed on your man, and just waited until it came back to you. And you promised yourself that you wouldn't lose it again, that you'd hold on to it this time.

WE HEARD THE CAR COMING UP THE DRIVEWAY, AND WE stopped shooting, watching it pull into the roundabout, right in front of the house. Bessie dropped the ball, and the two of them started sprinting to the car. I called out to them but then just started jogging after them, wondering what we were running toward, if we should have been going in the opposite direction.

I saw Carl hop out of the driver's side, looking ragged, his shirt untucked, and he ran around to get the door. By this time, I'd caught up to the kids, and we were just standing there, watching it all unfold like it was television, like it wasn't real at all.

Madison scootched out of the car, holding Timothy, who was wrapped up in this baby-blue towel. He was asleep, but as she stepped away from the car, he opened his eyes, gazed up at the mansion.

"Hey," I said, lame as hell. Madison looked at me, took a deep breath, and then nodded.

"Can we say hi?" Roland asked Madison, who looked so tired. She didn't say no, just stood there, and the kids came up to her.

"Hey, Timothy," Roland said.

Timothy seemed to regard them for a moment, placing them in his mind. "Hello," he said.

"You were amazing," Roland said, but Timothy just fell back against Madison.

"He doesn't remember," Madison said to me. "At least I don't think he does."

Jasper stepped out of the car and, seeing the children, said, irritation running all through his voice, "Madison, let's get him inside. Could we please go inside?"

What was the formal greeting for the secretary of state? Mr. Secretary? That sounded like a horse that finished last in the Kentucky Derby. He looked at me for a second, as if I were responsible for any of this shit, and then, once Madison went into the house, he followed her inside.

Carl took me by the hand, squeezing it tightly. "We're going to talk," he said.

"We saw it on TV," I told him. "Holy shit."

"It was . . . it was ill-timed," he admitted.

"What happened?" I said. "Afterward?"

He looked down at the kids. I told them to go ask Mary for something to eat, and they scampered into the house before anyone could stop them.

"It was chaos. Nobody else could really understand what

had happened, especially since Timothy was unharmed. Of course, we knew what had happened, but that's not a human being's first instinct, to assume that a child spontaneously combusted on the steps of the Capitol. It was all Madison. She moved so quickly, called media outlets, gave them updates. It was like two seconds after it all happened, she had a response ready. It really was impressive," he admitted.

"So, like, Jasper's going to resign, right?" I asked.

"Are you fucking crazy?" Carl said. "There's no way he's going to resign. Because his kid caught on fire? No way. And why would they take it away? They just confirmed him. They'd look like idiots."

"But if it happens again?" I asked. "Why risk it?"

"It's complicated," Carl admitted.

"Everyone keeps saying that," I told him. "It seems not that complicated to me."

"Let's go inside," he told me.

"What's happening?" I asked.

"Lillian?" he said. "Just try to think about it rationally. Try to consider the situation."

"I want to talk to Madison," I said. I ran ahead of him into the house. In the kitchen, Bessie and Roland were sitting at the counter, while Mary heated up some chicken nuggets. "Stay here," I told them. I went back into the living room, where I'd first had iced tea with Madison. Jasper was standing there, pacing around the coffee table, running one hand through his silver hair.

"Where's Madison?" I asked.

"She's putting Timothy to bed," he told me. Carl walked into the room and stood beside me.

"Lillian," Jasper continued, "as you can imagine, this has

been a very stressful few days. The confirmation hearing alone, good lord, but now . . . now this."

"It's crazy," I said, but Carl kind of leaned against me, a signal to keep quiet. I shut up.

"I want to thank you for your service," he said. "You have helped us immensely, and we are so grateful for that. I know that you have done everything in your power to make sure that Roland and Bessie have been cared for."

"It's okay," I said. Thanking me for *my service* seemed weird, but it also felt like something political people said to mean any number of weird things that you had to do for them.

"I'm afraid that the circumstances have changed, that we were perhaps naive to think that we could do this on our own, that you, without any training, could handle this."

I looked at Carl. "What's going on?" I asked.

Jasper kept talking. "We no longer require your services. We have found other accommodations for the twins."

"Boarding school? I know about that. Do you think that's such a hot idea, to send them away? To Europe?"

Jasper looked confused and stared at Carl, who then spoke. "They'll actually stay in Tennessee," he said. "There is an alternative school, a kind of ranch, where trained professionals work with troubled children. It's in the Smoky Mountains. It's very private. Very discreet."

"When did you decide this?" I asked.

"Carl found this place a long time ago," Jasper said, "but I was too stubborn to listen."

"You did this?" I asked Carl, who blushed.

"Early in the proceedings," he said, "I was tasked with finding as many options as possible for the care and treatment of these kids."

"'Troubled children'?" I said, and just hearing it made me angry.

"You don't think Bessie and Roland are troubled?" Jasper asked, dumbfounded. "This facility will work with them physically and mentally."

"This is bullshit," I said. "What is it? You said 'school' and then you said 'ranch' and now you said 'facility.'"

"It's multipurpose," Carl said. "It's kind of a rehab center."

"They call it an academy," Jasper said.

"Shut the fuck up, Jasper," I said. "Carl, you know this is bullshit. You're going to hide these kids and forget about them."

"We don't have many options, Lillian," Carl said.

"I'm the secretary of state now," Jasper said, his voice rising. "You cannot even imagine the sacrifices that I've made. My responsibilities—"

"I could honestly punch you in the face right now, Jasper," I said.

"Lillian," Carl said. "I don't like this any more than—"

"Then don't fucking do it, you moron. You fucking idiot," I said. "This is so unfair. And what about Timothy? How are you going to take care of him? Why do Roland and Bessie get punished?"

Carl looked at Jasper, who was shaking his head. Then he said, "For the next six months, Timothy will be checked in to a facility, to be observed."

"You're the weirdest person I've ever met, Jasper," I told him.

"There's nothing sinister," he said. "You think the worst of us. It's like the Mayo Clinic, cutting-edge medicine. But . . . private."

"That sounds really fucking sinister. It sounds . . ." I searched so hard for the right words, but I couldn't think straight. "Not good," I finally said.

"It does sound fucking sinister," said Madison, who was now standing at the foot of the stairs.

"We talked about this," Jasper said.

"Not Timothy," Madison said. "That's not what you said."

"It's temporary," Jasper said.

"Six months?" Madison said. "No fucking way, Jasper." She turned to Carl. "Where is this place?"

Carl actually gulped, way out of his depth. "M-Montana."

"No fucking way," Madison repeated, and she looked amazing. She shined with a kind of ferocity that you couldn't teach, that you had to be born with. "I'll go get Timothy right now." She turned to go up the stairs. "We'll stay with my parents. Did you hear that? I'll go live with my terrible parents. My brothers will drive up here and beat the shit out of you."

"What else can we do?" Jasper asked, almost crying.

"Why are you guys shouting?" Roland asked, walking into the room. Bessie was beside him, staring daggers at Jasper.

"Carl?" Jasper said, gesturing to the kids, as if Carl was going to bonk them on the head and stuff them into a sack. "Carl?"

Carl hesitated, staring at the kids. "Perhaps we need to rethink our plan of action, sir," he finally said.

"You have ruined my life!" Jasper shouted, his hair flopping over his face, which was red now. It wasn't clear who he was talking to, exactly. All of us, probably.

"You ruined our lives," Bessie shouted, and I ran to her, knelt beside her.

"Your mother ruined your life," Jasper said, softly, like he was pleading with her.

"You fucking idio—" I started to say, and I jumped up and grabbed his shirt, tried to claw his eyes, but Bessie was already on fire before I could do any damage. And then Roland was on fire. I shouted at Madison to go get Timothy, and she ran up the stairs.

When I turned back, Jasper pushed me so hard that I fell through the coffee table, glass shattering. Carl went to restrain Jasper, holding him in a full nelson, forcefully walking him toward the front door.

Madison came running down the steps, holding Timothy, and she looked at me for a second before she finally ran out of the house. Timothy looked at the fire through heavy lids, like he couldn't be bothered.

Bessie and Roland were simply touching objects, the sofa cushions, a painting on the wall, setting it all ablaze, calmly moving through the house.

Still lying there, I turned to see Mary, holding some expensive pots and pans, walk out the front door without looking back. I wished her all the best in the world, every good thing.

I pulled myself off the table. I was scratched up pretty bad, but no gashes, nothing too serious. I ran over to the children, who were now in the hallway.

"Let's go," I said. "We have to go."

They looked at me, confused. "You and me," I said. "We're going. We're going away."

"Just the three of us?" Bessie asked, and I nodded.

They closed their eyes, took deep breaths. I wanted to hold them, to pull them into my arms, but I stood there, as close as I could get to the heat, and watched as they slowly pulled the fire back inside themselves. There were all these little fires burning in the mansion, and we stared at them, dumbfounded at the mess we had made. It wasn't beautiful, but it was hard to look away from.

Just then, Carl ran back into the mansion. "Get out of here," he shouted. I grabbed the kids and we moved to the door, but then he stopped us.

"The back door," he said. "Go get some clothes, pack a bag. As quick as you can." He handed me a ring of keys and pointed to one of them. "The Civic is in the garage," he said. "Just take it. Don't tell me where you're going. Just go."

"Thank you," I said, taking the keys.

"I'm sorry," he said.

"It's okay," I told him. He ran into the kitchen for a fire extinguisher, and we were out the back door.

"Get some clothes," I told the kids the second we were inside the guesthouse. "Whatever, it doesn't matter." It took us five minutes, maybe less, the kids shaking off their burned clothes and putting on their Nomex. I grabbed my wallet, a candy bar, trying to concentrate and not succeeding. When we walked out of the guesthouse, we saw the inside of the mansion lit up, flickering from the flames. We crept around to the garage and piled into the Honda. I started it up, told the kids to put on their seat belts. I looked at Madison, who was still holding Timothy. As I drove off, she turned to look at me. I waved to her. She smiled. She waved back. And then she turned to the house, watching it.

Farther down the long driveway I saw Mary, and slowed to offer her a ride. She said that her boyfriend was coming to get her, and she waved me on. The kids said goodbye to her, and then I sped off, watching the mansion in my rearview the entire time; the children turned around to look, too. A few minutes later, two fire trucks, their sirens blaring, sped in the opposite direction, toward the estate.

In that moment, still nearly hyperventilating, I couldn't figure out just how bad things were. How illegal was it, what I'd done? Kidnapping? Arson? Physical assault against a secretary of state? I bet there were so many other charges that I wasn't even considering, that I wouldn't even know about until the judge read them off to me in court, while I was waving to the kids, telling them everything was real cool, just fine.

I honestly just drove for a while, no real consideration of where I was or where I was going. Part of the problem was that I didn't really know where to go. I figured we should get a hotel room, but that seemed suspicious. I was cut up from the coffee table.

I finally found the interstate and got on it, speeding up to merge with traffic. The kids had been so quiet, probably traumatized, but there was nothing I could do about that now. Setting your childhood home on fire, that seemed like some symbolically heavy shit. I looked in the rearview mirror and saw that both of them were wide awake, staring at me.

"Hey, kiddos," I said, smiling.

"Are we in trouble?" Bessie asked.

"Some," I admitted.

"What are we going to do?" Roland asked.

"I don't know yet," I said.

"Well, where are we going?" Bessie asked.

And I knew it, the way it clicked into place, the only option I had. The car was already going there. It was unavoidable.

"We're going home," I told them.

"Whose home?" they asked. They'd had so many over the last few months.

"My home," I said, almost crying, so fucking angry with myself.

"Okay," the kids said.

# Twelve

MY MOTHER OPENED THE DOOR, SAW BESSIE AND ROLAND on either side of me, and she just nodded, not saying a word. It was entirely possible that she had ignored pertinent details of my life for so long that she would accept the idea that I was the mother of ten-year-old twins.

"Hi," Roland said.

"Mm-hmm," my mother said. Even though she had given up smoking ten years earlier, she always looked like she was just about to take a long drag on a cigarette and blow the smoke right in your face.

"Hey, Mom," I said.

"You're bleeding," she said, gesturing to some blood on the sleeve of my shirt, from one of the cuts I'd received falling onto that glass table.

"I know," I said. "Can we come in?"

"It's your house, too," she said, which made me want to cry, but it wasn't clear exactly why.

"This is Bessie, and this is Roland," I said, tapping each kid softly on the head.

"You're their governess, right?" she replied.

"I don't know what I am to them, Mom," I said. "It's kind

of jumbled up at the moment. I'm taking care of them, though. We need a place to stay, to keep them safe."

"Are you in trouble?" she asked me, still looking at the kids.

"Kind of," I said. "Kind of yes and kind of no."

"Well, your room is still there," she said. "Haven't been in it since you left."

"Thanks, Mom," I said, but she waved me away with a flick of her wrist.

I hustled the kids upstairs, up to the attic, which was sweltering because none of the fans were on. I cursed and started plugging them in and getting them going. I set the kids in front of the two biggest ones, cranked up to high, which just blew all this dust around the room, little particles hovering in the air. There was an old piece of pizza sitting in an opened box, petrified. It was so embarrassing, to show these kids what my life had been like before them. It must have vaporized any confidence they had that I knew what I was doing. I kind of shuffle-kicked the pizza box under the bed, but they'd both seen it.

"We're hungry," Bessie told me. I realized that over the course of this summer they had become used to a lifestyle where someone simply reached into a refrigerator or cabinet and food immediately appeared. The pizza place delivered, but I was paranoid about the cops.

"My stomach," Roland said. "Listen to it growl."

"Okay, okay," I said. "I get the picture. Just sit tight, and I'll bring something up."

"Can't we come down there?" they asked. "It's hot up here."

"We kind of need to give my mom her space," I told them. "She's not good with kids."

I ran down the stairs, huffing. I reached behind me and touched a spot just above the waist of my jeans, and I felt a little piece of glass stuck in there. I tried to pull it out, but it was in there pretty good. It didn't hurt, but now that I knew it was there, it was all I could think about. It could not be good to have open wounds and hang out in that musty attic. I was losing my focus. I went into the kitchen and my mom was there, reading a magazine, listening to soft rock on the radio.

"Um," I said, so embarrassed. I hated needing things, and I hated it even more when I needed things from my mom. "The kids are hungry."

"That makes three of us," she replied, still looking at the magazine, which was about houses on the beach or some such nonsense.

"I've got money," I said. "Could you order all of us a pizza?"

She looked up at the ceiling, thinking about it. "I'm not really in the mood for pizza," she said.

"Anything," I replied. "McDonald's? Subway?"

She sighed, stood up from the table, and started going through the cabinets, snatching them open and then slamming them closed.

"I've got macaroni and cheese," she said. Then she looked in the fridge. "And hot dogs."

"That's great," I said. I reached for a pot and filled it with water. She threw the hot dogs on the counter next to the stove and went back to the table. While I waited for the water to boil, I stared at her. When I was a kid, there had been so many nights like this, usually my mother and one of her boyfriends watching TV on this little model they kept in the kitchen, while I made butter noodles or a wilted, soggy salad with Thousand Island dressing, cutting up cucumbers and green peppers like we were the healthiest people in the world because of me.

I walked over to the stairs, called out to see if the kids were okay, and they shouted that they were. When I stepped back into the kitchen, my mom said, "I knew you were coming."

"Is that right?" I said, feeling my skin getting itchy, my heartbeat picking up.

"A man called a while ago. Cal or Carl or . . . something like that. Asked if I'd heard from you."

"What did you tell him?" I asked her.

"I said I hadn't seen you all summer, that I hadn't even talked to you," she said.

"Okay," I said, because I knew there was more.

"He said that I should call him if you turned up with two kids," she continued, now finally looking at me. "Said he'd pay me for my trouble."

"So did you call him back?" I asked.

She shook her head. "He was so stiff, so formal. I didn't like his tone. So, no, I didn't call him back."

The water was finally boiling, and I poured in the macaroni.

"You're welcome," she said.

"Madison's husband," I said, "he's—"

"I don't want to know," she told me.

"Well, the kids, Bessie and Roland. Something you need to know—"

"No, I don't need to know," she said. "I won't keep you from what you want to do, Lillian. I've never kept you from what you want—"

I huffed, my turn to interrupt her.

"You do what you want, but just let me have my peace," she said after a few seconds.

When I looked over at her, she seemed so old, even though she was only forty-seven, and I knew that sometimes she adopted the mannerisms and posture of someone much older to avoid having to do things that she didn't want to do. If I'd been a man, if I'd been handsome, she would not have been reading a magazine about coastal living and yawning. I think, maybe, if I'd been anyone other than her daughter, she would have acted differently, but I made her feel old, because I was hers.

I stirred the pasta, started putting hot dogs in a pan.

"I never pictured you with kids," she said. "You didn't seem the type for it."

"That makes two of us," I replied.

"We're so hungry!" Roland shouted from the attic.

"Let 'em come on down," my mom said, indicating the table. She stood up and filled four plastic cups with water.

"Come down!" I shouted up at them, the rickety house letting sound shoot through the walls and floors, and then they were thumping down the stairs.

"Hi!" Roland said, again waving to my mom, who took her magazine and pulled her chair over near the window.

I heated up the hot dogs, nearly burning them because I was also straining the macaroni, and then I mixed everything together in a pot. I got some plates and served them.

"Don't you want some?" Roland asked my mom.

"I guess so," she replied, and she pulled her chair over to the table. She took a bite and nodded. "It's good," she told me. She always liked it when I cooked for her, whatever it was.

"You're quiet," my mom said, pointing her spoon at Bessie.

"I'm a little tired," Bessie replied.

"She's cute," my mom said to me, her spoon still fixed on Bessie, who brightened a little.

"We're on a trip," Roland announced, wanting my mother's attention.

"For how long?" she asked. I wondered how long it had been since she'd talked to a child. To anyone.

"We don't know," Roland said. "It's hard to tell."

"Just for a little while," I told the table, not hungry, pushing my food around my plate.

"We don't stay anywhere for very long," Bessie admitted.

"Well," my mom said, "it's better than just staying in one place for your entire life."

"I don't think so," Bessie said, looking at me now, like she wanted me to say something, but my mind was somewhere else, not in this house. This happened a lot, where my body was right here, in the house where I'd grown up, but my mind was hovering just outside it, waiting to see what it was that I was going to do.

**AFTER THE KIDS FELL ASLEEP, I WAS STILL TOO KEYED UP TO** do anything. Being back in this house, in the attic, felt like sliding down the biggest slide in the world, just an utterly cosmic joke. I tried to imagine my life before this summer, all the times I moved out and then moved right back. I had been so smart, and then when things didn't work out exactly how I'd hoped, it was like I pushed that curiosity way down inside myself. I'd wasted so much time.

I'd check out books by Ursula Le Guin, Grace Paley, and Carson McCullers. And then I'd hide the books from view when anyone walked by because I was afraid someone would ask me about them, like they might think I was showing off or trying to be someone that I wasn't. There were times when I felt feral, like I hadn't gotten the proper training right when it mattered, and now I was lost.

And here I was, and now there were these two children, their arms wrapped so tightly around me that I could barely breathe. And maybe, now that I had them all to myself, now that we didn't have the safety of that house on the estate, I worried that these kids had missed that opportunity, too, that they were lost. And I wondered if it was cruel to pretend that there was anything I could do for them. I knew there would come a time when I had to give them back. And, god, they would hate me. For their entire lives. More than their mother. More than Jasper, even. They'd hate me because I'd made them think that I could do it.

I pulled their arms off me, and they muttered, their bodies so sweaty in this humid attic. I rearranged the fans so they were closer to the kids, and then I walked downstairs, the steps creaking and squeaking loudly, until I saw my mom on the sofa in the living room. She wasn't watching TV or reading or doing anything. She didn't even have a drink. She was just staring into space.

Not long after I'd come back home after being kicked out of Iron Mountain, we were in the driveway, my mom about to take me to school. And when she started the car, smoke began pouring out from under the hood, this terrible grinding sound. More smoke. I ran to the house to get some water, and my mom used some rags to protect her hand while she popped the hood. I ran back outside with a pitcher of water sloshing around, and now the engine was on fire, the flames reaching pretty high. And I stopped a few feet from my mom, who was just staring at the fire, with that same look on her face that I was seeing now. It was like she could see something inside the flame, some prophecy. Or maybe she could see the span of her life up to this point, how she got to this moment, standing over her ruined car.

I'd walked over to her and held up the pitcher, but she just shook her head. "Look," she said, gesturing toward the engine, "just look at it." I didn't know what she wanted me to see, if we could even see the same thing. "It's kind of pretty," she finally said. And we stood there, watching the fire, until she finally took the water from me and dumped it on the engine, which didn't do much of anything. "You don't have to go to school today," she told me, sighing so deeply. "I'm not going to work." I nodded, smiling a little, because I thought maybe we'd spend the day together, go see a movie, but when we went back into the house, she lit up a cigarette and closed the door to her bedroom, locking me out, and I didn't see her until the next morning. And this was what I finally realized, that even as we sank deeper and deeper into our lives, we were always separate. And I wondered what it would feel like, to fall but to hold on to someone else so you weren't alone.

And now, here we were, back in this house. What I wanted to do, if this was a dream, was to walk into that room. I wanted to sit next to my mom. And I wanted to ask, "Why did you hate me?" And I wanted her to say, "You're looking at it from the wrong angle. I didn't hate you. I loved you so much. I protected you. I kept you safe from harm." And I would say, "You did?" She would nod. I'd ask her who my father was, and she'd say that he was the worst man who had ever been born. She'd say that she had given up everything in her life to get away from him. And she had raised me all alone, as best she could. And I would say, "Thank you." And she would hug me and it wouldn't be weird. It would be like the way somebody hugs another person. And the entirety of my life, everything that had come before, would disappear. And things would be so much better.

I stared at her for a few more seconds, and I could not imagine what was inside her head. I didn't hate her. But there was no way that I was going to sit on that sofa. There was no way that I was going to say anything to her. I turned around, the steps creaking so loud that she must have heard me; how could she not have heard me? And there were the kids, still curled into the shape of sleep, their bodies both rigid and loose at the same time. I crawled back into bed. And Bessie opened her eyes.

"What's going to happen?" she asked.

"I don't know," I told her. Because I had no idea, had barely made it this far.

"Will we have to go back?" she asked.

"Eventually," I admitted. "Yes, we will."

She thought about this. It was so dark in the attic. I couldn't really see her and I wasn't sure that I wanted to.

"Okay," she said.

"It's okay," I said. "It really is."

She kissed me, the first time either of the children had kissed me. I stroked her hair, her weird hair, this weird child.

"How much longer is summer?" she asked.

"A long time," I replied. "We still have a long time." And this was enough. She was asleep again. And then, soon enough, so was I.

WHEN I WOKE UP, CARL WAS STANDING OVER ME, HIS HAND lightly resting on his cheek, like I was abstract art, like he saw something that interested him but he wasn't sure what it meant, like he thought I was something a child could have made. And, honestly, I wasn't that shocked. He'd let us go, but I always knew that at some point he'd be the one to bring us back.

"Hello, Carl," I said, and he shook his head, observing my circumstances.

"There wasn't anywhere else that you could go?" he asked.

"I . . . I don't have many friends," I told him. "When did she call you?"

"Late last night," he replied. I wasn't even mad at her. I don't know what I thought would happen. Maybe I wanted it to be over with, had reached the limits of what I could do on my own. That it had taken barely a day seemed pathetic.

"So this is where you grew up?" he asked me, looking around the attic.

"No, Carl. I grew up in a normal room. Downstairs. This room is where I ended up."

"I see," he replied.

The kids heard us talking and opened their eyes. When they saw that it was Carl, they simply groaned, flopped onto their sides, and pulled the sheets over their heads.

I should have been more afraid, after all that had happened, but Carl, as much as he irritated me, didn't scare me. If it had been the police, then I'd have been scared. I realized that Madison and Jasper hadn't told anyone else about me, about the kids.

"Please tell me the mansion didn't burn down," I told him.

"It's okay," he said. "Some smoke damage, a month of renovations. It's fine. It could have been much worse."

"How did you explain it to the fire department?" I asked him, genuinely curious. My guess, if I had only one guess, was that money was involved.

"The fire chief is a close friend of Secretary Roberts," Carl said. Well, okay, I realized, favors. Rich-people favors were better than money. And then I noticed the title Carl had used, Secretary.

"He's not resigning?" I asked.

"I'm not here to talk about that," Carl replied. He held out a cellular phone.

"Who do you want me to talk to?" I asked him.

"Mrs. Roberts," he replied. "She's the one who set all of this up. She wants to talk to you."

"Carl, I don't know if I can talk to her," I said. "Legally, I'm not sure what—"

"Just talk to her, okay?" he told me. He put the phone in my hand. "Just press the green button," he said, and then he shook the bed, pulling the covers off the kids. "Do you kids want to get ice cream?" he asked.

"Not really," Bessie admitted.

"Well, do you want to get out of this awful attic and get some fresh air?" he tried next.

"With you?" Roland asked, sneering.

"It's okay," I told them. "Carl has been good to us. I just need to talk to Madison for a little while."

"You're not leaving us?" Bessie asked, cautious.

"Carl's just going to take you downstairs so you can hang out with my mom," I told her. "It's okay."

They got out of bed, adjusting their clothes. Carl held out his hands, and each kid took one, disappearing down the stairs.

I LOOKED AT THE PHONE. IF I THREW IT IN THE TRASH, IF I could sneak down the stairs and out a window, I could be back on the road, entirely on my own. I resisted this urge, which was pretty common with me, the slightest friction causing me to jump out of whatever it was that was in motion. I'd get a little banged up, would ruin my reputation, but it always seemed worth it for the escape. And then I imagined those kids sitting with Carl and my mother, such a sad fate. I put the phone to my ear and waited to hear that voice, one that I'd replayed in my mind for so many years.

"Lillian?" Madison asked.

"It's me," I replied.

"Okay," she said. "Thank goodness. Just tell me straight up, have you done anything stupid?"

"No," I said, a little aggrieved. "Well, I mean, I went back home to my mom's."

"Well, yes, that is stupid, but that's not what I'm talking about. You haven't talked to any reporters? You haven't drawn attention to the kids?"

"No," I said. "We drove to my mom's. We ate mac and cheese. We slept on the most uncomfortable mattress in the world. It's fine."

"Well . . . good," she said.

"How much did you pay my mom to tell you where I was?" I asked.

"A thousand dollars," she told me. I didn't say anything. "Why?" she asked. "Is that more or less than what you had hoped?"

"I honestly have no idea," I said. I didn't really know how money worked anymore.

"We never really got a chance to talk, Lil. It's been so crazy. It's been insane. I mean, yes, the confirmation, all that. But, you know, Timothy . . . catching on fire . . . being a fire child. All that."

"You protected him," I told her.

"Well, I fucking dropped him," she said. "Oh my god, he burned the hell out of me."

"But you protected him when it mattered," I said.

"When Jasper threatened to send him to some weird test site? Yeah, that was never going to happen. I would have destroyed him. It was such a sign of his own weakness that he was even going to consider it."

"But you were going to send the kids to that ranch, that whatever-the-fuck," I told her.

"It was up for discussion, Lil. That's all. I know you don't believe it, but I have a conscience. I feel bad about stuff. It may take longer than it does a normal person, but I do feel bad."

"But now that you have your own fire child," I said.

"Exactly," she replied. "Exactly. It happened, and it was terrifying, but then Timothy was still Timothy afterward. He was sweet. He was mine. And I felt like, okay, I can do that. However many times it happens, I can do it."

"That was pretty impressive how you covered it up," I said.

"It honestly wasn't even that hard," she said. "I had it all worked out before we even jumped into the car. There are a lot of nice things about being rich, but one of the best is that you can say almost anything, and if you do it with confidence, without blinking, people put a lot of effort into believing you."

"So Timothy is staying with you?" I asked.

"Oh, yes," she said. "I made Jasper understand that, and he's accepted it. We had a long talk last night—we had to stay in the guesthouse, by the way, which was pretty great, even though Jasper couldn't stop crying about his family home— and I had to make him understand a lot of things. I had to make him understand how much I could ruin him. How much all of us could ruin him. So he can be the secretary of state. Let him have it. It's as close as he'll get to the presidency."

"So you're gonna stay with him?" I asked, kind of already knowing the answer.

"Yeah," she said. "It's fine. I'm going to get what I want. At this point, Jasper gives me access to the things that matter to me, and I don't just mean money. I mean the freedom to have my own ideas and my own life. Plus, honestly, I still kind of like him. He's stupid, but I like him well enough. And, hey, guess what? Somebody talked to me about running for Jasper's seat in the Senate. I mean, wouldn't that be wild?"

"And if Timothy catches on fire again?" I asked.

"I don't know that it matters, honestly," she said. "I'll come up with something. Maybe I'll even tell the truth. Timothy is going to be fine. I'll make sure that he's fine. I mean, you did it with two kids; I can handle one."

"Maybe *he'll* be president," I offered.

"Absolutely not," she said. "Timothy is going to be a Tommy Hilfiger model. He's going to marry royalty. He's going to have it easy."

It was so nice to hear her voice, to hear her voice and listen to her talk about what she wanted. I never quite knew what I wanted, the letters I sent her so wishy-washy and pained. Madison, she fucking wanted stuff. And when she talked or wrote about it, with that intensity, you wanted to give it to her. You wanted her to have it. And it was so easy, I was in love with her again, the routine of our relationship, that she would hurt me, but I would allow it. I would live with it.

"What about the kids?" I asked, finally, waiting for bad news. "What about Bessie and Roland?"

"They are not going to that, whatever, that insane boot

camp. It's fine. Plus, honestly? It was going to cost like five hundred grand a year for both of them. That's bullshit. No way."

"But is Jasper going to take care of them?" I asked. "What will happen to them?"

Madison was quiet, and I could hear her breathing. I wondered where she was right now, if she was on the porch, a pitcher of sweet tea beside her. I wondered if she was on a private jet back to D.C. to go apartment hunting. I wanted to picture her clearly in my mind.

"Well, it's complicated," she replied. "Jasper wants to do the right thing, Lil, and he really, truly means it. He fucked up. He fucked up so bad that I don't think Roland and Bessie ever really need to forgive him. They'd be well within their rights. But they'll be taken care of."

"How?" I said. "Madison . . ." I was almost crying. "How?"

"Do you want them, Lillian?" she asked.

"What?" There was this little ray of light. I could almost touch it. It was so faint, but I could reach up and it would be right on my fingertips. And I could barely breathe. And I could barely move.

"You heard me. I know that you heard me," she said.

"Me?" I asked.

"Would you take care of them? Would you keep taking care of them?"

"For how long?" I asked.

"As long as they want you to. As long as you want to. For good. Permanently."

"How?" I asked. "Why?"

"It's not that complicated. Well, it is, but Carl walked me through everything. He's so smart. He's the best. I had the idea, but he worked it out. So, you wouldn't adopt them, okay?

Because that would, like, make you responsible for them. And Jasper, he's a good man, but it's nice if he has to *legally* be a good man. It's legal guardianship. You've heard of that, right? You'd be their legal guardian. But Jasper would make sure they were cared for. He'd provide for their upbringing. He'd pay their expenses. If you wanted Bessie to go to Iron Mountain—"

"Fuck no," I said, but I was kind of laughing. I was kind of crying, and I was kind of laughing. I must have sounded insane.

"Well, whatever, not Iron Mountain, but a good school. A good but normal school for both of them."

"They'd be mine?" I asked.

"Yeah," Madison said. "Would that make you happy?"

"I honestly don't know," I admitted.

"Lil, that is not what I'd hoped to hear. I've been working on this ever since you nearly burned our fucking house down."

"No," I said. "It would. It would. I'm just . . . I'm just afraid that I won't do a good job."

"Who would judge you?" she asked. "Who do you know who's done a good job? Name one parent that you think made it through without fucking their kid up in some specific way."

"I can't think of anyone right now," I replied.

"There isn't anyone," she said, getting irritated, wanting me to be grateful, wanting to make up for whatever she had done to me.

"Okay," I said. "I'll take them."

"Lillian?" she said. There was silence.

"Yes?" I replied.

"I think I fixed everything," she said.

"No," I said. "Not really. But you kept it from getting more messed up."

"That's fixing something," she said. "You stop it from getting worse."

"Okay," I said. "Thank you, I guess."

"I'll see you, okay?" she said. "We'll see each other. Timothy will see Roland and Bessie. When the time is right, Jasper will see Roland and Bessie. Just not often, not a ton. But it'll keep going."

"Okay, Madison," I said.

"I love you, Lillian," she finally told me.

"I love you, too," I answered, but what else could be said? What else could be done? "I'd better go," I told her.

"Bye, Lillian."

"Goodbye," I said, and I turned off the phone.

And how do I say this? How do I say it and have you understand? Maybe there's no way to say it. I was happy. I was happy that Bessie and Roland would be mine. But, can you understand me? I was sad. I was sad because I wasn't entirely sure that I wanted them. They had appeared, like magic, but I wasn't magical. I was messed up. I messed things up. And I knew that having two children, two children who caught on fire, would be hard. It would make me sad. It would be so easy to ruin them.

Something was ending. Even if it had been awful, my life was ending, and it felt like this wasn't my life anymore. It was someone else's. And I had decided that I'd just live inside it, see if anyone noticed, and maybe it would become mine. Maybe I would love it.

I'm just trying to say that I got something that I'd wished for. But I knew it wasn't a happy ending, no matter what Madison thought, no matter how much she convinced herself that everything would work out fine. It was just an ending. And

downstairs, there was a new beginning. And they were waiting for me. But I sat there in that attic, where I had never once
been happy in my entire life. I sat there and I held on to this
moment, before the new beginning started. I wondered how
long I could stay in this moment. I wondered how many times
in my life I'd come back to this room, to this exact moment in
time. I wondered what I would feel, looking back on it.

I got out of bed. I put on some shorts, a ratty T-shirt with
a Dominique Wilkins caricature silk-screened on it, the colors
faded. I put on my basketball shoes, which I loved and had
thought I might never see again. And under the bed, still there,
was a basketball, the grip nearly worn off of it. There was a
shitty court a few blocks away, weeds and no lines and not even
a net on the hoop. But I wanted them to try, to get used to a
life that could be all of ours.

DOWNSTAIRS, BESSIE AND ROLAND WERE SITTING ON THE
sofa. Carl was building a house of cards for them, but it kept
falling down. My mom was nowhere to be found, of course. I
imagined she was already on her way to Tunica to gamble with
the money Carl had given her.

"So you talked to her?" Carl asked, standing at attention.

"Yes," I replied. I didn't want to draw this out. I handed
the phone to Carl. I gave him a hug, which I could tell he either
did not like or did not expect. Either way, I just kind of hung
on him for a second. "We were a pretty good team," Carl said,
looking sheepish.

I nodded. "Say bye to Carl, kiddos," I said. And he was
gone, out the door. I wondered if I'd ever see him again.

"What's happening?" Bessie asked.

"Do you want to stay with me?" I asked them. "For good?"

"Yes," they said without hesitation.

"You don't have to," I told them.

"Yes," they said again. They were vibrating.

"It won't be like at the estate," I said. "It will not be fun all the time."

"It wasn't fun all the time there," Roland said. "It was awful sometimes."

"Well, then it'll be like that now, too."

They just nodded. They weren't smiling, exactly. They had a kind of dazed look on their faces.

"Do you want us?" Bessie suddenly asked.

"What?" I replied. My heart stopped.

"Do you want us?" Bessie asked.

I wanted to say yes immediately, but it was unnerving, the way she was looking at me. I felt like she knew what was in my heart, even if I didn't. And she wasn't blinking.

"Yes," I finally said. "I want both of you. I want to take care of you."

And she didn't smile. She didn't say a word. She just stared at me. I could see her skin starting to get red, blotchy. I could feel the heat coming off her. I knew that if she caught on fire, I would pull her close to me. I would let it come.

But she didn't catch on fire. Her skin paled; she took a breath.

"You do want us," she finally said. "Yes, you do."

"Let's get out of this house," I told them, holding up the basketball. We stood in the doorway, the whole world opening up before us. God, there was so much of it. We walked out of that house, and I led them toward whatever came next. I handed the ball to Bessie, and she bounced it on the sidewalk, that steady thump like a heartbeat.

Bessie had believed me. She knew that I wanted them, that I would always take care of them. And so I decided to believe her. I decided that this was the truth. It was this little fire. And I would hold on to it. And it would keep me warm. And it would never, ever go out.

# Acknowledgments

**THANKS TO THE FOLLOWING:**

Julie Barer and everyone at the Book Group, especially Nicole Cunningham.

Zack Wagman, an amazing editor, and everyone at Ecco.

The University of the South and the English Department, with special gratitude to Wyatt Prunty.

The Corporation of Yaddo and the Hermitage at St. Mary's for the time and space to write.

My family: Kelly and Debbie Wilson; Kristen, Wes, and Kellan Huffman; Mary Couch; Meredith, Warren, Laura, Morgan, and Philip James; and the Wilson, Fuselier, and Baltz families.

My friends: Aaron Burch, Manuel Chinchilla, Lucy Corin, Lee Conell, Lily Davenport, Marcy Dermansky, Sam Esquith, Isabel Galbraith, Elizabeth and John Grammer, Jason Griffey, Kate Jayroe, Kelly Malone, Katie McGhee, Matt O'Keefe, Cecily Parks, Ann Patchett, Betsy Sandlin, Matt Schrader, Leah Stewart, David and Heidi Syler, Lauryl Tucker, Claire Vaye Watkins, Caki Wilkinson, and Becca Wells Williams.

And, as always, with all my love: Leigh Anne, Griff, and Patch.

# Nothing to See Here

## Kevin Wilson

*A Reading Group Guide*

# Author Essay

## I Was Worried My Anxiety Would Prevent Me From Being a Good Father. My Sons Changed That

*Originally published in Time in October 2019*
*(reprinted with permission)*

EVER SINCE I WAS A CHILD, I'VE HAD THIS AGITATION. It seems entirely plausible that I could burst into flames. The thought began when I was 9 or 10 years old. I had a friend named Tony who had the Time Life: Mysteries of the Unknown books, which I read constantly. There was this small section on human combustion. It locked into my brain: the recurring image of people bursting into flames.

At first, I worried that it could happen at any time. But as I entered adolescence, I kind of wanted to combust. I thought it would actually make me feel better, would burn all the anxiety and worry out of my body, and I would be clean.

I was a very shy and anxious child. I kept everything in my head and tried to keep secrets from the people who loved and protected me the most. I didn't want them to know the things I was thinking, because they were scary. Holding it all inside eventually made me sick. By the time

I was finishing high school in Winchester, Tenn., my parents were driving me an hour and a half to see a therapist. I learned that being able to talk to someone was really helpful, but I knew from that age on that anxiety was going to be my life. I don't enjoy being in the world very much. I overcompensate by trying to be overly generous so people don't suspect there's darkness in my mind. But when my brain gets locked in and obsessive, it's almost impossible to break out. It's on a loop and the loop gets so loud—I want to do whatever it takes to shut it off. I've learned that when a thought won't stop looping, I've got to hold on to it and touch it and, sometimes, make something with it. The best way I navigate it all is by writing. Creating a story is a way for me to connect to the world—to situate my anxiety in a way that can be understood and that I can move forward from.

Before my wife, Leigh Anne, and I had children, I never thought I would be capable of caring for someone because of my own circumstances. We had to seriously evaluate whether we wanted to have children when I had to go to McLean Hospital in Massachusetts after having a nervous breakdown in 2006. But we decided that the positive things we could offer a child would outweigh those concerns, and Leigh Anne believed that children would teach us to become the people we needed to be. Now, we have two boys, ages 11 and 7. When my oldest, Griff, was born, I felt this kind of wonder that I had brought a child into the world—replaced almost immediately with anxiety-ridden questions: *How am I going to do this? How am I going to keep this child alive? And not just keep him alive, but turn him into a person?*

The only thing I knew how to do, because I have always been pretty isolated, was to reach inside myself and give my sons all the things that had kept me going. I would read my boys every story I could find. We would make our own stories. I would try to get them to appreciate that when the world is overwhelming, a narrative can be sustaining and can help you survive. I gave Griff comic books—I loved the ideas in those, the magic of them, and he did too. My younger son, Patch, and I would listen to rap music, which might have been inappropriate for a 4-year-old, but I couldn't help myself. I loved it, and it made sense to share it with him. Again and again, I tried to show them my ways of coping with the world through the beauty of art.

When Donald Trump was elected, there was all this talk about how great art was going to come from these trying times and that felt like such bullsh-t to me. Great art can come from anything. I don't want the world to have to be ravaged in order for art to exist. And I don't think art can change the world—but I do believe art can help you survive it. Books, movies and music can make life tolerable. They allow you insight into the way the world works, in the way people work; and with that insight, you can manage life a little bit better.

I used to really struggle with how I could live life with my children. I would think, *How am I going to take care of them when I can barely take care of myself?* I started to think about the saying, "the strong protect the weak." That's the way a society should function. Those in power, the people who are strong and able, should protect those who can't protect themselves. But my worldview has changed radically since I've had kids. I've realized that the strong don't protect the weak. They'll do it, if it's in their best interests, or if they feel like it. But people who are strong and in power find weakness repulsive. They don't want to be around it. They can't understand why it exists. I came to understand that the weak protect the weaker. I might feel like a damaged person, but I am always going to reach into myself and do as much as possible to protect my children, to give them a safer world. I can become slightly stronger to protect the people who need me, even when I feel like bursting into flames.

My children are aware of who I am and how I operate. They know that I don't like to go into the city—that I don't like going to their schools when they have performances or parent-teacher conferences. I don't want to be in a building full of people. But now, when my sons recognize anxiety and feelings of weirdness in themselves, they know they're not alone. I'm grateful that my children live in a time where people are more open about mental health. Their teachers and friends are sensitive and understanding. Griff has friends who are anxious in completely different ways than he is. My children think anxiety is not that big of a deal, whereas for me, it was the biggest deal in the world.

Every day that passes, I see that I've made it another day, that our family has made it another day—and I've realized that maybe my fear that I was going to ruin my children was self-important. Maybe my sons won't let me ruin them. Because they're strong and interesting and their own people. Griff just started middle school and immediately signed up for theater. He has a part in the play and he's memorizing all of these lines. I would never have done that. Before I had children, I always thought that the best way to keep safe was to bunker down and make myself as small as possible, to disappear from the struggles I faced. But when we brought Griff and Patch into the world, I understood that the world would continue after I died, which didn't matter to me before—I wanted to get in and get out. Now I can imagine the world after me, and my sons are in it, as well as all the amazing people who I've met because of my family, and I want to stay here as long as I can, to try and make it better. I have to survive and figure out how to take part. And I owe that understanding to my sons. They have taught me that we're stronger and better if we connect.

# Questions for Discussion

1. The twins in *Nothing to See Here* spontaneously combust when they get agitated. The fire they generate can burn others but leaves the twins unharmed. What does the nature of this condition represent? Did your perceptions of the condition change at all throughout the book?

2. This novel offers a unique perspective on the complexities of love and what it means to look beyond a person's differences. What sort of preconceived notions does Lillian bring to her role as the twins' caretaker? How do Bessie and Roland challenge those notions?

3. Lillian works hard to establish and maintain a bond with the twins. What is it about Lillian that makes her uniquely equipped for this job? Why is she able to connect with them while others have failed?

4. Throughout the book, many characters look for ways to control or cure the twins' condition. Think about the variety of methods put forward. What did you think of each method? What might the methods reveal about each person who suggested them?

5. At the end of chapter three, Lillian expresses surprise that the children's hair remains unsinged after they burst into flames: "I don't know why, with these demon children bursting into flames right in front of me, their bad haircuts remaining intact was the magic that fully amazed me, but that's how it works, I think. The big thing is so ridiculous that you absorb only the smaller miracles." Do you relate to this sentiment? What other "smaller miracles" are present in the story?

6. The novel offers examples of how class dynamics can shape an individual's experience: Lillian's and Madison's differing experiences at their elite boarding school, for instance, or Lillian's early days as an employee on the Roberts estate, alongside Carl and Mary. How do wealth and privilege shape the story? Which characters most feel the impact of this?

7. How does Lillian's dark sense of humor amplify the book's themes of love, acceptance, and parenting? Did you enjoy the use of humor throughout the novel? What does it tell you about Lillian's character?

8. Lillian makes a big life change at the end of the novel. What are your thoughts about her transformation from being Madison's boarding school roommate to becoming the eventual caretaker to her stepkids? What do you think she ultimately saw in Roland and Bessie that led her to make such a change?

9. Madison and Lillian have a complicated relationship that veers from deep affection to intense rivalry and from bitter resentment to uneasy allies. Do you think

they're foils for each other or something else? How does their competitive edge play into their relationship? And do you think their relationship will live on after the events of the novel?

10. *Nothing to See Here* explores different representations of family structure and dynamics. How do the family units presented at the beginning of the book evolve and change? What does Lillian value in family? Which characters share those values, and what are some of the values of the characters who don't?

# About the Author

KEVIN WILSON IS THE *NEW YORK TIMES* BESTSELLING AUTHOR of the short-story collection *Baby, You're Gonna Be Mine* as well as the novels *Perfect Little World* and *The Family Fang,* which was made into a film with Jason Bateman and Nicole Kidman. His story collection *Tunneling to the Center of the Earth* received an Alex Award from the American Library Association and the Shirley Jackson Award. Wilson teaches fiction at the University of the South in Sewanee, Tennessee, where he lives with his wife and two sons.